THE
IMMORTAL
MUSE

THE
IMMORTAL MUSE

MANDY JACKSON-BEVERLY

CRICKET PUBLISHING / U.S.A.

Copyright © 2019 by Mandy Jackson-Beverly

All rights reserved. Published by Cricket Publishing, established 2015.

Jackson-Beverly, Mandy.
The Immortal Muse / by Mandy Jackson-Beverly. — 1st ed.
https://mandyjacksonbeverly.com

Library of Congress Control Number: **2019900224**
Hardcover ISBN: 978-1-7335906-1-7
Paperback ISBN: 978-1-7335906-0-0
E-Book ISBN 978-0-9965088-9-6

Cover Design: Damonza
Formatting: Damonza

For Suesie

thanks for being there

The Motto of the Allegiance
SINE VIRTVTE OMNIA SVNT PERDITA
(Without courage, all is lost.)

Creatives: Artists who paint truths within paintings, secrets only visible to a few. Their images share the gift of prophecy. All Creatives have amethyst-colored eyes

The Allegiance: An ancient organization that protects art and Creatives and gives sanctuary to those threatened by religious zealots

Members of the Allegiance

The Lady and the Rose: Goddess and protector of the Allegiance

Freyja: Immortal Nordic goddess of the Underworld **Ravinka:** Kenan's human lover

Hakon: Nordic fae prince, creator of the Allegiance, father of Prudence, Sonja's beloved

Sonja: Ancient immortal Nordic seer, mother of Prudence, Hakon's beloved

Prudence/Astridr: Immortal seer, head of the Allegiance, Stefan's beloved, mother of Gabriel

Stefan: Serbian vampire, warrior, poet, Prudence's beloved, father of Gabriel

Gabriel: Italian half-vampire, half-warlock, second-in-command of the Allegiance, Coco's beloved

Coco (Colombina): American half-vampire, half-human, Creative, Gabriel's beloved

Alessandro: Italian vampire, warrior, member of the Allegiance, Chantal's beloved, father of Christopher and Coco

Chantal: American vampire and Creative, Alessandro's beloved, mother of Christopher and Coco

Christopher: American half-vampire, half-human, lawyer for the Allegiance, Layla's beloved

Kishu: American human, father of Chantal, grandfather to Christopher and Coco

Nikandros: Ancient vampire, Luciana's beloved

Sabine: Ancient vampire, warrior, doctor

Pelayo: El Salvadoran vampire

Frederico: Italian vampire, warrior

Ignacio: English vampire, Louisa's beloved

Jeremy: American human/fae, Arianna's twin brother, son of Katja and Elion

Arianna: American human/fae, Jeremy's twin sister, adoptive parents are Isabel and Steven

Sylvia: Owner of adoption agency in LA **Illona:** Fae, Elion's sister, aunt to Jeremy and Arianna

Jason: American human, mathematician/economist, friend of Christopher

Layla: Italian human/fae, Christopher's beloved

Louisa: Italian vampire, Ignacio's beloved

Luciana: Creative, Nikandros's beloved, mother of Flora

Flora: Creative, Kenan's daughter

Antonia: Italian human/fae, mother of Layla, mediator for the Allegiance

Eduardo: Italian human, art professor, Caprecia's husband, father of Louisa

Maria: Italian human, café owner

Isabel: American human, Arianna's adoptive mother

Elion: Deceased fae, father of Jeremy and Arianna, Illona's brother

Caprecia: Deceased Portuguese vampire, Louisa's mother, Eduardo's wife

Sam: Vampire, lawyer, works for Sabine

Protected by the Allegiance

Marilyn: Human, Gabriel's ex, Marco's wife

Marco: Human, Marilyn's husband

Frances Reed: Human, journalist, works for Sabine

Steven: Deceased human, Isabel's husband, Arianna's adoptive father

Helen McCarthy: Young pregnant mother, wants to tell her story

Isabella Romola de' Medici: Daughter of Cosimo I and Eleonora de Toledo, related to Lorenzo the Magnificent

Marguerite: friend of Isabella Romola de' Medici

Other Characters

Leonie: Seer, Alessandro's grandmother

Beatrice: Seer, betrayed by the church, given power by the devil

Birgit: Seer, Illona and Elion's mother, captured by Domenico

The Holy Father: vampire equivalent of the pope

The Devil Incarnate:

Kenan: Italian vampire, third and strongest incarnation of the devil, determined to destroy all Creatives and the Allegiance

Domenico: Italian vampire and Kenan's maker, second incarnation of the devil

Vinicio: Vampire, Domenico's maker, first incarnation of the devil

THERE HAS BEEN no sign of Kenan, but his darkness continues to spill across borders, into homes and places of worship. His evil demeanor enters uninvited and comes to rest upon the shoulders of the tormented. It begins with a sense of sorrow, morphs into doom, and takes root as indignation. From there, hatred grabs hold of one's soul and leads it willingly into temptation.

Coco senses a seductive pull, the allure of her old life fed by her inherent need for freedom. Spurred on by her lover's dishonesty, she questions her present life and the purpose of the Allegiance. But is this reality or part of Kenan's plan to destroy her?

To save his beloved, Gabriel must revisit his past and a spell he would rather forget. But in order to destroy Kenan, it is the world of the dead he must enter.

The darkest depth of winter has arrived,

and the voices of the dead are calling.

Whispers of torment and anger,

distrust and pain.

They beg to rest,

to sleep without horror.
They seek justice,
answers,
and accountability.
They gather in strength,
remembering their dignity,
their grace,
and their purpose.
Take heed,
for they are approaching,
a force of fury
in a river of blood.

PROLOGUE

Kittery, Maine

THE YOUNG GIRL stared through vacant eyes at the small strip of paper on her bed. She reached for a strand of her unwashed hair and twisted the lock around her fingers, finding comfort in the silkiness of the smooth texture. The nightly news drifted from the TV in the living room, reminding her of the doom of the world. She shoved her feet into her snow boots, grabbed her parka, and opened the bedroom door. The smell of fried chicken drifting up the hallway made her stomach turn, and she covered her mouth with the back of her hand as she slipped out a side door and into the biting wind of a New England blizzard. Pulling a pair of gloves out of a pocket, she slipped them over her hands, walked across the front yard and onto the snow-covered road.

She glanced at the houses in the neighborhood—mostly working-class, single-family weatherboard homes with the occasional two-story newer addition that catered to the younger, wealthier couples moving into the area, people with plans for a bright future. A shiver ran down her back, and she turned to see if she was being followed. Nobody, just the ghostly silhouettes of barren trees and snow-laden wires crisscrossing the street. She continued walking, turned left at the next road, and pressed onward until she reached an intersection. This was where she waited for the school bus, always perky, for she was, if nothing else, a virtuoso of hiding her pain. The wind sent a flurry of snowflakes on the path before her; they danced in a circle, coaxing her forward with a soft murmur of a message. *Keep walking.*

At the end of the road, the young girl stared ahead, her fate hovering in the direction she would decide to take. With a quick glance back along the way she had come, she turned around and jumped a chain-link fence. She walked briskly across an expanse of freshly snow-covered ground and under a row of tall cement pylons. Grabbing hold of a thick tree limb, she hoisted herself up and onto the main highway. To her right was the green curve of the bridge. Stepping up her pace, she walked forward, looking over her shoulder every so often, still wondering if she was being followed. A shiver ran over her body, causing the hair to lift on the back of her neck. She stopped for a moment and grabbed a steel girder to keep her balance. The swirling, icy waters of the river captivated her, offering tranquility and an end to her torturous life. Her shoulders relaxed, and a sense of calm wrapped around her. She thought of Homer and the book she kept hidden in her bedroom…

"Nevertheless, I long to reach my home and see the day of my return. It is my never-failing wish. And what if one of the gods does wreck me out on the wine-dark sea? I have a heart that is inured to suffering, and I shall steel it to endure that too. For in my day I have had many bitter and shattering experiences in war and on the stormy seas. So let this new disaster come. It only makes one more."

❧

On the shore, a journalist named Frances Reed snapped photographs of the bridge with her camera and a telescopic lens. As she panned over the massive arc, a shadow caught her attention. A man dressed in dark clothes and a long black coat strode in a smooth, even pace along the bridge as if he was following someone. Frances panned out and saw a young girl standing midway on the bridge, clutching a girder. The girl turned toward the dark-clad man, who now stood beside her, but it was as if she did not see him. She turned and gazed into the water. Her lips were moving, and when they stopped, she climbed over the iron railing. Frances gasped and watched helplessly as the young girl fell from the edge of the bridge and into the frigid water below. She scanned the area for the man but saw no one. With a shaking hand, she reached for her phone and dialed 9-1-1. The next call she made was to the woman funding her research, Dr. Sabine Fiore.

CHAPTER 1

Casa della Pietra, Northern Italian Alps

MUD-COLORED WATER SPRAYED into the air as Coco hurled a ceramic jar across the room and hit her target—a painted canvas displayed on an easel—before watching it crash onto the hardwood floor.

"Fuck you, Gabriel!" Coco yelled. She leaned back on her heels and stared up at the painting. The image of the botanical garden on the UCLA campus seemed innocent, a far cry from the sensual scene behind it. Coco grabbed hold of another jar, but as she went to hurl it, a familiar hand grabbed hers. She looked up at her mother whose amethyst-colored eyes mirrored her own. "Let me destroy it, Mom!"

Chantal eased the jar from Coco's hand and placed it back on the table beside the easel. "Will destroying the painting—rather than considering what you saw from a rational point of view—make you feel better?"

"Maybe," Coco said. Her shoulders slumped, and her long dark brown hair that earlier had been twisted and held in place by a pencil now fell in strands over her face. "Probably not, and in retrospect, I'd rather throw the damn jar at Gabriel."

"Why? What did you see?"

Coco shook her head and squeezed her eyes shut.

Chantal headed to a large worktable filled with assorted frames, scissors, and staple guns. She placed a twenty-four-by-thirty-six-inch maple picture frame on top of a piece of canvas, stapled one side, and used stretching pliers to bring tension to the material while stapling the edges to the wood. Using the pliers was purely out of habit as she could easily have stretched the fabric using her immortal strength.

The all-too-familiar art studio sounds told Coco that her mother was keeping herself busy, no doubt giving Coco time to calm herself and gather her thoughts before speaking. Coco wiped her eyes with her shirtsleeves and did her best to control her temper by taking a deep breath. When she finally spoke, it was as if she were talking to herself. "There are moments when I want to go back to my old life. To paint from my heart, not create horrific images." She paused as another wave of emotion hit her. "The image behind the painting showed Gabriel with another woman. It was another era, but I could tell he loved her. I know there have been other women in his life—a shitload, no doubt—but he told me I was the only woman he'd loved. That was a lie, Mom. He lied to me." The loud clunk of the staple gun in action made her jump. She turned to Chantal.

"Confront him, Colombina. Let go of the emotional baggage. I've no reason to doubt Gabriel's love for you, and experience has taught me the perils of hiding emotions. Without honesty, relationships linger on the verge of crisis, and I'm fairly sure that's not Gabriel's intent."

Chantal, Gabriel, and Prudence—head of the Allegiance—preferred to call Coco by her birth name of Colombina, and although the name was new to her, she found it endearing. "Did Gabriel share his past relationships with Dad? I mean, he must have—they've been friends for centuries."

A knowing smile pulled at the edges of Chantal's mouth and spread to the corners of her eyes. "Oh, I've no doubt they had some wild times together, but they're not my stories to tell, and quite frankly, the past is done; it's history." She pushed the trigger of the staple gun a couple more times, leaned against the table, and gazed at Coco's painting. "I've learned that what we see is not always real. Images can be bent and molded."

"You mean through magic?"

Chantal nodded. "During the twenty-eight years that Kenan kept me prisoner, he used to have me watch footage of you. But always in my heart, I knew the young girl in the videos wasn't you but rather manipulated images of another child. Kenan hoped that if I saw my daughter, I'd submit to his demands, that I'd be terrified by his threats of hurting you. He hoped to emotionally blackmail me into giving him information about the Allegiance. He was always testing me, hoping to wear me down. But I saw behind his game; he thought you were dead, and for a long time so did I."

Coco considered her mother's words. "What I saw behind this painting was not a lie."

"How would you know?" Chantal asked. "You need to open your eyes and see the image for what it truly is. Observe like the artist you are. Now, what did you see?"

"Gabriel was… intimate with a woman. And I heard him tell her he loved her." She pinched her lips tight to stop them from trembling. "Something disturbed him, and he turned around. That's when I saw it was Gabriel."

"You know as well as anyone that Gabriel is not a cruel man," Chantal said. "He would never intentionally hurt you. I'm sure he wants nothing more than to be with you now and explain what you've seen."

"You think he saw what I saw?"

"I'm sure he sensed your anger and pain even though he's hundreds of miles from here, and with his innate connection to you, it's possible he saw the scene in its entirety. But I sense there's more to your anger," Chantal said. "What else has made you so upset?"

"There were letters too," Coco blurted out. "Proclaiming their love for each other."

"Letters were how people connected in the past," Chantal said. "How would you feel if you thought Gabriel had access to emails from your past lovers?"

"Like he hasn't already seen them? I've no privacy anymore. I can't even do my job… something that I love."

"So this isn't only about what you saw in the painting but also about needing your autonomy."

A flush of warmth brushed Coco's cheeks; she turned to Chantal and nodded.

"Your safety is of the utmost importance to all of us, Colombina," Chantal continued. "I'm fairly sure that what you saw in the painting was connected to dark magic, and until we find Kenan, you're safest here. Do you understand?"

"I'm trying to, Mom, but it's breaking my heart. Is it so wrong to admit that I miss my old life, teaching, and my students?"

"Of course not," Chantal replied. "But if you choose to ignore the reasons why we protect you, then not only are you acting impulsively but Kenan will win because breaking you down—and destroying the Allegiance—is what he wants. Remember your power; you're not only a Creative but you also have the essence of magic shared through your father's bloodline. That's why you can travel through paintings, a trait I do not have, nor do the more experienced and older Creatives among us—Luciana and Flora. You can choose to either embrace this talent or not. The choice is yours."

She glanced at Coco's recent painting, then returned to her work. "However, before you make your decision, I suggest you consider other female members of the Allegiance who have fought for justice before you. Immortals such as Sabine, whose life's purpose is to protect women from abuse at the hands of men. When she became a vampire, Sabine accepted her fate without question and used it to better this world."

"I understand." Coco rested her forehead on the palms of her hands. "You think Kenan's getting at me through my paintings and dreams?" She sensed an instant change in the air and realized her mother had stopped what she was doing, and when she looked at her, she seemed agitated.

"You've dreamed of him?"

"Yes," Coco said. "Dark dreams. Of young boys being brutally attacked while Kenan stands over them watching… urging his men to bring the boys to their knees in submission."

Chantal walked over to Coco and knelt before her. "That particular dream is not Kenan in your head. It represents your fears coming to the surface. The boys are an aspect of you. The you that allows others to control what you do. In this dream, Kenan is your animus, the male aspect of your psyche." She held Coco's hands in hers. "Pick yourself up and express to Gabriel your need to continue teaching. I'm sure that when Kenan's dead, Gabriel will want nothing more than to nurture what you love, what makes you happy."

"How will I know when the Kenan I see in my dreams is not another side of me but rather him inside my head?"

Her mother's eyes darkened. "You'll know. Every cell in your body, mind, and spirit will be tested. Kenan's darkness will bring you absolute terror."

"But how do I stop him from entering my mind?"

"If Kenan's in your head, make no mistake that he'll do everything he can to control you. And if you resist, he'll do his best to drive you to insanity."

"Then I'm screwed," Coco said, "and I'll let down the Allegiance."

"That's not true. Maybe my father can help."

"Kishu?" Coco asked. "How?"

Chantal stood and held a hand out to Coco. "He learned certain gifts from our ancestors. If he hadn't taught me those traits as a young woman, I would not have made it through the years of Kenan's mental torture."

Coco accepted Chantal's hand and rose. A soft chime had Chantal reaching for her cell, and her brows knitted into a frown as she read a text.

"What's wrong?" Coco asked.

Chantal's fingers moved quickly as she wrote a reply. She dropped the cell back in her pocket and returned her attention to Coco. "A group text from Jason. The apparent suicide of a young girl has been reported in Maine. It's an area where Sabine suspects Kenan has a compound, but as yet she's been unable to track it down. She has warriors there who report unusual behavior to Jason who forwards us the information. I'm going to meet your father in the library."

"I'll see you there shortly," Coco said. "There's something I need to do first."

CHAPTER 2

FOR A BRIEF moment, a dark memory from Gabriel's past flashed before him, catching him off guard. He turned away from his fellow immortals—Alessandro, Sabine, Pelayo, and Frederico—and concentrated on the source of his uneasiness. His eyes narrowed, and instantly their golden hue dissolved to black as an image of Coco appeared in his mind. Through his blood connection with her, he watched in real time as she reached a hand toward her most recent painting of a garden. As the pigments lifted from the canvas to reveal a scene, he understood why this particular dark shadow from his past had called to him.

A tall man wearing a cloak pushes his way through a crowd. The dome of the Cathedral of Santa Maria del Fiore is visible in the distance. Women in long dresses with puffed sleeves and full skirts accompany men wearing buckled boots and stockings tucked into velvet bloomers, worn with doublets and jackets. The tall man in the cloak makes his way to a sturdy iron gate between two stone buildings. He opens it and stares at the figure of a woman standing on her own in shadows. He walks up to her, pulls her to his chest and kisses her, then tucks her protectively under his arm. They walk to the end of the alley, stopping in front of a sturdy-looking wooden door. The man bangs his fist on the wood in a musical rhythm. The door opens, and he ushers the woman inside. In one swift movement, he lifts her into his arms and heads toward a wide stone staircase, taking the steps three at a time. On the landing, he strides along a hallway to an open door and enters a room void of light. He waves a hand, and the remains of the dead fire spring to life and flames light up the fireplace.

He lays the woman on a bed, and she grabs at his clothing. Her unbuttoned jacket reveals the flesh of her bosom and the hint of pink nipples from beneath a lace bodice. She loosens her skirt, and the man tugs it down over her hips and thighs and tosses it to the floor. He pulls at the ribbons of her bodice and watches as she runs a hand over her skin from her breasts to her mound of dark hair before tugging at the man's pants. He lifts her so she sits on his thighs, and she wraps her legs around his body and pushes back the hood from his head.

"I love you," he says.

A sharp hissing sound causes the man to turn around. It's Gabriel.

The words Coco screamed as she fell to her knees stabbed his heart like a hot dagger. *"Fuck you, Gabriel!"*

The low-toned and heavily accented voice of Pelayo drew Gabriel back to the present. "Do you sense anyone in the house, *amigo?*"

Gabriel momentarily ignored the question and fought the urge to dematerialize to the art studio and explain to Coco the truth about what she had seen. He reached for his phone. "How is this possible?" he mumbled. A hand on his shoulder instantly snapped him out of it.

"*Amigo?*" Pelayo asked. "*¿Estás bien?*"

Gabriel ran a hand through his dark hair. "No, I'm not okay!" He contemplated calling Colombina but decided that under the circumstances, it would be best to discuss in person what she had witnessed.

Returning his phone to a pocket, he focused instead on the matter at hand. Gabriel's unique magical skills derived from his mother, the seer Prudence, although where her strengths lay in the future, his lay in the past, present, and dark arts. His vampire assets were handed down from his father, Stefan Lazarevic, and because of the age of his father's maker, Gabriel's vampiric blood amplified his supernatural talents.

From where Gabriel stood in the tower of Sant'Eugenio Catholic Church, he looked out over a sea of bisque-colored, curved roof tiles. Behind him, Alessandro, Frederico, and Sabine were evaluating blueprints belonging to a particular villa owned by a group of investors involved with Kenan. The villa was barely visible behind a stone wall and a forest of trees. Gabriel agreed with Jason, the Allegiance's most recent member and Christopher's longtime friend, whose initial observations were that the villa itself might be considered on the smaller side considering the vast size of the property. However, the overgrown garden gave Kenan what he wanted: privacy. It wasn't the villa that interested the Allegiance but the ancient tunnels that ran beneath it.

Gabriel pushed his anxiety aside, ran his fingers over his aged set of runes, and tossed them into the air. "Show me the interior of the villa," he whispered. The stones froze on their descent; he closed his eyes, and the rooms of the villa emerged before him. Gabriel used his magic to remotely roam through the house, similar to exploring via a virtual-reality tour.

He began his tour in an empty attic, situated the same as it was on the blueprints. From there he wandered to the third floor, moving quickly through each room and noting that, like the attic, this floor was empty. He walked down a wide marble staircase to the next level where he found five bedrooms, each with a private bathroom. One of the bedrooms contained a king-sized bed made up with white bed linens. An archway led to a library, and Gabriel observed that most of the books looked to be leather-bound editions and well-worn. Matching plush leather armchairs and a sofa were arranged around a fireplace, and to the right were windows and a door that opened up to a terrace overlooking the Eternal City.

Gabriel exited the bedroom, returned to the marble staircase, and made his way to the ground floor. There the décor of parquet floors and dark, wood-paneled walls was in high contrast to the stark white interior of the rest of the villa. The kitchen mirrored any chef's dream, with a restaurant-sized gas stove, refrigerators, and new appliances. The entire villa looked more like it had been staged by a real estate agent rather than lived in for any period of time.

At the back of the kitchen, Gabriel found what he was looking for: a narrow spiral staircase that led to a basement. As he descended, strands of pain and death reached out to him in the form of wisps of dark, thin fingers, and the atmosphere changed from stark to dense. He searched the basement, looking for trapdoors—anything that resembled an entrance to a lower level. His search ended when he detected a strand of blond hair on the stone floor behind the stairs. He knelt and saw that the stones there were of a different age than the rest of the basement floor.

He ran a hand over the old section, stopping at one particular area where a hairline crack in the mortar between the stones breathed a story of a different kind. "Found you."

He opened his eyes, stared up at Pelayo, and acknowledged his friend's earlier question. "The villa's empty, and the entrance to the main tunnel is located behind the staircase in the basement. I don't sense any beings directly below the villa, but best to use caution—we know better than to underestimate Kenan."

Gabriel caught the runes as they fell into his waiting hand and returned all but one to his pocket. He extended an arm toward the villa and flicked the rune into the air. Seconds later the church tower sat empty.

Gabriel, Alessandro, Pelayo, Frederico, and Sabine appeared in the basement of the villa and quickly located a section of wall that acted as a façade. Frederico pulled at an edge until a part of the wall opened like a door. The immortals moved down a narrow wooden staircase, landing on solid ground a hundred feet below the basement floor. They stood in a grotto-like area about sixteen by twenty feet with walls built of small bricks and a floor of dirt and well-worn stone. Faint electric lights brought to life this part of the ancient city that lay beneath modern-day Rome. Archways framed what appeared to be an endless covered passageway made up of bricks and rocks belonging to different periods of time.

"The laser scans showed a series of rooms up ahead and to our left," Frederico said. He pointed to LED lights set into the wall every twenty feet. "The addition of electricity makes me think that vampires are not the only visitors to these parts. Perhaps the ring of conspiracy is wider than we first thought. It's not as if we immortals need light to see."

"And yet we have been blind to all this," Sabine said.

"The Holy Father found it difficult to accept that Kenan has been performing atrocities so close to his sanctuary," Gabriel said. "And that he was unaware of the depth of Kenan's debauchery."

"He consciously elected to be oblivious to Kenan's actions," Sabine said, her voice pragmatic with no sign of emotion. "The Holy Father chose ignorance over fact."

Gabriel considered Sabine's words. "Yes, that's true, and he realizes now that because of his ignorance it's as if he had slain the innocent."

"Because of his ignorance, my beloved suffered," Alessandro mumbled.

"The Holy Father had best let go of his Catholic guilt—it's a useless weight to carry." Sabine ran a hand over the old wall of the tunnel. "This is not about faith. Kenan is evil incarnate and must be killed. There's no place for religion in this war. The Holy Father needs to hang up his collar and concentrate instead on the here and now. We are at war with the devil residing in an immortal's body. However, if the god he honors would care to aid us, then now would be as good a time as any for him to step forward."

Since she'd witnessed the recent cruelty forced upon young women in the United States by Kenan and his tribe, the warrior side of Sabine's demeanor had intensified along with her unfavorable views of monotheism. Gabriel's thoughts were interrupted when he caught a ghostly ripple of fear belonging to a human deceased long ago. He looked ahead. To the left stood a thick metal gate, secured with a chain and padlock.

"Want me to break it open?" Frederico asked.

Gabriel stepped forward and shook his head. "No need." He waved a hand over the padlock, a click sounded, and he removed the lock from the chain and pushed open the gate. "I don't sense any physical beings here, only whispers from the memories of the dead. Look around, we need information—anything that might help us find him." He strode over to a corner of the room where the walls showed remnants of faded frescoes. He readied to place both hands upon a wall.

The ghostly voice of a woman called out to him. He knew her well, but the pain of this part of his personal history was something he preferred to keep buried. To have it flaunted before him twice in an hour sickened him. He waited until the others had left the room before lowering his hands onto the cold stones.

A woman appears. A tight caul made from lace and encrusted with small jewels covers her auburn hair. She addresses Kenan. "I am to meet again with Gabriel this evening."

Kenan runs a finger along the side of her face and the outline of her lips. "You have performed well, Isabella, and for your loyalty, I am happy to offer you a gift. A few drops of my blood, enough to take away the ailment of gout that has caused your family members so much suffering."

Isabella's face holds a stoic expression. "An idea to ponder, but that would not take care of what ails me."

"And what is it that ails you, my dear?"

"My husband."

Kenan waves a hand in front of his face as if flicking at an insect. "Then perhaps to seal our relationship, I can offer you my assistance in that area."

Isabella walks toward a door that opens as if beckoned. "And so, sir, when will you make good on your part of our deal?"

Kenan's lips curl into a sadistic grin. "Soon, my dear, and I look forward to giving you an end to your suffering."

Isabella exits the villa.

Kenan chuckles and watches the door close behind her. "And unbeknown to you, dear duchess, my witch has captured your passion with Prudenza's son in a web of magic." He turns and stares directly at Gabriel. "Yes, Gabriel, if not through death, then you will suffer great heartache."

Gabriel dropped his hands and clenched them into tight fists by his side. He looked up to see Pelayo staring at him.

"What did you see, *amigo*?"

"That bastard is always a step ahead of us," Gabriel said. "After he killed Domenico, he must have spent centuries alone, planning the demise of the Allegiance." He paused and shook his head. "I believe Kenan set me up to lose Colombina centuries ago."

Pelayo leaned against a wall, his arms crossed. "How's that possible?"

Alessandro appeared in the doorway. "It all comes back to that business with the duchess, doesn't it?"

"I believe so."

Alessandro motioned his head toward the tunnel. "There's a scent I'm familiar with drifting in these hallways, not only Chantal, but another from my past."

"The duchess said she'd heard mention of a seer," Gabriel said. "One who captured moments with her powers—pictures in motion. Perhaps that was the magic the old witch spoke of to the Holy Father before she died."

"What happened to this duchess?" Pelayo asked.

"Her husband murdered her," Alessandro cut in.

"She was a Medici," Gabriel continued. "And the whole scenario was a ploy to help both her and her children escape to the north. There were two women; at times, both appeared to be the duchess. One was her confidante—a brave woman named Marguerite—who vowed to keep the duchess's illegitimate son, whom she'd had with her lover, safe from those wanting to end her lineage. I wove a spell to have Marguerite appear as the duchess and the duchess appear as Marguerite."

"A twin image," Pelayo said. "Was her son saved?"

"Yes," Alessandro replied. "And so was Marguerite."

"But if that's so, then—"

"The Medici lineage is still strong," Gabriel said, interrupting Pelayo. "But I've made a grave mistake in not sharing this information with Colombina."

Alessandro frowned. "How so?"

"Because, somehow, she's seen me with Marguerite, and I can only surmise she believes I lied about her being my one true love."

"Get back to the fortress and explain the truth to her," Alessandro said.

"That's my intention," Gabriel said. "But first we need to see what's here. And the fact that you sense your family's blood is a curious circumstance. I'm guessing your heritage is the reason Colombina is more than a Creative?"

Alessandro nodded. "No doubt. But that part of my family's story remains unsolved."

CHAPTER 3

New York City, New York

SABINE POURED THE remains of a bottle of whiskey into a glass and handed it to her friend. She didn't need her preternatural senses to figure out that since witnessing the young girl jump to her death, Frances had barely slept. The dark shadows beneath her eyes told Sabine everything she needed to know. She had met Frances when she was a junior in college, where they had been introduced by one of Sabine's immortal warriors, a criminal investigative lawyer named Sam. Realizing the need for legal assistance for female victims of abuse, Sabine set up a legal office in New York.

When Frances gained her MA from the School of Journalism at City University of New York, Sabine had been quick to offer her a job researching and reporting on specific cases that resembled the gruesome work of Kenan. Frances had accepted the world of immortals with ease, and whenever possible used their traits to gather information unavailable to her. But it had been the apartment above the office that signed the deal for her. Since then, Sabine had seen to it that Frances's stories made it into major newspapers.

Sabine's cell pinged. She stared at the text. *Got something you need to see—it's regarding the young girl. On my way.*

She texted back: *Frances is out of whiskey...*

Twenty minutes later, Sabine opened the door to Sam, a petite woman dressed in a tailored two-piece skirt suit and carrying a briefcase and a brown paper bag that she promptly handed to her boss.

"I'll take mine over ice, thanks," Sam said.

Sabine grabbed a whiskey tumbler and a few cubes of ice and joined her friends in the living area. "What did you find?"

"Seems you've stumbled onto something big, Frances."

Frances drained her glass. "Meaning?"

"The young girl kept a detailed diary," Sam said. "And the police found a positive pregnancy-test indicator on her bed."

Frances rested her head on her palms. "She was pregnant?"

"Yes. Showed up in the autopsy report."

"They did an autopsy?" Frances asked. "She jumped from the fucking bridge, Sam—surely that's the cause of death!"

"She was thirteen and pregnant," Sam replied. "The autopsy also revealed she had bruising caused by forced entry... multiple times." She handed both women a couple of photocopied pages. "These are excerpts from her diary."

May: Confirmation

His hand smelled of cigarettes and it was sweaty. It covered my mouth. He told me to keep quiet. I knew who it was. I'd heard him talk every Sunday morning since we moved here about how we should be kind and help each other. He pushed me over a pew and then kicked my feet apart. I saw the tips of his shiny black shoes and my new sandals, the ones Mom bought to go with my long white dress. All I could hear was my heart thumping in my ears, I wanted to hit him. I felt sick. He lifted up my dress and pulled down my panties. It was cold in the church, I remember that. I wanted to get out of there. I wanted it to stop, like when there's a scary part of a movie and I grab the remote and hit Fast-forward. I felt dirty. I was scared. I stared up at the stained-glass window and saw Mary. I squeezed my eyes shut and grabbed the wood when the pain got too much. I wanted to hit him, but I don't think Mary would have done that. I couldn't breathe. I looked at the floor and watched the tassels from his robe go back and forth.

I don't understand.

What did I do to deserve this?

I turned twelve today…

October

I HATE my life.

I HATE him.

I HATE that I have to lie to everyone.

I HATE that my parents think he's a nice man.

I HATE the dark circles under my eyes.

January

Mom asked me why I'm always late home after religious education class, so I told her. Her face looked weird, and I was scared she was going to get really mad at me like it was my fault. But instead she said nothing. Later that night she came to my bedroom and called me Mary. I guess she means the Mother Mary, but I don't feel special or anything. I feel dirty and angry. One day I want to go to college and get out of this place. At least next year I'll be in high school, and that's one step closer to being a scientist, something else I have to hide from Mom and Dad. They would be so angry if they knew I wanted to study science. I'm sick of hiding stuff from them. I'm sick of that dirty old man doing things to me and making me feel bad.

I hate him.

May

I feel horrible. I've got stomach cramps. Mom said I don't have to go to religious studies class tonight… BEST NEWS EVER!

I turned thirteen today…

August

Two more weeks until I start eighth grade, then I'm off to high school, then college.

February

Missed my period… I HATE HIM!

Frances placed the papers on the table and poured herself another drink. Sabine sensed her push her anger and sadness aside and clear the way for logical thinking.

"What else do you have?" Frances asked.

"Something's off here," Sam replied. "And I'm pretty sure it has something to do with the figure you saw on the bridge standing beside the girl. That and the fact that the priest who presides over the church the family attended has been relocated to a church in Boston. This is his third move."

Frances opened her laptop. "So the church likely knows about this asshole's problem, but instead of calling him out, they relocate him. Let the shit settle, pray to God—literally—that his victims keep quiet and that he won't repeat his pattern of violence against children. Which he does, and so they move him again."

Sam handed her another paper with information regarding the priest.

"Thanks," Frances said. "And I have to ask, is this information from a legitimate source?"

"Of course," Sam said. "The police found the diary in the girl's bedroom; it's being held as evidence."

"So I can't use it."

"Not yet," Sam replied. "But that doesn't stop you from researching the priest, the family's connection to the church, her friends, et cetera, et cetera. It wouldn't be the first time a story like this brings other victims out of the woodwork with personal stories to tell. This is why we love this work, remember? To encourage others to tell their stories. We do the research, get solid proof, and hopefully see justice follow through."

Frances stretched her arms over her head and cracked her knuckles. "I saw this kid jump, Sam, that's all the encouragement I need to write this piece." She glanced at Sabine. "It's up to you and your warriors to find the unworldly creature I saw on the bridge. Apparently no one else saw him, so I'm guessing he's immortal. He disappeared the second she jumped. And as for that priest, well, I've no doubt you have something planned for him."

Sabine walked over to the window and regarded the street below. "You needn't be concerned about him. He'll get what he deserves."

"What else can I do to help?" Sam asked.

"See what you can find regarding the priest's previous locations," Frances said. "Complaints, pregnant teens, suicides, marriages where parental consent is needed."

"Christopher has a guy working with him. His name's Jason," Sabine said. "Kind of a nerdy numbers type. Let me know if you need specific figures and I'll ask him what he can do to help us."

"She was just a kid," Frances said.

Sabine turned to her. "Her diaries may be what's needed to bring justice to a fucked-up system."

The doorbell rang.

"I ordered pizza," Sam said. "Figured it's going to be a long night."

CHAPTER 4

**From the diary of Isabella Romola de' Medici
Florence, Italy—Summer, 1576**

I have not been well of late. My husband believes I am of weak constitution, but in truth my health suffers from the strain of hiding the many secrets of my personal, political, and financial life. At times these areas seem no longer black and white, for more than ever there is now gray in my shadow... It hovers above me like a dismal cloud. Oh, how I wish I could run away with my beloved or, better still, send those who betray this city of my forefathers, this city of life and love and artistry, and take them to a place worthy of their sins. Yes, I have sinned in the face of God, and I pay for my misdoings every moment when my beloved and I are apart. But I will never betray this city, for she is the true duchess, not me, and my love for her and her people runs in the blood of my veins.

⚘

Rome, Italy—Present Day

GABRIEL'S THOUGHTS LINGERED between his past with Marguerite and Isabella and how the consequences of his actions were affecting his present life with Coco. With any luck, the current distance between them would give her time to calm herself so that she would listen to his explanation.

He glanced again around the dingy room where he stood with Alessandro and Pelayo. As they moved farther along the underground tunnels, the essence of evil would grow thicker.

"There's more to see," Sabine said. "I suggest we keep moving and catch up with Frederico."

They followed her along a narrow passage with rooms on either side until they entered an area that contained a refrigerator, bed, and desk. At the far end of the room stood another thick wooden door. Gabriel could already hear the long-ago pleas for mercy from Colombina's mother, Chantal, seeping through the ether.

"I hear her too," Pelayo said.

Gabriel placed a hand on his friend's shoulder. "Another trait you've inherited from me, and one that is not always welcome. Anytime you're overwhelmed, focus on breathing. As cliché as that may sound, it funnels your vision and you'll find the voices will gradually disappear." He dropped his hand. "Are you ready?"

Pelayo snorted. "As ready as I'll ever be."

Sabine pulled open the thick door with ease, and immediately the air smelled of decomposing matter. Gabriel walked through the doorway and into another tunnel, one that lacked lighting.

"The devil's lair," Gabriel said. "This is where Kenan brought Chantal. I can hear her crying… hoping to talk sense to him."

"For once I'm grateful that I don't have your abilities," Alessandro said. "If I heard her cries, it would drive me insane."

They continued on, following Frederico in silence until Gabriel stopped at another door. He waved a hand and the door opened, grinding like old joints in pain from occasional use. Gabriel muttered a flurry of ancient Nordic words and a soft glow illuminated the room, revealing the source of the stench of putrefaction that saturated the dense air. On the stone floor lay a decaying human body, as if tossed aside without a second thought for the life that once was. Rats scattered away from bones and rotting flesh, disappearing through a nearby crack in the rocks.

Gabriel surveyed the room while Frederico and Sabine shoved a single bed away from a wall.

"According to the schematic, there's another door here," Frederico said.

Sabine kicked at the stones, ran her hands upward from the floor, and stopped momentarily. She turned to Gabriel. "As much as I'd like to kick this door down, perhaps a less aggressive way would be best."

Gabriel gave Pelayo a confident nod.

Pelayo held his hands in front of his torso with his palms facing the wall. *"Abierto!"* A section of the wall—about two feet by five feet—slowly slid back. He extended his right hand toward the chasm of darkness. *"El toque de luz."* Light flooded into the gloom.

Frederico stooped down and stepped through the doorway, offering a hand to Sabine.

She smiled at the gesture and accepted his hand. "Your chivalry does not go unnoticed and is always appreciated."

The corners of Frederico's mouth turned upward.

The group of immortals stood on a landing at the top of a steep and narrow stone stairway, bordered by high walls that formed an arched ceiling. With Gabriel in the lead, they hastened down the stairs and proceeded along a tunnel that had been carved from volcanic rock. Here the atmosphere thickened, marred not only by Kenan's aura but also the dark and sinister persona of Domenico. There was another too, but Gabriel could not place the scent. He wondered if it belonged to the devil's first victim, Vinicio.

Up ahead, the tunnel funneled out into a cavernous space with arches leading into various rooms. He approached Sabine. "I know what I sense. But before we search this area, I'd appreciate your logic and wisdom. What can you tell me about this place?"

Sabine surveyed the subterranean area and walked over to a wall where an image lay buried under years of dirt. She blew dust from the wall, and a faded fresco emerged that told a story of an ancient time. Gabriel stepped closer and examined the scene.

"As a young woman, I once visited what is now known as the Tunnel of Wonders and marveled at the intricate mosaics depicting Apollo and the Muses." She turned to Gabriel. "It's difficult to remember exact years, but I recall my visit coinciding with the death of Tiberius."

"Around 37 AD," he said.

"Yes, that seems about right," she said. "There were whispers of the new god, although it would be a while before Christianity became more than its original intention, which was a group of people helping those less fortunate. I'd heard rumors of a sadistic cult with followers here in Rome. It was said they worshipped a daemon. Some believed that worshipping such a being was a step toward higher consciousness."

She traced a finger over the frescoed wall and stopped at an image of a man holding a blade above a young woman. "A sacrificial act, the taking of life. And see here? A stream of blood disappears through a crack in the rocks until it flows into an underground river." She studied the entire fresco. "This is an evil place. We can only be thankful that it was hidden from the general public. The devil spent centuries devising his plan, waiting for the manifestation of greed and power to corrupt the Catholic Church. He waited and watched while an innocent woman—a woman who gave her life to God—was raped by a man whom she and others believed to be of the highest order."

"The devil stepped in, and his charade began," Alessandro said. "Fuck knows how many other women he tormented before Beatrice became his earthly tool."

"She was deceived by the church she loved," Sabine said. "Then offered unimaginable power to hold the devil's fate in her hands. Everything was so well planned."

"There must be something here that'll help us get one step ahead of him," Gabriel said. He looked across at Pelayo and Frederico. "Search every corner of this place. If we're correct and this has been the devil's hideout for millennia, we'll find something."

The two vampires headed for the rooms leading off the main part of the cave.

Alessandro stared at the wall. "My grandmother was a seer. It's from her I inherited the flecks of amethyst in my eyes."

"You spoke of her years ago," Gabriel said. "What happened to her?"

Alessandro shook his head. "She disappeared. Some say it was the devil who stole her, for only he was her equal in power. I said earlier that I sense the blood of my family here—what if she's the one who guided Kenan to Chantal?"

"The past is gone. Chantal and Coco are safe," Sabine said. "You are good and kind, Alessandro, and so was your mother. If there's something on these walls to enlighten us to Kenan's whereabouts then no matter how we're linked—through good or evil—we must endure."

He pressed his lips together and gave her a quick nod.

Gabriel tossed a rune into the air, and it froze in front of the wall. Years of dirt and dust fell away to reveal a series of haunting images. "The devil's story," he said, taking in the timeline before him. He observed every figure and concept laid out on the wall and stopped when he saw the name Benedict followed by the numbers IX. Underneath the name were images of rape, bestiality, and murder. "Benedict IX."

"Known as the demon from hell," Alessandro said. "One of many corrupt individuals to acquire the chair of the pope. Perhaps such men were driven to heinous acts through mental torment by the devil himself, or maybe he just urged them to live out their darkest thoughts—"

"Either way is wrong!" Sabine cut in. "We all experience dark thoughts, but most of us have a strong moral compass that allows us to keep our dark side under control. Benedict IX had no morals."

Sabine and Alessandro walked beside Gabriel, stopping at a place where the word Primus had been written above the image of a beach. The sky appeared a wash of black and gray, and white-tipped waves were captured as they gathered momentum, ready to crash with fury onto the sand. In the foreground, two men had been immortalized in the throes of sexual relations. Another painting showed a close-up of the couple: one male appeared to be an adolescent, the other in his midthirties. The next image showed the young boy laid out on the ground—a pool of blood seeped from a gash in his neck. Beside him, the older man held a dagger covered in blood, his face twisted in pain.

Gabriel took stock of the next scene. The older man lay beside the boy, one hand clutching the boy's wrist, the other on the handle of a blade that stuck out from his own chest. Gabriel's gaze lingered over the portrait of death. He held out a hand toward the image, which began moving like a clip from an old movie.

A dark shadow hovers at the side of the slain man; the dagger in his chest is removed by an invisible force. The bloody wound magically heals. Gradually, color returns to the dead man's face, and with a rattling gasp he inhales. The dark shadow seeps into the man's flesh like dye into cotton. The man pushes himself up, and when he opens his eyes they are flooded with blood. His lips draw back in a snarl. "From bloodstained fields I shall rise," he says. "For I am Vinicio."

Gabriel lowered his hand. "One would think he's been expecting us."

"*Merde!*" Alessandro said.

Gabriel pointed to the first image of the couple on the beach. "See this rocky outcrop?"

Sabine looked at the scene. "It could be anywhere."

"No," he said. "My bet is it's somewhere near this villa. Jason's fairly sure Kenan's money trail has ties to an abandoned monastery on the coast of Lazio. According to Freyja, that particular part of Lazio is where she last saw Kenan while she was in her human form as Ravinka." He took out his phone and took multiple photos of the image and forwarded them to Jason, asking him to look for a geographical match along the coast of Lazio. He slipped his cell into a pocket and returned his focus to the next part of the wall. The word Secundus told another story.

The scene revealed hundreds of men lying dead on a blood-soaked battlefield, some with lances and swords still clutched in their hands. Horses with open wounds, arrows in chests, men with sun-baked skin and heads wrapped in fabric, their dark eyes pained with death. Others wore the surcoat of crusaders. Among the scene of war stood a pale-faced man dressed in a white cape bearing the red cross of the Knights Templar. At his feet lay the man from the previous fresco, a blade protruding from his chest. Gabriel stretched a hand toward the image, sickened with the truth he was about to unveil.

The warrior stares at the dying Vinicio and watches while the vampire's face changes into that of a human: the color of his eyes turn from black to blue, and a tinge of color blossoms on his cheeks.

He smiles up at the warrior who had struck him with the blade. "Domenico… you discovered my witch," he says. "I taught you too well. But you must find your own witch to take over the cave of our doom. For mine is nearing the end of her time."

"How is this possible?" Domenico staggers back. "I killed you!"

"You freed me of the demon… Now he dwells in you."

"No!" Domenico screams. "I killed you so I may be my own master!"

"Go to Rome—your answers are in my journals." Vinicio's head rolls to the side and blood runs from his open mouth.

Domenico buckles over. He stumbles toward his horse, mounts, and falls forward, grabbing the animal's mane as it gallops across the battlefield.

Another figure caught Gabriel's attention.

At the edge of the field is a man on horseback. The rider surveys the carnage. He turns his horse and rides away.

Gabriel dropped his hand and stared back at the wall. "*Secundus*—this was Domenico."

Alessandro cursed. "A crusader, no less."

"My grandfather may have been there," Gabriel said. "When I was a young boy, Prudence told me that upon seeing the carnage after one of the battles of the Holy Wars, Nikandros shelved his life as a warrior and lived for many years as a recluse. For a while he sought refuge at the fortress, burying himself in the writings of the Greek philosophers. Later, when his heart was able to appreciate things of beauty, Prudence introduced him to the gallery of art that the Allegiance saved from destruction. In time he left Casa della Pietra and returned to the country of his birth, promising to repay my mother for her kindness. She explained that in the future there would be a time when she would reach out to him. That happened later, when she had the premonition of my father's death." He looked at Sabine, whose expression had saddened. "What is it?"

"Do you think Nikandros knew what happened that day?" she asked.

Alessandro placed a hand on her back. "That's a question for Nikandros." A ripple of air made him reach for his sword.

Nikandros appeared before him. "There's no need for your sword,

Alessandro. The others have returned from Tuscany, and Prudence urged me to join you here. She said there is something I need to see."

Alessandro sheathed his sword.

Nikandros stepped closer to the frescoed wall and stared at the image of carnage. "I remember this day well, for it was the last time I joined people who used the name of God as their war cry. This was a fierce battle that took the lives of many great warriors." He shook his head. "And unbeknown to me, among the carnage lay Vinicio and Domenico."

Gabriel laid a hand on his shoulder. "Grandfather, I think Kenan knows we're here and there's more to see. Best we do this quickly."

Nikandros nodded.

The next image showed a man dressed in a robe embellished with embroidery and medallions, standing over a woman whose habit and scapular were ripped. Her face was bloody, her chemise pushed up over her buttocks. With his hand clutching her red hair, the man stood between her legs, his robe parted at the front. His corpulent flesh fell in folds over her bruised skin. In the corner of the room, men in priestly robes stood together, their heads lowered, holding the jewelry and garments of the holy man. One young priest stood out from the others.

Gabriel placed a hand over the image, and the scene came to life.

The priests watch as the cardinal rapes the red-haired nun. Her screams are masked by church bells announcing mass. One of the priests lowers his eyes and clutches the cross that hangs from his waist; it's the Holy Father.

Sabine was the first to break the silence. "The Holy Father confessed to me what happened that day. He said, 'It seemed the devil had penned a play, and we were all players. And dear Beatrice, who gave up her earthly possessions—a chance of ever being loved—was raped by not only the cardinal but also the church.' He also admitted that after witnessing the cruelty the cardinal had inflicted upon her, he felt he had no right to question why she accepted the devil's gifts, for Beatrice was already living a life of hell."

The immortals were silent.

Alessandro walked to another part of the wall. He knelt and brushed away dirt that had piled up in a corner, beneath which he found a paintbrush. "My grandmother was a Creative and the daughter of a prominent seer." He looked at Gabriel. "Could it be that it was Domenico who stole her? Can you tell if she painted these images?"

Gabriel picked up the paintbrush and placed his other hand on the painting on the wall. An image sprang to life.

> *Kenan stands over a woman with long, silver hair.*
>
> *The woman speaks slowly. "Gabriel will find great love. But trickery will bring deceit and destruction to the relationship. The deceit will take root soon... in the city of the artists."*
>
> *"Florence?" Kenan asks.*
>
> *"I see them together... He is bedded with her." She gasps. Her head falls back against a stone wall.*
>
> *Kenan yanks her up and turns her so she's facing the wall. "Show me!"*
>
> *The seer reluctantly accepts the brush and palette from Kenan and paints. A familiar bedroom scene emerges.*

Alessandro hung his head. "It was Domenico who took her. He forced her to betray us all."

"He would have used the threat of death to her loved ones to force information from her," Nikandros said. He placed a hand under Alessandro's elbow and hoisted him to his feet. "I'm sure there's more to her story. Sometimes what parents do to protect their children and loved ones can appear cruel, but it has been my experience that often what seems cruel or unkind at the time is later realized to be love." He shared a momentary glance of tenderness with Sabine.

Pelayo entered, carrying an armful of books. He handed one

to Gabriel. "This is one of many. There are three sets. I'm guessing each was written by one of the three different incarnations: Vinicio, Domenico, and Kenan."

Gabriel opened the book and regarded the first page, then handed it to Nikandros.

"Are they all written in Latin?" the ancient immortal asked.

"Yes," Pelayo said.

"We'll take these back to the fortress and analyze every page." Gabriel returned his gaze to the frescoed walls. "Kenan knows we're here."

Nikandros placed a hand upon Gabriel's arm. "Have you seen anything regarding the death of Prudence's friend, Birgit?"

"No," Gabriel replied. "However, if you feel it's important, I can cast a spell and see if there's anything of her essence dwelling in this place."

A quick nod from Nikandros gave Gabriel his answer. He walked to the center of the cave and tossed his runes into the air. The aged, flat stones formed a circle before him. "Odin," Gabriel whispered. In answer to his call, a stone without a symbol drifted to the center of the circle—the Unknowable rune, the rune of the Divine.

"I seek the essence of the great seer Birgit." A sharp gust of air shot through Gabriel's body. He steadied himself and raised his left hand. Upon the wall before him, a scene appeared…

A woman with white hair and striking blue eyes lies on a floor. She is naked. Her face and body are marked with open wounds and bruises. The stones beneath her are stained with blood.

Domenico stands at her side. Blood drips from his mouth. "What spell did you cast over your daughter?" He grabs her hair and yanks her up off the floor. "There are rumors of a ghostly woman around these parts. She fits the image of your delicious daughter, Illona… I heard you whisper her name."

"My daughter is dead…"

Domenico snarls. His fangs descend. He tears into Birgit's neck, ripping open her jugular vein. His head falls back and he licks his lips. He draws a sword and in one clean swipe, Birgit's head falls to the floor. He sheaths his sword and stares up at the strange twin image drawn on the stone wall.

"Brother and sister… I must find Illona's brother and kill him too." He yanks open the cell door and shouts orders to a guard. "Burn her body!"

Gabriel lowered his arm, and the runes fell into his open palm. "Birgit sacrificed herself so her daughter and son would live." He turned to Nikandros. "You knew her."

Nikandros stared at the wall with a calculating expression. "Yes, and apart from me, she was your mother's dearest friend. When the time is right, I'll tell Prudence what happened."

"I understand," Gabriel said.

"We must leave here." Sabine gathered a stack of books in her arms. "There's work to be done."

Chapter 5

Tuscany, Italy—Present Day

PRUDENCE, THE MATRIARCH of the Allegiance, surveyed the area around her. A canopy of trees hid the place well, and unless one knew a cave stood just a few feet away, they would have no reason to linger. She heard the crunching of leaves under deer hooves on a nearby blanket of vegetation, but the animals' sharp senses had alerted them to the arrival of vampires, and with that knowledge, they fled the area. The robust smell of rotting compost thickened the air, clinging to Prudence's sleek white hair, which framed her ethereal beauty and fell in locks of starlight over the satin of her floor-length silver gown. She shivered, not so much from the chill of predawn but from the obscurity of light and goodness.

Whispers of devilry reached out as if woken by the allure of the supernatural. Spirits hissed curses at her as she followed the Holy Father through a thick curtain of overgrowth steeped with the acrid smell of decay. Hakon, Sonja, and Stefan had insisted on accompanying her, and Prudence had not fought their wishes, for now as the stagnant air became tinged with dark magic, she knew her father— the fae prince, Hakon—would be apt at unraveling spells cast by the deceased witch. For it was the witch who had helped the devil enter the bodies of three men, the latest of which was Kenan. Prudence maneuvered her slender body forward and through the low entrance, straightening to her full height upon entering the cave.

As the darkness clamped down upon her, she fought the compulsion to run, to be far away from this place of evil. Her mother, Sonja—the great Nordic seer—stood at her left, her delicate white hair drawn back from her face in a braid that fell to her waist. The softness of her mother's hand grasped Prudence's fingers.

"Running away is not an option," Sonja said. "We'll confront this darkness together."

"*Lys,*" Hakon said. No sooner had the word left his lips than an eerie glow radiated from his palms, spreading throughout the cavern and bringing the witch's lair to life.

Stefan and the Holy Father stood with swords drawn and ready in case Kenan had decided to return to this place, and although nothing gave rise to another immortal or human close by, they strode across the dirt floor, checking the smaller antechambers that were situated around the outer rim of the cavern.

Sonja released her tight grip on Prudence's fingers. "There are no other creatures here," Prudence said. She wandered over to a fire pit in the center of the cave. Picking up a handful of cold coals, she watched as the fine dust slipped through her fingers. "This is where the witch held her strength, her youthful persona."

"From ashes scorched with evil, she will rise in all her beauty and strength," Stefan said. He turned to Prudence. "It may be advantageous to keep a small portion of this dust from the coals."

Prudence stared into the fire, and an image of Gabriel popped into her mind. She smiled at Stefan. "Yes, my love, I agree." In her hand appeared a leather pouch. She gathered a handful of ashes, placed them inside, and tied the pouch to her waist, then rose and turned her attention to an outcrop of stone where yellowed papers lay in disarray among pieces of animal bones and fur. She walked over, brushing a hand across her nose as the stench of carrion became stronger than the already fetid air. But the color drained from her face when another scent caught her attention.

The Holy Father stood beside her and stared past the rotting carcasses to three vials balanced on a cloth of black velvet. "These vials contain the blood of the three men the devil embodied. With each incarnation, his strength has multiplied, and now, with Kenan as his instrument, his capacity for destruction has grown infinitely stronger."

Hakon joined Prudence. He picked up each vial individually, held them in his hand for a moment, and then returned them to the velvet. "Kenan's story differs from the two victims before him. He came to the witch, hoping to destroy Domenico because he had fallen in love. He wanted to end his tortured life as Domenico's attendant, to start a new life with Ravinka. Domenico craved absolute power. Love is Kenan's weakness. He changed over to the devil incarnate with one thought—his beloved Ravinka." He walked over to Sonja and caught hold of her hand. "Humans speak so often of love overcoming evil, but we have only to look at events in history to know that is not always the case, and it was not true of Kenan's fate."

Stefan sheathed his sword. "You speak with unsurpassed knowledge, Hakon, but like the Holy Father and Kenan, I was once human, and even in the midst of war, it was love that powered my sword. Love for my people and my country. I would not have chosen this life had I not fallen deeply in love with Prudence." He eyed the vials. "But I agree that all men have a weakness, and everything points to Kenan's weakness being Ravinka."

Hakon nodded. "And yet Freyja said she is certain that not one memory of her as a mortal remains within Kenan's mind."

"She sensed nothing?" Stefan asked. "Not one thread of his love for Ravinka?"

Hakon shook his head. "Only darkness and hatred. No one has escaped the devil's fury."

"Perhaps someone did escape," Prudence said. She glanced at her father, whose golden eyes mirrored her own. "Someone I once thought of as dead has begun to surface in my dreams. And as I stand here, I am able to perceive the part she has played in all this. You see, Gabriel and I knew that someone outside the Allegiance had done an excess amount of work to cover up the birth of the twins—to separate Arianna from her mother and twin brother Jeremy—and leave no trace of her adoption." She paused for a moment, and a hint of a smile touched her lips. "There is only one who would care about the fate of Arianna and Jeremy as much as their parents, Elion and Katja, and I believe it is Nikandros who can lead me to her."

Sonja closed her eyes. "You speak of Elion's sister… She has two faces: one is Illona, the other she holds secret." Her eyes fluttered open and she turned to Prudence. "She's waiting for you."

"It is imperative that we find her," Prudence said. "She may be the only magical creature to have escaped Kenan's clutches. How she pulled off such a feat is valuable information."

"Whatever your plan, Prudence," the Holy Father said, "I made a vow that we would destroy the objects in this place."

"Yes, of course, that is my intention." She took in the sight of the cave. "I need every object in this place, no matter how trivial it may seem. Bring everything to the fire pit."

"And what of the vials of blood?" the Holy Father asked.

"Have you done as the witch ordered and dipped the tip of the hallowed blade into all three vials?" Prudence asked.

"Yes, it's done."

"Then the vials must also be destroyed, for they hold only darkness. We have only one chance of destroying the evil within Kenan. We must not falter."

The Holy Father joined Stefan and Hakon as they gathered whatever items they could find and brought them to Prudence. She held her hands above the cold ashes and repeated ancient Nordic words until a spark appeared and grew into glowing embers. She nodded to Sonja, who tossed pieces of animal hides, bone, bedding, and cooking utensils into the burning blaze. The flames reached out, pulling each item into the heart of the fire as if it welcomed death. Smoke curled like gnarled fingers as each timepiece of the witch's life spat and gurgled its final cries.

The Holy Father laid a set of leather-bound journals on the ground at Prudence's feet. "They are her diaries," he said. "Must we destroy them too? I need to know her story."

"These books are more than the witch's diaries," Hakon said. "They are her grimoire, pages filled with spells and curses. Allow me to pull her story from the pages and share them with you later. We cannot afford to waste time, and I feel the witch's aura beckoning us to finish this." He studied Prudence. "I know you can feel the darkness bound within the pages—do not let sentiment blur your thoughts."

It was then that Prudence saw in her father the strength and wisdom that was his birthright. He stood in the uniform of an elfin warrior, carrying his sword with its hilt emblazoned with the rune *teiwaz*. She placed the first grimoire on her palms and watched as he held a hand a few inches above the aged leather. A small, crystalline clear ball appeared and hovered between the book and Hakon's palm. A stream of illumination flowed from the book into the ball. When the light disappeared, Hakon nodded to Prudence, who tossed the grimoire into the flames. She repeated the act until every volume had turned to ashes.

As the flames softened, Prudence walked over to the rock out-cropping and took the vials, wrapped them in the black velvet, and returned to the fire. Together with Hakon, Sonja, Stefan, and the Holy Father, she stood in a circle around the fire pit.

"If you wish to say a prayer over the souls of these three men, Holy Father, then so be it." She tossed the vials into the flames, and screams for mercy shattered the silence before dissipating.

The Holy Father pulled a small bible from his robes. "In the name of God, the merciful Father, we commit the blood of your three sons to the peace of the grave. From dust you came, and to dust you shall return. Jesus Christ, our Savior, is the resurrection and the life. *In nomine et Filii et Spiritus Sancti.* Amen."

The flames rose, hissed, and died, leaving the ashes cold, just as they had been when the group first entered the cave. Prudence and Sonja circled the interior of the cave, walking in opposite directions, making sure not one strand of the witch's magic lingered.

When they were finished, the group exited the cave, and Prudence waved a hand across the entrance. "Be at peace, dear Beatrice."

The fissure closed, and vines crept over the rocks until all traces of the witch's lair vanished. Mist surrounded the group of immortals, and moments later they disappeared.

CHAPTER 6

Italian Coast

A GLASS FELL FROM Kenan's hand and shattered on the terra-cotta tiles. He dropped to his knees, ripped open his dark gray shirt to free his chest, and watched as the small white buttons tumbled in slow motion through the air and bounced across the floor. Heat rushed through his veins like flames of Greek fire. He gagged on old blood that rose in his throat and wiped a hand across his lips. His hand had swollen, the pink skin blistered and withered to a blackened clawlike appendage.

"What magic is this, Prudenza?" he sputtered through cracked lips before he collapsed, his face smashing into shards of glass.

He awoke in darkness.

Heavy rain pounded on the terrace, and long silk curtains fought with the wind as it broke through the half-opened doors, bringing the storm inside. Kenan raised his head off the floor and surveyed the area around him. He remembered the broken glass and intense burning sensation that had caused him to pass out. Pushing himself off the floor, he strode over to the doors, slammed them closed, and returned some semblance of peace to the room.

He held his hands out in front of his body, checking to make sure they no longer resembled blackened claws. Vanity caused him to run a hand over his face, knowing full well the glass that had pierced his skin had disappeared. Next, he retrieved his cell and sent a text.

Shortly after, two young men—one a vampire, one human—entered. The human knelt before him, pushed back his hair, and exposed his pulsing jugular vein. Kenan hauled him to his feet and sank his fangs into his neck. When Kenan had fed, the attending vampire hoisted the unconscious human over his shoulder and exited.

Kenan surveyed the room. The spilled wine and broken glass were gone. A shadow passed to his side, and he turned toward it but saw nothing. He bolted across the room and into a large en suite bathroom where he stripped naked and stood under a steaming hot shower.

He contemplated his anxiety and questioned a sudden yearning to be on the beach near the ruins of Domenico's ancient villa in Lazio. The sensation was not one he had experienced recently, and as such, he pushed it away, turned the faucet to cold, and returned his attention to destroying Coco and Gabriel's relationship. Which, in turn, would bring about the collapse of the Allegiance.

The Creative, Coco, was a weak victim. One glimpse of her dear, beloved Gabriel in the throes of passion with another woman and she had been putty in Kenan's hands. He had felt her anger, so immature and expected. As yet, she had not sensed him taunting her in her dreams. He sneered at how easy it had been to corrupt her love and could only imagine the anger brewing within Gabriel's soul. He wished he could access Coco more easily, away from her paintings and dreams. But soon she would come to him and willingly do as he asked.

Another sudden urge to be in Lazio purged his thoughts, and this time he could not ignore it. He turned off the shower, dressed, and made his way to the basement.

Driving was not something Kenan often chose to do, but there were times when the act itself distracted him and allowed him time to revisit memories, of which there were far too many. He wove in and out of the Livorno traffic on his MV Agusta F4 1000 R with the precision of a Grand Prix driver, noting the similarities between riding this machine and riding his favorite stallion, Barios. Both emoted a sense of power and freedom. Kenan glanced at the side mirror and merged from the SS1 and onto the E80 highway. Seeing the absence of cars, he switched gears and headed south to Lazio.

Tonight his body did not crave lust but rather the sting of salt from the ocean, along with the only place on the planet that gave him a sense of solace. But he would need to be wary, for he did not doubt that the Allegiance would be searching through records to find him. No matter, there were a few places they would never discover, places he meticulously kept hidden.

When he found who it was who had guided them to his place in Rome, he would take great joy in personally overseeing their elimination. Unfortunately, he had not had time to remove the journals from his underground library, and now the Holy Father would have insight into his past. The thought of their next confrontation sent a rush of excitement throughout his body.

Remembering his private library and journals brought forth the memory of one of his so-called tools of the trade. Each incarnation before him had kept a seer prisoner, threatening to kill her family and friends if the woman did not share her visions. Kenan had inherited Domenico's seer and for centuries had kept her hanging between life and death. The seer's perceptions of the geographical changes in the areas where his previous incarnations had owned property had made it easy for him to stay hidden for so many years. During that period, he read through the journals, memorizing Vinicio's and Domenico's strengths and weaknesses and the assets they had gathered across Europe.

As explorers forged into new worlds, Kenan had been quick to purchase property using alternate names, and thanks to the foresight of his seer, the land had proved to be valuable real estate. He kept her with him in his underground hideout in Rome, and because of the violet tinge to her eyes, he had provided her with brushes and paint. Like those before her, she had frescoed the walls with mirror images of her visions, giving clarity to Kenan when she seemed overcome with emotion and could not speak. He remembered her words after the death of the second Cosimo di Medici.

Florence, 1574

"GABRIEL WILL FIND great love, but trickery will bring deceit and destruction to the relationship," the seer said. Her eyes closed, and her breathing grew erratic. "The deceit will take root in the city of the artists."

"Florence?" Kenan asked.

"I see them together," she continued. "He is bedded with her." She gasped, and her head fell back against the stone wall that encircled the main cave of Kenan's underground quarters in Rome.

He yanked her up and spun her around so she faced the wall. "Show me!"

Her eyes sprang open. She reluctantly accepted the brush and palette from Kenan and began to paint. As Kenan watched a bedroom scene emerge on the wall, he knew that the offer of eternal youth was not something the familiar woman in the painting could refuse. Vanity was her downfall. In time, Kenan sent one of his men to deliver a message to her.

The following day, the duchess arrived at Kenan's villa, and although at first she was reluctant to believe what a stranger was telling her, all it took was a few words about her indiscretions—information Kenan drew from his seer—and the famous beauty of Florence could not refuse him.

As the days progressed, Kenan's captive seer shared with him the news that Gabriel and the duchess had fallen in love with each other. His plans were set. And so, once more, Kenan met with the duchess.

This time he offered her an exchange for the knowledge she shared; a few drops of his blood, enough to take away her fear of suffering from her family's ailment of gout and early death.

He remembered their final conversation.

"And so, sir, when will you make good on your part of our deal?"

"Soon, my dear, and I look forward to giving you an end to your suffering." He waved her off, and with a swish of her skirt, she exited his villa.

"Eternal health in exchange for my indiscretions," the duchess whispered as she exited the villa, shaking her head and slipping her hands into her gloves.

Kenan's mouth turned into a sadistic grin as the image of her final moments drifted into his memory.

The duchess walked toward her husband, stopping when she realized they were not alone. She gasped, but a hand over her mouth quickly shrouded her screams. Her gaze went from her husband, who was approaching her with madness in his eyes, to the figure of Kenan standing in the shadows.

Upon the duchess's death, the duke—in his madness—had happily agreed to whatever he could do to support Kenan in his endeavors. Kenan left the estate and headed for Rome. He hurried along the tunnel and unlocked the door leading to his private quarters.

Next Kenan questioned the seer, demanding to know when Gabriel would receive news of the duchess's death and return to Florence. He asked when Gabriel would be alone, away from members of the Allegiance, so that he would be easy prey. But the seer shook her head; all threats of killing her family and friends were useless as she feigned that her kin were long gone. She refused to give Kenan further information and begged that he release her from his hold.

"Tell me!" he ordered, wrenching her arms behind her back until her screams told him her shoulders were dislocated.

"I have nothing more to say."

Kenan's anger exploded. He grabbed her hair, yanked back her head, and sank his fangs into her vein, drinking until every last drop of her lifeblood was gone.

❦

A car sped by, bringing Kenan back from his past. He thought of Gabriel scrutinizing his underground quarters. He would have enjoyed seeing the shock on the immortal's face when he realized it had been the seer who had orchestrated Kenan's shrewd actions with the duchess. Kenan knew he would need to be careful while enacting the rest of his plan to destroy the Allegiance. He remembered the pain he had suffered last night—the burning sensation that coursed through his veins. *Prudenza will pay for the part she's played in wanting me destroyed. Yes, Prudenza and every woman who chooses to defy the rules laid down by men of God.*

His thoughts turned to a set of amethyst eyes that burned his memory. *And that fucking whore of a woman who calls herself my daughter—Flora, born to a Creative—she'll die too. I'll kill her myself!*

He downshifted and veered onto the coastal road. An hour later he drove up a narrow, steep dirt road that ended at a tall stone wall and a thick wooden gate. Kenan pulled up to the gate and turned to a face-recognition panel. The gate opened, and he continued up a long driveway until he came to what appeared to be an outcropping of large boulders. On his approach, they slid across to reveal a dimly lit garage area, immaculate in appearance. He parked the bike, turned off the ignition, and lifted the helmet off his head.

Soon. Soon his plans would come to fruition.

CHAPTER 7

From the diary of Isabella Romola de' Medici
Florence, Italy—Summer, 1576

Once again, I have managed to sell pieces of my jewelry, this time to pay for the children's care and the heavy debt my husband has incurred with his life of debauchery in the city of sin. My trust in the members of my household grows thin, and I sense that Paolo has spies watching my every move, as does my coldhearted brother, Francesco. This does little to calm my frazzled nerves. I had hoped to gather all my children and flee with my beloved to France where we would live under the protection of Cathérine de' Medici. But I cannot do this on my own, and it is this challenge I ponder as I hold my sweet newborn son in my arms. Soon I will have to let him go, and that thought stabs my heart. I marvel that even at birth this little babe resembles his handsome father.

Present Day: Florida

HELEN MCCARTHY SET the plastic indicator on the bedside table and hugged her knees to her chest. She had known before she bought the test that she was pregnant. This was not her first child.

She caught a memory as it flickered by; blowing out candles on a birthday cake, all eleven of them with just one breath. Her first confirmation class had followed shortly after. That night, Helen had been the last to leave, or so she thought.

She would never forget the agony of his intrusion.

His breath smelled like her parents' when they returned to the pew after communion. His hands were rough and large—she remembered that about him because one of his hands had covered her entire face, and his palm in her mouth made her gag. He told her not to tell anyone or something terrible would happen to her cat.

Running home, a hot shower, pain, blood.

Puberty had come early for her; swollen breasts and pubic hair were not the only events to mark the end of her childhood as she knew it. Months later, when she could no longer hold down food and the blood of her periods ceased to flow, and her belly swelled with new life, her mother finally sought out the family doctor. Her parents told her she was pregnant, then they went to the church, and unbeknown to her, a decision about her future was made.

Her eyes brimmed with tears as she remembered her wedding day…

From somewhere beyond her secret place—the place of puppies, her happy space—the young girl heard a man say her name. The image of puppies instantly dissolved, replaced by something that frightened her even more than the strange things happening to her body—her growing tummy; feeling sick; the strange looks people threw her way, people she didn't know, even her friends.

The old man standing beside her grabbed her hand; she hated when he did that. She reacted as she always did; she did nothing. She didn't care about the pretty white dress her mother had made her wear, and she hated the way her hair looked, piled high above her head like scoops of vanilla ice cream. Her mother told her the dress and the hair and makeup made her look elegant, but Helen didn't want to look that way.

The priest standing in front of her had told her to say something; she did what he asked and repeated his words although they had no meaning. The man who made her scared put his lips on hers, and she wanted to throw up all over her white dress. She had always thought of this man as a bad person, but her parents told her he would take care of her. She couldn't hold back her tears anymore.

"Why are you crying?" the priest asked. "This is a happy day."

She looked at the uncomfortable shoes her mother had made her wear and shrugged her shoulders. She didn't feel happy.

Earlier that morning her mother had taken her belongings from her bedroom and stuffed them in two boxes and a suitcase, then explained that from now on she would be living in the man's house. But how long would that be? Her mother's words made no sense. Why would her parents make her leave her home? Helen loved her bedroom, it was her hideout, the one place the bad man didn't enter.

As she was leaving her bedroom, she noticed that her favorite stuffed animal still sat on her bed. She grabbed the long-eared fluffy puppy and carried it to the car, but her parents told her she couldn't take it into the church, so she refused to leave. Only after her mother put her precious stuffed puppy in the suitcase with her other belongings did she agree to get in the back seat. But now, with the wicked man's lips on hers, she wished she had run away.

He said something to the priest, grabbed her hand, and pulled her down the aisle. Helen spotted her mother and looked at her with pleading eyes, and for a split second, she thought she saw a tear roll down her face. But then she was in his car, so were her suitcase and boxes. He drove down the road near her school, and that made her think of her friends; they'd be in math class now. She didn't like missing classes, especially math, even though she hated it—she wanted to pass with a good grade before she entered high school.

"I've saved you from that hellhole," said the bad man. He looked across at her, lifted his right hand from the steering wheel, and rested it on her thigh. His hand felt hot and damp even through her dress. "I'll teach you the stuff 'at's important."

As he drove by the school, Helen looked at the buildings and the parking lot and the soccer field. "But I like school," she said. "Why would I leave?"

He patted her stomach, and she worried that his hands would dip farther, between her thighs. "You're mine now. You're gonna have my babies, clean my house, and cook me food. Well, there's more too, but I'll give you a taste of that a little later." He pulled the car into a driveway and turned off the ignition. "Welcome to your new home."

Helen stared at the double-wide, the dried-up garden, the overflowing trash can, the boxes of empty beer cans. The man handed her the suitcase and hoisted the two boxes under his arms, dumping them at the side of the trailer, close to the trash can. She followed him along the side of the trailer to a barren backyard bordered by a chainlink fence, up a couple of steps and through a squeaky screen door. She stood in a kitchen that smelled of burned cheese. Dirty dishes were stacked on the sink with hardened bits of gravy stuck to plates.

Her hand flew to her mouth. "Bathroom," she said. The sour taste of vomit tainted her mouth.

He pointed to a door at the end of a hallway. She ran to the bathroom, closed the door behind her. Another smell lingered, but she pushed that away, lifted the toilet seat, and vomited. When she had emptied her stomach, she flushed away her breakfast and took a moment to look around. A wet towel hung over the side of the bathtub, another lay on the floor. A razor, like the one her dad used, sat on the sink next to a can of shaving cream. On the floor next to the toilet, she noticed a magazine. She picked it up and stared at the glossy images that filled the pages. Naked women and men, a woman with her legs open wide and another woman kissing her.

The door opened. She dropped the magazine.

The man stood over her with a weird grin on his face. His gaze moved from the magazine and over her dress to her face. "I'm goin' out. Have the house clean when I get back. Maybe I'll bring home a new magazine." As he walked away, his abrasive laugh left her chilled.

Helen studied the image in the mirror, hardly recognizing herself. She understood now why her mother had insisted on putting makeup on her face—she appeared older, like a grown woman on her wedding day, not a young schoolgirl barely in her teens. She walked out of the bathroom, looked around the run-down, dirty trailer that was now her new home, found her case and a bedroom, and began unpacking. She hung up her white wedding dress and swore that one day she'd burn it, but for now she had to clean the house. She was well acquainted with the force of the wicked man's hand and knew better than to make him angry…

Looking back, Helen realized that all along her husband had been free to do as he wished, but from the moment he had slipped the ring on her finger, she was the one who became enslaved.

Since that day she'd had four children, and now she would endure the pain of childbirth again. But this time would be different. This time she would be on her own. She picked up the newspaper and reread the headline: Young Girl Jumps To Her Death. The tragedy of the girl's suicide was not all that drew Helen to this story. It was the fact she had been pregnant, and up until her death had attended church regularly. Helen had snooped around and discovered the name of the priest who resided at the church. She could read between the lines, and that fueled her anger and gave her courage. She reached for the phone and called the newspaper. Her time for keeping silent had passed.

❦

New York, New York

WHEN HELEN ENTERED the office where the journalist worked with her team, she had a sudden urge to turn and run. The only thing keeping her there was the image of the young girl falling to her death. But something was nagging her about this story; the girl's friends had insisted she was smart, kind of a nerd, and that she was straight edge. As she looked around the room and at the photos pinned on the walls, Helen knew that, like her, the journalist sensed there was much more to the young girl's story than what the family was saying.

The journalist introduced herself as Frances and motioned Helen to a chair. She sat and fidgeted with her purse.

When Frances spoke, her tone was congruous to her profession—direct, but with an edge of empathy. She gestured toward a woman who entered from the main entrance. "This is Dr. Sabine Fiore; she's funding the research for this story."

Sabine closed the door behind her and sat opposite Helen, then held out a hand. "Good to meet you, Helen."

Helen noted Sabine's firm grip and the chill of her skin, but the woman's air of kindness and the slight European accent put her at ease. "I want the marriage laws changed," Helen said in a soft voice. "The girl who died… I understand what was going through her mind. I nearly did the same thing." The room seemed to close in around her, but she took a deep breath and continued. "Sometimes, when I lie in bed surrounded by darkness, lonely and frightened, my body hurting from another assault from my shit of a husband, I wish I'd dared to kill myself." She clenched her jaw, grabbed a piece of paper and a pen that lay on the desk, scribbled down a name, and turned the paper toward Frances. "Here's another person you need to be investigating. He's the asshole who raped me and married me off to a member of his congregation."

Frances placed her cell on the table and tapped the recorder app.

"What's said in here is between us," she said. "Are you okay with me recording this meeting so I don't miss anything?"

Helen stared at the phone, nodded, and relayed her story in horrid detail. By the end of the second hour, Frances had filled a notebook and was on to another. At some point the reporter had twisted her long blond hair into a bun on top of her head and shoved a pencil through it to keep it in place. She stared at the notebook and tapped her pen against the table.

"Do you think your husband's gone for good this time?" Frances asked.

Helen nodded. "Yes. Word is he's shacked up with a woman somewhere in South Carolina."

Frances leaned back in her chair. "Do you know of other women, like yourself, who've been forced to marry at a young age or are connected to this priest?"

"I'm not an anomaly if that's what you're thinking." She stared at Frances. "While the liberal elite condemns other countries about underage marriage, rape, and female genital mutilation, the holier-than-thou right-wing religious nutcases here in the United States are marrying off their own girls when they're just kids. And nobody's talking about it! That has to change. I'm doing this to protect my daughters. I want my girls to be able to go to high school and maybe college—to get a good education. The publicity doesn't interest me— in fact, it will cause me harm. When I made the decision to call you, I knew I'd have to take my kids and leave home forever. Do you have any idea how they'd be ridiculed? What would happen to me if I stayed?"

"No," Frances said. "Tell me."

"I'd most likely disappear off the face of the earth, and my kids would be adopted by some subservient couple. Yeah, I know a few big words. I didn't stop learning just because I couldn't go to school. Whenever possible, I packed up the kids and went to the library. That place became my sanctuary."

Frances drummed her fingers on the table. "Are you safe where you're staying now?"

"For a while. Until the people searching for me find where I'm hiding."

Sabine had also been taking notes. She placed her pen on the table and looked at Helen. "Why don't you and your children come and stay with me? I travel often, but you wouldn't be alone as a couple of my cousins also live in the house." She leaned in closer. "There's a guest house too if you'd prefer your own space. We all work long hours, and actually, it'd be really nice to have a family around. What do you think?"

Frances raised an eyebrow. "Sabine forgot to tell you that one of her cousins is an ex-marine and the other is a lawyer and that the place is more secure than the White House. I think moving you and your kids in with Sabine is a good idea. I'll know where to find you, and hey—it might help remove some of my liberal-elitism guilt. So, what do you say?"

"Will you tell my story?" Helen asked.

Frances nodded. "Oh yeah, and I'll introduce you to some politicians who've been dancing around this issue for years. They could do with a kick in the ass."

"Then it's a deal," Sabine said. "How about I drive you over to the house now? You can take a look around, and if you like it, we'll help you and your children move in immediately." She pushed back her chair and smiled at Helen. "What do you think?"

Doing a quick calculation of the cost of rent in New York, Helen shook her head. But as if reading her mind, Sabine's next words made the decision for her.

"It won't be completely rent free. You can keep the place in order," she said. "Maybe trim the roses... You'll be doing me a favor."

Helen was suddenly at a loss for words. It had been a long time since anyone had been kind to her.

"Thank you for having the courage to speak out," Frances said.

"Let's plan on meeting up again, same time next week. That'll give me time to research. I know how difficult it is to discuss personal issues, but things don't change unless we stand up, speak up, and fight for what's right." She handed Helen a canvas bag. "There's a tablet ready to go, and your new cell number is on a sticky note inside the box. I suggest you smash the phone you have now and toss it in the trash. From here on, you and your children's safety is a priority."

CHAPTER 8

Casa della Pietra

GABRIEL MATERIALIZED IN the main library and immediately headed to his study. He sensed Coco's anxiety building and imagined how he would feel in her situation—if he had been shown intimate images of her with her ex-lovers. A guttural rumble resonated through his pursed lips. He hastily shoved the thoughts aside, for more than the visions Coco had seen, he knew it would be the letters that would break her heart, for she would undoubtedly think they were written to him.

He opened the door to his study and slipped inside. Coco sat in one of the oversized lounge chairs. She seemed petite, fragile, and distraught. In her lap, an aged leather book lay open, one that for centuries had kept secrets hidden. Gabriel had planned on telling her about the duchess, and now he wished he had done so earlier, for the pain emanating from his beloved was unbearable, and he had caused it.

She raised her head and stared at him, her face flushed and wet with tears. "I had to check," she said. "I had to see if it was all true… the vision of you and her together and the letters. I dreamed about them, and here they are." She paused for a moment and sniffed. "She loved you, Gabriel, and you loved her. I'm not your first love, and perhaps I'm naïve to think I'll be your last." She wiped her eyes on the sleeve of her sweatshirt and read the first letter out loud.

My Dearest Beloved,

I write in haste as I have had word that the duke is to return soon to Florence. Do not despair, for in his presence I shall feign illness and excuse myself. My heart breaks when I think of our little one who has not yet met his father.

How I yearn for the warmth of your mouth and the taunting of your flesh against mine. But for now, catch the whispers within the trees. Each dancing leaf carries the essence of our hushed passion and my eternal love for you.

Until next time we are together…

TD

Gabriel closed the door, walked over to Coco, and sat on a nearby chair. "I wanted to tell you about her, about these letters."

"And yet you chose not to. Instead, you repeatedly told me that I was your only love, how you'd waited so long for me. I'm not stupid, Gabriel, I expected you'd had lovers, but you lied to me." She glanced at the letter she held in her shaking hands. "People don't keep letters like this from a casual affair."

"Yes, I kept the letters as a reminder," he said. "But not because I loved her. I kept them because of a promise, and also to remind me of betrayal."

Coco waved the letter in his face. "Betrayal? This letter doesn't speak of betrayal, it speaks of deep love. She loved you, and I'm guessing you loved her. Don't insult me by denying that."

"There's more to this story than you've seen. The situation was complex, and as you saw, my name is not on the pages. Please, let me explain."

A pained silence hung between them.

"Go on," Coco said.

"First of all," he said, "there were two women."

Coco glared at him, and he sensed her heartbeat speed up.

"TD stands for The Duchess," he continued. "She was a Medici who was murdered by her husband. She had a lover, and together they had children. The Allegiance hoped to get the duchess and her children out of Italy. It wasn't until today that I had confirmation of who was behind the whole charade."

Coco held up a hand. "Please, don't use Kenan as a scapegoat. Don't make me hate you as I hate him."

He glared at her. "You hate me?"

She shook her head. "I don't know how I feel, but I hate lies. You know that! I was fed them most of my life, and now I find out that the man I gave my heart to played me."

"Can't you see that Kenan is behind this?" He sprang up and glared at her. "I hate him. He wants to break us apart. He knows that if I lose you, I'll question my very existence."

Coco folded the letter and returned it to the book safe. "Then explain why you kept this relationship hidden from me. And while you're at it, you may as well tell me about any other women in your life who meant more to you than a casual fuck!"

In a flash, Gabriel was across the room at the window, his body shaking with rage. "Is that what you think you are to me, a casual fuck? Christ, Colombina, you haven't exactly lived the life of the Virgin Mary, and yet I've not asked you about your previous lovers or questioned your love for me."

The book safe went flying in Gabriel's direction. He caught it in midair.

"I've never been in love until now," she screamed. "Why did you lie to me?"

He held the book safe above his head and gave it a quick shake. "First tell me how you found out about this?"

Coco stood, wiped her eyes with the palms of her hands, and stared into the fire raging in the fireplace. "I dreamed about the letters and the book safe." She tucked her hair behind her ears. "When I woke up in the main studio, I saw I'd completed a painting... It pulled me in. That's when I saw you making love to her." She turned to him. "It seemed like she knew someone was watching."

"Someone *was* watching," Gabriel said. "You must believe me, Colombina. There is nothing happenstance about what you saw. Seeing me with her was preconceived by Kenan. As for the duchess, she was not who she seemed but another woman... her friend, a woman named Marguerite. I used magic so she would appear as the duchess. We needed time to get her out of Florence and to lure Kenan out of hiding. I will admit that for a while I wondered if I was in love with the woman behind the mask, and I believe that some part of her was in love with me. But, in truth, Marguerite and I loved each other as friends."

He lowered his arm and acknowledged the ache in his heart that the memory sparked. "The Allegiance hoped to save the duchess. Sadly, we did not. Her husband was a greedy, deranged man, and he wanted her out of his life. What I felt for Marguerite—the woman disguised as the duchess—was not in any way measurable to the love I have for you."

He strode across the room, placed the book safe on his desk, and studied Coco. "Before you say another word you may come to regret, I suggest you hear me out."

"This is the only chance I'll ever give you to tell me of any other lovers who meant more to you than a casual girlfriend."

He grabbed her wrist. "I'll do better than that." He leaned in so that his lips grazed her neck below her ear. "I'll introduce you to the only other woman I've loved."

He tossed a rune into the air. The flames instantly died down, and the room lay empty.

CHAPTER 9

From the diary of Isabella Romola de' Medici
Florence, Italy—Summer, 1576

Marguerite and I are once again in Florence, but hiding the pregnancy and recent birth has weakened my body and spirit. I pine for the scent of my newborn child and the tight grip he held on my fingers. The thought of him lifts my fragile spirit, and I pray that he not forget me. Marguerite's mother is caring for him while I nurse the soul of the city I love.

I have asked Marguerite for her help in a sensitive matter. I must gather my children and leave this place, for I will not go to Rome as Paolo demands. Marguerite has spoken of friends who would be willing to help me should I ever be in need, and so I have asked if they will meet with me. I offered to pay for their services; however, Marguerite insists they are not in need of my money. It is due to their past ties to Lorenzo that they offer their assistance, for they have concerns over the Medici lineage and this city.

I explained to Marguerite that my solicitude is not without warrant and showed her the note I received this morning, stressing that I do not know from where it came. The mysterious note reads as follows…

Isabella,

Does your husband know of the child you gave birth to last week? If you wish me to keep quiet about your indiscretion, then I suggest we meet and discuss a way to protect your… integrity. Tomorrow, at dusk, I shall send a coach for you.

✒

Florence, Italy—Summer, 1576

AS SOON AS Gabriel read Marguerite's note asking him to come to Florence, he mounted his horse, departed from his property on the outskirts of San Gimignano, and rode toward the city in darkness. At the eleventh hour, he sat in his tower residence not far from the Bargello and stared at the burning logs in the fireplace. He listened while Marguerite explained Isabella's dilemma, and finally she handed him the note. Gabriel lifted it to his nose and sniffed the paper.

"And as far as you are aware," he said, "this is the first time Isabella has received anything from this individual?"

"Yes." She nodded. "Do you recognize the scent?"

His answer was interrupted by the sound of chatter and the front door closing. He grinned and jumped to his feet. "Alessandro! Where have you been?"

The two men grasped each other's elbows. "Chasing down another Botticelli for your mother."

"Any luck?" Gabriel asked.

"Of course!" Alessandro let go of Gabriel's elbow, walked over to Marguerite, and kissed her hand. "Always a pleasure to see you, Marguerite."

"Likewise."

Alessandro motioned to the note in Gabriel's hand. "That stinks of Kenan." He held out his hand, and Gabriel passed him the letter. "So, the rat has finally come out of hiding. But for what?"

"My thoughts exactly," Gabriel replied. "He claims to have an interest in the duchess, Isabella."

Alessandro raised an eyebrow. "This is Florence—everyone has an interest in the duchess."

Marguerite drummed her fingers on the arm of the chair. "I swear, there was no one else apart from myself and the midwife at the birth of Isabella's child, and we trust the midwife implicitly. Isabella dismissed the staff upon our arrival at Cafaggiolo, and they did not return until we had departed. So how does the person who wrote this note know about the child?"

After pouring himself a goblet of wine, Alessandro sank into a chair. "There is another scent lingering on the paper." He ran the paper once more under his nose.

"I caught that too," Gabriel said. "It is laced with dark magic. Any thoughts as to who that might be?"

A muscle in Alessandro's jaw twitched, and the flecks of amethyst in his eyes disappeared into darkness. His friend's gaze mirrored a sincerity one only shows to a family member. "No," Alessandro replied. "And that bothers me, because it smells familiar."

"Are you saying that another immortal knows about Isabella and Troilo's children?" Marguerite asked. "And if so, then what can we do?"

"Who are her enemies?" Alessandro asked.

"She has many," Marguerite replied. "While her husband enjoys her money and the title that came with their marriage, he prefers the decadence Rome has to offer, and the bed of a particular prostitute. But since the death of Isabella's father, it is Francesco who makes Isabella's life difficult. I doubt he would grieve if she were to die an early death."

"And with Isabella's death, Francesco's wife would hold the title of the lady of Florence," Gabriel added.

Marguerite sipped her drink. "Adultery may be a sin punishable by death, but in all honesty, if such crimes were upheld, then a vast majority of the population of Florence would be behind bars, waiting for the executioner." Her eyes narrowed, and she gave a quick, disgusted snort. "I would not put it past Francesco to call upon this law to bring down his sister. While Isabella's affair with Troilo may not be a secret, many see her as a victim of her bloodline, forced to marry a man she did not love. The poets and musicians who perform at her dinners speak of the melancholia she keeps hidden behind the mask she wears."

Gabriel considered Marguerite's words and mulled the situation over for a moment. "The question still remains. Why is Kenan blackmailing her?"

Alessandro leaned forward. "If he is in Florence, then he knows you are here, my friend. I am guessing it is you he wants."

"It is my mother he desires, not me."

"Blackmailing Isabella seems as good a way as any to draw out the Allegiance," Marguerite said. "And what better way of snaring a mother than using her son as bait?" She moved forward in her chair. "There's more I need to ask of you, and this comes from Isabella. She wants to escape with her children, for she fears their lives are in danger. Paolo is set to arrive in Florence soon, and rumor has it he expects her to return with him to Bracciano, his villa in Rome. And if that happens, she will be trapped. While her father was alive, he protected her. Paolo's escapades were no secret to him. Cosimo adored Isabella and wanted her near, but now, without his protection, she has no stand here in Florence. And after receiving this letter, she is concerned for her newborn son."

"Where is the child now?" Alessandro asked.

"With my mother. What else could I do?" Marguerite stared at her glass and twisted it slowly in her hand. "I have an idea. A way that Isabella could see her child, although I am not sure it is possible. I need your help. Both of you."

"We're listening," Gabriel said. He noticed the elevation of her pulse and how she nibbled on her bottom lip.

She stared directly at him. "Is there a way to make me look like Isabella—only for a short while?"

"Possibly. Why?"

"A distraction. While I'm with you—as Isabella—Alessandro could take her to see her child, disguised as me. If this works, then we can plan her escape. Move Isabella and the children away from here so she and Troilo can live as a family under the protection of Cathérine de' Medici."

Alessandro shrugged his shoulders. "Can she ride?"

"Like the wind," Marguerite said.

"I'm in," Alessandro said. He looked at Gabriel with a raised eyebrow. "Can you do this kind of magic?"

In answer, Gabriel tossed his runes into the air and stared at Marguerite, muttering a string of words under his breath. Her hair changed from dark brown to auburn, and the blue of her eyes became tinged with brown. Shortly after, Marguerite appeared as Isabella. "Yes, I can, but it is not something I care to do. Wearing the mask of another is a serious decision." He snapped his fingers. The runes fell into his waiting palm, and Marguerite's appearance returned to her own.

"While that may take care of freeing up the duchess to see her children, what do we do about Kenan?" Alessandro asked.

"Let's give him some bait," Gabriel said. He placed his glass of wine on the mantel and handed Marguerite her shawl. "Go to the duchess. Have her dress in your riding habit, and you in her evening dress with a hooded cape. I shall explain everything when I see you."

"When and where?" Marguerite asked.

"In Isabella's drawing room, in an hour," Gabriel replied. "And Marguerite…" She turned to him. "Tonight we play as the lovers we once were."

She gave him a lopsided grin. "One of my favorite characters." She departed hastily.

"She is your Calypso," Alessandro said.

Gabriel chuckled. "Ah, but I am not blind to her trappings, nor she to mine. And my destiny lies within another's arms."

"Tell me more, my friend."

"One day, perhaps," he said. For a moment a shadow of sorrow fell upon his heart. "But not today."

❧

Gabriel had met the duchess on one other occasion. She had been a young child, besotted with her brother, Giovanni, whose early death would later leave her deeply saddened and without her dearest companion and moral compass. But even as a child, Isabella's playful antics toward her father had charmed Prudence, Stefan, and Gabriel while they met with Cosimo and his wife, Eleonora di Toledo, at Palazzo Vecchio.

But the woman who stood before him now would have shocked the people of Florence, who saw her as a fashionista—an educated woman of beauty and elegance, a duchess who adored the city and her people. For now the stresses of her life were mirrored in dark shadows below her eyes and the telltale strands of gray peeking out from her well-coiffed hair.

She held out a hand toward Gabriel. "Thank you for your willingness to help me."

Gabriel lowered his head and kissed her hand. "The honor is mine, Duchess. I only ask that everything that happens this evening is kept secret. My family has a long history of friendship with your Medici lineage, but that has always been based on trust. If this information is something you feel unable to bear, then it would be best for you to bow out now. Spies and magic are not new to this city, and my mother and Lorenzo di Medici were the best of friends."

This time it was the duchess who bowed her head. "You have my trust, sir, and my gratitude. My wish is that my children are kept safe and that we are placed under the guardianship of Cathérine in

France. And if my life is taken, I beg that you save my children and keep them hidden from my husband and other family members. In particular, my brother, Francesco, for he is not to be trusted with the Medici heirs."

"I understand," Gabriel said. "In regard to the threat you received, I suggest you go forward with the meeting. See what Kenan desires. I will send men to watch over you."

"Who is Kenan?" she asked.

"An immortal of the worst kind."

"An immortal?" she asked. "I have heard rumors of such creatures. And yet you think it is wise I meet with him?"

"Better to know your enemy's demands than ignore them."

Isabella nodded and her eyes sparkled. "I can see why Lorenzo trusted you. I shall send a note saying that I agree to meet him tomorrow evening and will inform Marguerite of the outcome."

Gabriel did not doubt her sincerity, for he sensed an underlying fear around her. "Then let us proceed." He looked up as Marguerite entered. "Have you explained what will transpire?"

Marguerite nodded. "Yes. Alessandro is waiting at the back entrance with two horses, and there are kitchen staff who will see the duchess leave, believing it is me, which is nothing out of the ordinary."

"And what will you do while disguised as me, Marguerite?" Isabella asked. "Discretion is requested."

Marguerite turned to Gabriel.

"Of course," Gabriel said. "We hope to draw out your enemy, for we believe it is not you that he wants, but me. Now, ladies, if you are ready?"

Both women nodded.

Gabriel tossed his runes into the air where they hovered while he whispered words of magic. Gradually, the faces of the two women before him changed into one another. He placed the runes into his pocket and gazed at Isabella, whose face and hair had now morphed into the image of Marguerite.

"I trust Alessandro with my own life, for he is a good man, and you are now under his protection," Gabriel said. "You had best depart and return by the fourth hour."

The duchess nodded and hugged Marguerite. "My sorrows show on your face, dear friend. Stay safe, and I cannot thank you enough for your courage."

"Without courage, all is lost," Marguerite said.

The duchess clasped Marguerite's shoulders and kissed her cheeks. "Truer words I have not heard."

She exited the room, and Marguerite walked over to the window and watched as Isabella, dressed in her riding clothes, mounted the horse Alessandro held for her and galloped away from Villa Baroncelli with the vampire riding his horse beside her.

Marguerite turned to Gabriel. "So, what do you have planned for us this evening?"

"Have your driver drop you off at my lodgings, and wait for me outside," he said. "With a bit of luck, Kenan will have someone watching both of us."

"Will this gamble place Isabella in more danger?"

"The only eyes who will see us are those of an immortal," Gabriel replied. "And if, by chance, anyone does see us together, then it will seem that Isabella has forgotten Troilo, and that will work in her favor. Call for your driver—I'll see you soon." He tossed another rune into the air, and his image dissipated.

As he strode across Piazza della Signoria, Gabriel caught a glimpse of the dome of the Cathedral of Santa Maria del Fiore in the distance. He thought of the woman he was on his way to meet, of their history together, of her courage. The first time he had seen Marguerite perform was at a small theater in Florence. She was part of an acting troupe that had gained a select following by performing the works of playwrights such as the satirist Pietro Aretino. Tonight she would play the part of her dear friend Isabella, whose present life was far from that of a comedy.

A group of well-dressed revelers mingled together outside a restaurant, the women in long dresses with puffed sleeves and skirts, accompanied by men wearing buckled boots and stockings tucked into velvet bloomers worn with doublets and jackets.

A little farther along, Gabriel turned into an alley, stopping in front of an iron gate that separated two tall stone buildings. He stared at the figure of Isabella standing on her own in shadows as the heavy thud of the gate closing echoed up and down the narrow alley. Knowing it was Marguerite, he walked over and pulled her to his chest. The two players kissed, and when they parted, Gabriel tucked her protectively under his arm.

They continued to the end of the alley, stopping in front of a sturdy wooden door. Gabriel banged his fist on the wood in a musical rhythm. The door opened, and he ushered her inside. In one swift movement, he lifted her into his arms and headed toward a wide stone staircase, taking the steps three at a time. On the landing, he hurried along a hallway to an open door and entered a room void of light. Gabriel waved a hand, and the remains of a dead fire sprang to life and flames lit up the fireplace.

He laid Marguerite across the bed, and she grabbed at his clothing and pulled him to her.

"How long do we have?" he asked.

Unbuttoning her jacket, Marguerite revealed the flesh of her bosom and a hint of pink nipples pushing up from a lace bodice. "The duke is expected to return to Florence any day."

She loosened her skirt, and Gabriel tugged it over her hips and thighs and tossed it to the floor before pulling at the ribbons of her bodice. She ran a hand over her skin from her breasts to her mound of dark hair and then tugged at his pants. Gabriel lifted her so she sat on his thighs, and she wrapped her legs around his body and pushed the hood away from his head.

"I love you, Gabriel."

"And I love you."

Suddenly the flames from the fire flared up and quickly extinguished. Gabriel turned around as a strand of magic reached toward him. He thrust a hand into the darkness, trying to grasp the remaining motes, but the strand disappeared and the fire in the fireplace rekindled. Gabriel leaped out of bed and surveyed the room. His nostrils flared as he sniffed the air, catching a faint, familiar scent.

"What was that?" Marguerite asked.

"Dark magic." He pulled on his clothes. "We were being watched. Get dressed—we need to get to your mother's immediately."

Marguerite dressed quickly, and Gabriel held her close.

"No need to be scared." He tossed a rune before him.

⁓

Marguerite shivered, and Gabriel ran a hand along her shoulders, instilling a rush of heat over her. He had not used his magic to travel with her before, but he needed to speak with Alessandro urgently.

She caught his hand in hers and kissed it. "I'm fine."

Alessandro stood by the front door of a stone cottage located in the foothills on the outskirts of Florence. "What happened?" he asked. "I thought we had planned to meet after I dropped the duchess off at Villa Baroncelli."

Gabriel motioned for Marguerite to enter the cottage, and after he closed the door behind her, he turned to Alessandro. "The scent on the note from Kenan to the duchess… it lingered in the room while we were together earlier. It was momentary, but I know someone was watching us." He ran a hand through his hair. "The air was tinged with powerful magic. Think, Alessandro. Can you remember where you encountered this scent before, perhaps from somewhere in your past?"

Alessandro shook his head and turned away. "I've not thought of much else since I left your lodgings, for the scent triggered something from my childhood. But I cannot place it."

"Perhaps the scent belonged to a grandparent or a family friend," Gabriel said. "The flecks of amethyst in your eyes are a reminder that you have Creative blood in your veins. What do you know about your lineage?"

"My grandmother was a seer," Alessandro said. "As was my mother and my sister. I remember there was something about Grandmother's face that, as a little boy, I found somewhat enchanting. In retrospect, it could have been that she had the eyes of a Creative. But I only knew her for a few years as she disappeared early in my life."

"Disappeared?"

"Yes. One evening her house burned to the ground, and as far as I know, my parents found no evidence of her body. I grew up alongside the birth of the Inquisition. To safeguard my sister and me, my parents learned it best not to enquire about my grandmother's whereabouts."

"So, in retrospect," Gabriel said, "there's a chance she may still be alive."

"Are you suggesting she took off with Kenan?"

Gabriel shook his head. "No, the time frame doesn't fit. She went missing when Domenico was alive. According to Prudence, Domenico hated seers, but she wondered if he had kept a few alive, not just for the taste of their sweet blood, but more for their gifts of prophecy. If Domenico were to find a seer with the eyes of a Creative, such as your grandmother, then I do not think he would kill her."

Alessandro sat on a wooden bench, his elbows resting on his knees. "So you think she's still alive?"

"Perhaps," Gabriel answered. "Although for her sake, I hope she is not. I cannot imagine her life if she's been forced to continually give in to Kenan's demands."

"Then what is he planning?" Alessandro mused. "And what does he want with the duchess?"

"All good questions," Gabriel said. "But for now, we'd best get both women to their respective homes. And I need to inform Mother that Kenan has surfaced."

CHAPTER 10

Florence, Italy—Present Day

A SUDDEN JOLT REVERBERATED through Coco's body. Caught off-balance by Gabriel's immediate need to leave the warmth of his study and prove his love, she did her best to calm her erratic breathing and control her fierce temper, which was close to exploding. In a futile attempt to shake her arm free of Gabriel's hand, she cursed under her breath when his grip tightened.

She stared at the ground, noting terra-cotta tiles before her gaze was drawn to a nearby wooden door with carved panels and framed with gray stone. Champagne-colored walls led up to a ceiling of multiple scalloped arches. Coco glanced at Gabriel, who was staring at something over her shoulder. She turned in the direction of his eyeline and saw a familiar red-bricked dome set against a striking blue sky and fluffy white clouds. Her view of the dome was accented by simple architecture. Arches framing a hallway were held up with Ionic columns surrounded by layers of stone and brick buildings, making Coco feel as if she stood on the bottom tier of a wedding cake. She observed the area before her—the inner garden, simplistic in design, the Medici coat of arms, covered walkways, Brunelleschi's cloister, the Chapel of the Princes, and the dome that marked the entrance to the Museum of the Medici Chapels.

"Why have you brought me to Florence?" she demanded.

Gabriel ignored her and strode briskly along the walkway to an open doorway with Coco in tow. They entered the vestibule leading up to the Laurentian Library. Even amid the drama unfolding, Coco was immediately overwhelmed with the intensity of Michelangelo's work. The masculine brackets, the swirls of the capitals, the drama of perspective. But there was no time for her to marvel in length at the creativity of the artist's work; instead, determined not to allow herself to seem weak in any way, Coco kept up with Gabriel, taking the stairs at the side of the grand staircase two at a time. At the landing, the doors opened and a seemingly young intern was stopped midstep by an elderly gentleman as she started to ask to see Gabriel's tickets. The man gave her a quick shake of his head, and the intern stepped back to allow Gabriel access.

Gabriel's gait didn't miss a beat. He continued walking, keeping to the carpet runner that ran the full length of the reading room. The warmth of the coffered wooden ceiling and rows of carved desks did little to ease Coco's fast-beating pulse. Once through the reading room, Gabriel veered away from the visitor area and yanked open a door marked Private. Another hallway lay before them, but Gabriel entered a door to his immediate right that opened up to a small office where a woman sat at a desk, typing at a computer. One look at Gabriel and she reached for the phone on her desk. Gabriel ignored her and instead opened a door opposite, then slammed the door behind Coco.

He stopped abruptly, and so did Coco.

An exquisite woman who appeared to be in her early sixties sat at a desk, pen in hand and taking notes. She wore a gray silk shirt, her blond hair wound into a french twist that showed off high cheekbones, large blue eyes, and lips created by Botticelli. The woman seemed somewhat familiar to Coco as she eased herself out of her chair and gestured politely to the three men sitting opposite.

"Gentleman," the woman said, her voice mellifluous, like honey falling in a single stream from a spoon. The hint of her American accent made Coco immediately feel at ease. "No need to introduce Gabriel." A few polite chuckles followed. "But it's my pleasure to present Ms. Coco Rhodes, an art professor at the University of California, Los Angeles."

The woman walked over to Coco, a draped silk skirt a few shades darker than her shirt clinging to her hourglass figure. She glared at Gabriel's hand on Coco's wrist, and he immediately let her go. Tucking Coco's hand into the crook of her arm, she escorted her over to meet her guests, all of whom carried the word *Professor* before their names. Coco's face flushed with embarrassment when she remembered she was dressed in paint-splattered, faded jeans and a similarly decorated Bruins sweatshirt.

"Will you excuse us, please, gentlemen," the woman said. "Coco is presently on a well-earned painting sabbatical, and I promised I'd not take too much time away from her work."

Coco immediately liked the woman and admired her grace as she accompanied her guests to the door, gliding seamlessly across the wide wooden floorboards in pure elegance and stiletto heels. Coco looked down at her own footwear—a much-loved pair of UGG boots, a far cry from the shoes she had worn the last time she was in Florence. The thought prompted her memory, and she suddenly remembered where she had seen the woman before.

"You were at the fancy-dress ball," Coco said the moment the door closed. "Layla's mother, Antonia, she introduced us… Professor Marilyn Scott-D'Angelo."

The woman smiled. "Call me Marilyn." She guided Coco to a chair and urged her to sit, then motioned to Gabriel to take the chair beside her. He held Marilyn's hands and kissed her cheeks before sitting in the chair she offered. Marilyn took her place behind her desk and looked across at Gabriel with a raised eyebrow.

Gabriel's fingers were clasped around the arms of the chair, his knuckles showing white. "I need you to explain to Colombina about our relationship."

The woman nodded and turned to Coco. "Gabriel told me a few years ago about you," she said. "He's been in love with you for a long time. As for my relationship with him… Well, yes, we were lovers once, and we still love each other, but not in the sense of life partners or two souls who are bound to each other. We're more like brother and sister. We tried many times to make our relationship work, but in truth, his world is not my cup of espresso."

Coco wondered if Gabriel also intended her to introduce him to her past lovers, and that thought brought a snort from him.

Get out of my head. Now!

His shoulders stiffened.

Marilyn sat back and drummed her fingers on the arms of her chair. "Gabriel, it might be best if you give Coco some space. In fact, perhaps if you waited outside?"

Gabriel glared at her. "I'm not leaving—"

Coco leaped out of her chair and turned to him. "You dragged me here without telling me where we were going!" She rubbed her wrist. "And now you don't even have the courtesy or sensitivity to give me what I need more than anything."

Gabriel stared at her.

"Empathy," Coco said through pursed lips.

The muscles in his neck tightened, his lips formed a hard line, and his eyes darkened. "I thought you wouldn't want me near you after what you'd seen." He looked away. "We can discuss this when we're back at the fortress. I don't wish to be separated from you, but I need you to hear what Marilyn has to say."

Coco lowered herself back into the chair. The door opened and closed—Gabriel was gone.

Marilyn walked around to Coco and handed her a box of tissues. "He may be a vampire warlock, but he's also a male," she said. "Perhaps you need to cut him some slack."

Coco pulled a tissue from the box and wiped her eyes. "He lied to me."

"Anything you want to talk about?" Marilyn asked.

"First, tell me about your relationship with him," Coco said. "When did you meet each other?"

Marilyn sat in the chair Gabriel had vacated. "November 5, 1966," she said. "I was thigh deep in mud, water, and God knows what else, retrieving manuscripts and artifacts—anything I could find—from Palazzo Medici Riccardi. For a young university student in Florence during a semester abroad, the scene unfolding before my eyes was terrifying; the loss of life, literature, and art was unfathomable."

Coco's frown dissolved. "*Angelo del Fango...* the Mud Angels, I read about that years ago in an art history class. Student volunteers stayed in Florence after the flood to help with the recovery."

"Yes," Marilyn said with a grin. "Although some of us stayed longer than expected. Anyway, back to how I met Gabriel. He stood with Prudence and Stefan, surveying the damage with officials and a team of conservation specialists, and in all honesty, I didn't take much notice of him. None of us had slept much, but we were wired with adrenaline. I had a stack of manuscripts in my hands and tripped over something hidden by water. The next thing I knew, strong hands had a tight grip around my waist, pulling me to a standing position. One look into Gabriel's golden eyes and I was putty in his hands, and luckily the manuscripts were saved from the spill." She smoothed a wrinkle from her silk skirt. "Because of Stefan's knowledge of literature, he worked with the conservation specialists, historians, and librarians to catalog what we could save, and Gabriel worked alongside his father."

"Were you in grad school?"

Marilyn chuckled. "Oh no. I was a senior, doing my BA in

literature. It was the sixties, Coco! I was in Italy, single, and being wined and dined by an extremely sexy Italian male. A Southern California girl with the mindset of bikinis, surf guitar, and sun-bleached blond surfers. To be courted by a man such as Gabriel, well, I thought I'd won the lottery!"

"Did you know about him?" Coco asked. "About his family and their unusual traits?"

"Oh, I had my suspicions," Marilyn said with a smirk. "At the time I studied European folklore and mythology. It was Gabriel's strength and abstract sense of the world around him that gave him away, not to mention his deep knowledge of art and history. We'd been together for about six months—which for a twenty-one-year-old seemed like an eternity—but one day everything changed." She stared past the window across the room where a hint of the dome from the Medici Chapels was visible.

"What happened?" Coco asked, noting the faraway look in Marilyn's eyes when she turned to her.

"I was assigned to work with a group that was testing new concepts in historic preservation," Marilyn continued. "When I arrived at the National Library of Florence, I made my way to the area where the team had set up shop and was introduced to a few of the archivists. While surveying the room, I noticed a young man in a lab coat leaning over a microscope; he looked up, and our gaze met. Dark curls hid most of his face, and he raked his hair behind his ears. He gave me a quick nod and pushed back his round-framed glasses... They were always falling forward. My heart beat so fast that I almost lost my balance. He nodded at me and said, *'Ciao! Sono Marco. Lavoro con manoscritti antichi.'*—I'm Marco, and I work with ancient manuscripts. To which I apparently answered in my worst Italian, 'Yes, I'm Marilyn, and I'm a book!'" She grinned. "Goodbye, Gabriel; hello, Marco. We've been together ever since."

"That's a long time," Coco said. "I mean, you don't look to be in your seventies."

Marilyn crossed her legs and ran a hand over her perfect hair. "Marco and I were in a terrible car accident; it happened a few days after our daughter's wedding. We should both be dead, but, thanks to Gabriel, we're still here. You see, he came to the hospital and gave us both a few drops of his blood. We recovered from our injuries—much to our doctor's surprise—and it seems Gabriel's blood added a few years to our lives."

Coco leaned forward. "Wait a minute. You're saying that his blood has lengthened your lives?"

"Yes. Oh, we'll die soon enough, but we've been able to see our grandchildren born and discover their own lives, and also continue with the work we both love."

Coco tucked that new information away and returned to her questions. "What work do you and your husband do now?"

"After the flood, I stayed in Florence and continued my studies in literature," Marilyn replied. "And Marco did the same but also added science to his portfolio of knowledge. He's an expert in the field of literature, Latin, and art conservation. Our work has taken us to different parts of the world for months at a time, but Florence is our home. We both love this city."

Coco thought for a moment. "Does your husband know about Gabriel and the Allegiance?"

Marilyn nodded. "Yes, and we'll take their secrets to our graves. Antonia and I are the best of friends—Gabriel introduced me to her before I met Marco. Thanks to her, I managed to navigate my way around the Italian language and lifestyle." She took hold of Coco's hands. "Gabriel and I were lovers, Coco, but we were not meant to be. Marco is my true love, just as you are Gabriel's. Of course Gabriel has had many other lovers—he's ancient for God's sake, and a handsome man—but he's been waiting for you for centuries. You must trust him and ask the same of him. Don't let anyone tell you otherwise, and question anyone's rationale who tries to deny Gabriel's love for you."

Coco shifted in her chair. "There was another woman, a duchess."

"Yes," Marilyn said, "but you must know that in reality Gabriel never loved her as you might think. The Allegiance was concerned for the duchess's life, and also for her children; not only the children she bore with her husband but also those with her beloved, Troilo Orsini."

"You've lost me," Coco said.

"The duchess, Isabella, was a Medici," Marilyn explained. "Her children were heirs to the Medici name. Had they died, an active fragment of the Medici lineage would have been lost. The rest is for Gabriel to share with you, not me." She squeezed Coco's hands and turned toward the door as male laughter drifted through to her office. "Marco's here." She leaned over her desk and pushed a button on her phone. "Please ask Marco and Gabriel to join us." She looked into Coco's eyes. "This relationship is new for both of you—be patient with each other and set rules. Let Gabriel know what you need. Perhaps you might consider teaching here in Florence." She took a business card from her desk and handed it to Coco. "I'm here for you."

Coco tucked the card into a pocket of her jeans and tensed as she heard the door open and felt Gabriel rest his hands on her shoulders. She reached for his hands. *We need to talk.*

He squeezed her shoulders, and when he spoke his lips grazed the side of her neck. "Yes, we do*, mi amore.*"

Marilyn embraced a tall, lanky man with an angular face and salt-and-pepper hair that fell across his temple and over a pair of round-framed glasses. He looked immaculate in dark dress pants, a white button-down shirt, lace-up leather shoes, and a tweed sports coat.

He turned to Coco and held out a hand. "*Ciao*, Coco," he said with a strong Italian accent. "I'm Marco. It's good to meet you."

"Good to meet you too," Coco said. As she shook his hand, a line of poetry popped into her mind, and the words slipped from her mouth. "She had a heart—how shall I say?—too soon made glad, too easily impressed: she liked whate'er—"

"—she looked on, and her looks went everywhere," Marco joined in. "'My Last Duchess.' Robert Browning."

Coco stared at Gabriel, and he shook his head. "Browning supposedly wrote his poem about Lucrezia, not the duchess."

"Supposedly," Marco said. "Although I'm not sure I agree with that hypothesis. Let's face it, there was more than one member of the elite who died under curious circumstances. I'm open to the possibility that he wrote the poem with more than one woman in mind. Perhaps he intended to open a conversation about the collective feminine persona rather than the delicate Lucrezia. Isabella and Leonora also died under questionable situations, and noticeably after they'd lost the protection of Cosimo I."

"What made you remember those particular words?" Gabriel asked.

"I heard them spoken in a dream a few nights ago," Coco replied. "And just now I felt compelled to repeat them when Marco's hand touched mine. What does that mean?"

"Was there anything else in your dream?" Marilyn asked.

Coco nodded. "Yes, I was standing in water… nowhere in particular, but it was a woman's voice who spoke the words to me."

Marco placed an arm around Marilyn's shoulders and kissed her forehead. "Tell them, *tesoro*."

Marilyn placed a hand on his cheek, where it lingered for a moment through unspoken words. She gave him a loving smile and then addressed Coco and Gabriel. "Before meeting Gabriel on that fateful day in '66, I stood in an alley near where I was living at the time, staring at the chaos around me. I noticed a book stuck in a crevice of the stone building beside me. I reached out, dislodged it, and held it in my hands. Remarkably, the book seemed to be in a reasonable state—only a few pages had become dislodged. I gently pried the book open to where the pages were detached and stared at the words on the first page: 'That's my last duchess painted on the wall.'"

Marilyn walked over to a small glass cabinet and retrieved a book. She handed it to Coco. "Every February fourteenth since that fateful day, I've had the same recurring dream where I'm standing in water and the words of 'My Last Duchess' are being spoken to me in Italian by a woman whose voice sounds like that of a young Italian aristocrat."

Coco ran a hand over the book and handed it to Gabriel. "And I dreamed the same dream," she said and looked at Marilyn. "But why do you think your dream falls on Valentine's Day?"

"Lucrezia de' Medici was born February 14, 1545," Gabriel said, with a tinge of sadness. "She was the second Lucrezia this city loved, and we lost them both far too early in their youth." He smiled at Coco. "The woman who wrote the letters you read was indeed Isabella, but her words were not meant for me. Isabella asked me to keep the letters for her—some were written by Troilo. You saw how the duchess's confidante, Marguerite, and I played the part of a couple in love—she was an actress after all. It was your father who rode alongside her and protected her on her journey to see her newborn son."

"So what happened to her?" Coco asked.

"I knew we were being watched," Gabriel said. "But it was difficult to prove without evidence. I had made a vow to Isabella, one that I would honor above all else." He handed the book back to Marilyn.

"What was the vow?" Coco asked.

Gabriel contemplated the view beyond the window and seemed to stare at something in particular.

Coco followed Gabriel's eyeline to a stone wall, a wall that held the Medici crest. "I don't understand."

"Isabella's marriage was not one of love," Gabriel said. "And it was well known that while she did not want to spend time in Rome, her husband Paolo craved the city. He had no intention of giving up his life of self-indulgence, sexual escapades, and overspending purely because he was married. Ironically, he encouraged his cousin to check up on Isabella when he heard he was headed to Florence."

"Troilo," Coco said. "And they fell in love?"

Gabriel nodded. "Yes, deeply. There were rumors that she bore his children, and this is where my vow to Isabella was born. In the latter part of her short life, she feared not for her own life but more for her children. She began to plan her own escape, but when word of her cousin's death reached her, it seems the duchess succumbed to her own imminent demise."

Coco held up a hand. "I'm sorry, but my knowledge of history—apart from art—is somewhat limited. Who was Isabella's cousin and why was she killed?"

"Her name was Leonora," Marco cut in. "Married to a madman, Isabella's brother, a man with many ghosts in his closet. He craved power and snapped at the thought of his wife's indiscretions. The city of Florence had rules about adultery; not so much for men, but for most women it meant death. The only reason Isabella and Leonora were protected for so long was because of Isabella's father, Cosimo I, but once he was gone and the Medici power was handed over to the eldest brother, Francesco, time was not a friend to the Princess of Florence."

Coco pushed on. "And what happened to Isabella and Troilo's children?"

"One died as a child," Gabriel replied. "Isabella requested that I take her son, born to Troilo far from Florence, which I did with the aid of Alessandro, Marguerite and her mother, for although the child was considered a bastard, he was a Medici heir and a child born of love. So, now can you see the importance of my vow?"

"Yes," Coco said, she fixed her gaze on Gabriel. "And what of Marguerite and the Medici heir?" The anger she had felt earlier began to melt away and had been replaced by an emotion she did not fully understand, but at least the fury of betrayal had dissolved.

"From the beginning, the child was the reason Marguerite and I played the charade for Isabella. Yes, we loved each other, but it was a love of loyalty, not of the soul and heart," Gabriel answered. "Because of a pact Prudence had made with Lorenzo de' Medici to protect the heirs born of love, we relocated Marguerite, her mother, and the child to the north, where they were protected by a family we trusted, and the Allegiance. The last time I saw Marguerite was on the night of her passing. She had married a kind man who raised the boy as his own. But the boy's story is long and significant, and not one I can speak of at this time."

Coco walked toward Gabriel and into his open arms. "And the letters?"

"Written by Isabella and her beloved Troilo," he said. "She feared that one day they would be found and asked me to keep the most profound letters safe."

The room was silent, and while Coco relished the rush of love from Gabriel, she did not push his silence but instead turned and spoke to Marilyn.

"Are there portraits of Isabella, Lucrezia, and Leonora here in Florence?"

Marilyn walked over to a bookcase and pulled out a hefty tome and handed it to Marco, who continued the story. "After Isabella was murdered by her husband, her brother, Francesco, sought vengeance, not only against his sister but anyone connected to her. Most of her portraits were destroyed, and many of her workers were either murdered or hauled off to prisons and never heard of again." He opened the book to a series of pages that showed members of the Medici family. "We have a few portraits of the Medici women at the Uffizi, and I'd be happy to show them to you."

Gabriel guided Coco over to the desk. She turned the pages of the book, searching for a hint of recognition or impulse to explore a portrait. "I was hoping to feel drawn to one—something that could help unravel what's going on—but I feel nothing."

"Give yourself time, *mi amore*," Gabriel said. He squeezed her hand and turned to Marco. "We've discovered a collection of old journals written in Latin, and the Allegiance would value your input in translating the volumes. Stefan and Nikandros will help, of course, and explain more about the people who wrote them."

Marco raised an eyebrow. "How can I resist such an invitation?"

"I must warn you," Gabriel added. "This collection contains graphic descriptions of torture and of evil beyond the realms of human thought."

"A challenge then," Marco said.

"That it is. Where's the best place for you to work?"

"We can set up here," Marilyn said. "We've everything we need, and I'll make sure we're not disturbed."

Gabriel nodded. "I'll have Prudence cast a layer of protective spells around the building, and I'm sure she'll want to be here with you too. When can you begin?"

"Give Marco and me a few hours to set up and clear our calendars."

"*Perfetto*! I'll return shortly with Stefan, Prudence, and Nikandros." Gabriel and Marco grasped each other's elbows.

Coco stepped forward and held her hand toward Marilyn, but the stylish woman placed her hands on Coco's shoulders and kissed her cheeks. "We'll see you again soon."

CHAPTER 11

**From the diary of Isabella Romola de' Medici
Florence, Italy—Summer, 1576**

This evening I had an encounter that I will not easily forget, and I shall do my best to convey the strangeness and details of the event.

The night air offered a slight respite from the heat of the day, and I patted my brow with a linen handkerchief while I sat in the luxurious coach sent for me by the author of the strange letter. I noted the softness of the black leather uphol-stery, the gilded artistry that decorated the interior, the likes of which I had not seen before. In another time, I may well have been envious of such wealth, but with the impending threat of relocating to Rome nagging at my mind, such things were of little importance. The safety of my children is all that matters now.

I looked out at the familiar surroundings, and a sense of longing passed over me as the carriage passed by the Pitti, the villa of my childhood. The gardens where my beautiful Spanish mother, Eleonora, had watched over my siblings and me as we played, and where she had garnished me with the attributes of knowledge and social graces I would need in my later years.

The carriage veered left, down an alley, and came to a stop in front of an austere stone building. A uniformed man opened the carriage door for me, and I accepted the offer of his gloved hand as I stepped down and onto the cobblestones where he motioned me toward a set of steps. As I approached the landing, a thick wooden door opened, although even as I entered the drawing room, I did not see a footman.

A single candle sprayed fragmented shards of light onto multiple scenes: grotesque horned beings torturing naked men and women, and another revealed the fires of hell. The moving light seemed to make the frescoed walls come alive with motion. The door closed behind me, and I caught my breath.

"What frightens you more, Isabella, death or damnation?" The words were spoken by a male, his voice condescending.

I gathered my courage and thrust back my shoulders. "Neither, sir, and if that is why you have called me here, then consider this meeting over. I do not play games with such issues."

"But we both know that to be untrue," he said. "For you bed other men while married. A sin in the face of our Lord, a sin worthy of both death and damnation."

"Is this why I am here? To be judged by a man I do not know, one who hides in the shadows rather than show himself?" I caught the edge of my skirt, and with a swish of fabric I turned to leave; however, standing before me was a tall, pale man with a scar across his forehead. When our gaze met, a shudder ran over my skin. I took a step back but did not lower my gaze from his cold stare. I knew instantly that this man, or creature, was of evil descent.

"And how is your newborn child, Duchess?" he said. "So strange that you hide him from your husband."

I was instantly struck by an edge of panic and caught the

words that lingered in my throat, sensing instead that it would be best to remain quiet, for I needed to hear his demands.

"It is odd, don't you think, that your husband is not aware that you have given birth, and to a son no less," he said. "Perhaps what is stranger is that the time frame between his visits with you do not tally with your pregnancy; however, I do seem to remember that Troilo visited Florence around nine months ago. Perhaps he is the child's father? Am I correct?"

My dear father had taught me the subtler points of negotiation, especially when the odds are not in one's favor. I smiled at the pale-skinned man. "To speak of such important issues without having more information would be disingenuous. So I ask of you, sir, two things—one is your name; the other, your price."

The edges of the man's mouth curved into a devilish smirk, and he dipped his head and motioned for me to follow him. He crossed the vestibule into a large, stark room where the only furniture consisted of two chairs placed in front of an oversized fireplace. Embers glowed but sprang to life when the man fed them dry wood. I sat on one of the chairs and removed my kid-leather gloves, placing them on my lap, and watched the man, who seemed to take pleasure in tending the fire with a large iron poker. When flames licked at the logs, he placed the poker against the thick stone wall and turned to me, then leaned casually against the mantel.

"My name is Kenan, and I have an interest in your latest lover, Gabriel."

"What kind of interest?" I asked.

Kenan shrugged. "My interests are no business of yours, Duchess, and under the circumstances, you might consider refraining from asking questions, for I do believe I hold the upper hand."

I smoothed the wrinkles of my skirt.

"Send word to me when you are meeting him next," Kenan said. "And do not think to cheat me, Duchess, for I know where you have hidden your bastard son."

"Why should I believe you?"

"Oh, come now, Duchess, surely as the lady of Florence, you know too well that there are more ways of viewing the world than what we see through our eyes."

I did my best to remain calm and lifted my chin. "To what do you refer, sir?"

"The world of magic," he said. "A world that you cannot begin to fathom, of seers who capture moments with their powers—indiscreet moments—pictures in motion, and dark creatures of the night."

The fire hissed.

I slid my gloves over my hands, rose, and headed toward the drawing room. An ominous chuckle from Kenan made me shiver. The front door magically opened on its own, and as I exited, it closed behind me. The footman guided me to the carriage, and it wasn't until I heard the clip-clop of horses' hooves that I allowed my tears to fall.

When I arrived at Baroncelli, Marguerite was waiting for me. I dismissed the servants, poured two glasses of wine, and recounted everything that had transpired that evening, including that Kenan asked I alert him the next time I planned to meet with Gabriel. Marguerite left shortly after to relay the events of my evening to Gabriel.

❧

Florence, Italy—Summer, 1576

PRUDENCE AND STEFAN had joined Gabriel and Alessandro in Florence shortly after hearing of Isabella's secret children. This would not be the first time the Allegiance had taken on the task of protecting children born to lovers, but it was one of a kind in such that the children's mother was a Medici. During the Renaissance, it had been Prudence who had asked Lorenzo di Medici to protect an infant born to their dear friend Sandro Botticelli and his beloved, Colombina. Prudence had woven a shield of magic to hide the amethyst color of the infant's Creative bloodline from the likes of the Inquisition, but not from those who loved her. However, the girl had long since disappeared, and that hung heavily on Prudence's conscience.

"How many times has Isabella met with Kenan?" Prudence asked.

"Once," Gabriel said. "He sent word today that she meet with him later this evening."

"And the newborn," Stefan asked. "Where is he now?"

Gabriel went to top off his mother's wineglass, but she placed a hand above the rim and shook her head. "The child is with Marguerite's mother," he said. "I've placed protection spells around her home."

"I am impressed at your ability to undertake the masking spell," Prudence said. "A difficult task for me, and yet not so for you… A skill you have inherited, no doubt."

"Do not be concerned, Mother. The masking spell is not one I have used often. However, the situation warranted its use. I am sure you agree."

"So, as I see things," Prudence said. "Kenan knows about Isabella's son with Troilo, and he believes that you are currently involved in an affair with her. Is this correct?"

Gabriel drained his glass. "Yes. Sadly, their first child died early on, which is why Isabella is determined to keep this son safely hidden."

"And to think she has had to suppress her grief," Prudence said. "Such are the woes of her lineage."

"Gabriel, you do realize that if Francesco were to suspect that his sister is involved with you, your life could be in jeopardy?" Stefan asked.

"No mortal saw us together," Gabriel said. "But there was a seer there—I am sure of it. Threadlike strands of dark magic reached out to us."

Prudence rose and walked over to the fireplace. "Did the energy seem familiar?"

"No, I've not sensed this particular presence before," Gabriel replied. "But I can tell you that the being seemed feminine in nature, and the scent left in the air after she departed matched the scent on the original note Kenan sent to Isabella."

Prudence looked at Alessandro. "And this scent was familiar to you?"

"Yes," he said. "But I cannot place it."

"You mentioned that you were a child when your grandmother died," Prudence said. "While our sense of smell is strongest, our sense of recall can be more difficult as we age. Not impossible, but slow to surface, especially in a stressful circumstance. Perhaps in time you will remember more."

"Was it here that you brought Marguerite—as the duchess?" Stefan asked.

"No," Gabriel said. "We met at my lodgings near the Bargello."

"I suggest meeting with others," Stefan said. "And in a more public place where your relationship with the duchess be seen as no more than friendship, and stay beside Marguerite, for it is imperative that others are witness to your friendship with both women." He motioned to Alessandro. "You had best join them. Prudence and I will be close by should Kenan enter the scene, but far enough away that he will not sense us should he decide not to make an entrance."

"And the matter of her infant son?" Gabriel asked.

"He must be moved tomorrow evening," Prudence said. "We cannot take a chance with his life."

"Isabella has asked Marguerite to act as the child's mother," Gabriel said. "She has accepted the request, and her mother will also travel with her. I would rather Marguerite's family stay under our protection."

Prudence leaned forward and reached for Gabriel's hand. "From whichever way I view Isabella's life, all I see is darkness. We can protect her son, but of Isabella's fate, I am not sure. I see a dark cloud approaching this city. We must warn those we can—anyone connected to Isabella—to leave this place."

"I shall ask Isabella to send word to Kenan that she is meeting with me this evening. Alessandro will take you to Marguerite's mother's home. I think that under the circumstances, hearing the plans for her sudden move will be better served coming from you, Mother."

CHAPTER 12

Casa della Pietra

FTER LEAVING HELEN and her children to get comfortable in a wing of her New York home under the watch of her warriors, Sabine headed back to Northern Italy. Sam and Frances had tracked down the priest who had raped Helen as a young girl and forced her into marrying a member of his congregation, an abusive man three decades older. The priest had been transferred to New Hampshire shortly after the incident, but the change of location had not quelled his need to take advantage of young girls—the only habit that had changed was that his taste now included boys.

But there was also the matter of the shadowed figure Frances had seen with the young girl on the bridge before she jumped to her death. Sabine had picked up the immortal's scent, and he reeked of Kenan. She had caught a similar scent on Helen's skin, and that did not sit well with Sabine, another reason she wanted the young mother and her children within the safety of her fortified villa and protected by immortal warriors.

Meanwhile, it seemed that the priest was descending into madness. Perfect for the scenario Sabine had planned for him. But Sabine's long life and experience had taught her the importance of gathering information before enacting even the best-laid plans.

A thumping bass guitar riff drifted along the hallway as she made her way to the main library. The spacious three-level room was currently being used as the center of operations for the Allegiance while they worked to break down Kenan's network of debauchery. She opened the door and entered.

Dark wooden bookcases carved with twisting forms of tree roots, vines, and roses lined every wall of the vast room. The ceiling was in itself a masterpiece of art, with paintings depicting specific subject matter indicating the topics of the books in that area: a globe represented exploration, a time line showing cave paintings and Egyptian hieroglyphics and letters of the alphabet marked the literary section.

Sabine gazed across the room at massive floor-to-ceiling windows that framed a set of glass doors leading out to a *terrazza*. Two semicircular reading areas mirrored one another on either side of the doors where Gothic-style lancet windows graced the space between tall bookcases and a dome-shaped apse painted with cherubs reading books.

The beauty of the artwork on the ceiling continued in the intricate, parquet-inlaid expanse of floor, which exploded with earthy colors to form a beautiful compass rose in the center of the vast room. Ancient, illuminated Islamic and European manuscripts displayed under glass marked the entrance to a different section of the library.

While the kitchen at Casa della Pietra was often considered the heart of the fortress, there was no doubt in Sabine's mind that it was this room—the library—where a sense of divinity, in the form of knowledge, resided. She took in a deep breath and recognized the scents of rosewood and mahogany that hung in the air—scents that brought back memories of her own youth and that of her maker. She scanned the room until she found one of the twins, Jeremy, working at a computer. As if sensing her presence, he looked up at her, picked up a remote, and turned down the volume.

"Hey," he said. "What's up?"

"I have a meeting with Jason and Christopher."

"They'll be back in a bit," he replied. "They went to the kitchen to get coffee. Anything I can help you with?"

"Not unless you're offering a vein."

Jeremy gulped and turned slightly pale.

"I'm kidding," she said. "Pelayo would kill me. I'll just help myself to the hidden stash."

She wandered over to a bookcase, pulled a copy of Bram Stoker's *Dracula* forward, and waited as a panel of wood slid back to reveal a large refrigerator and freezer. After helping herself to a bag of B positive and drinking the entire contents in a few gulps, she tossed the empty plastic bag into a nearby trash can and turned back to Jeremy.

"I'm glad you and Pelayo have found each other," she said. "He's a good man."

"Thanks," Jeremy said and looked toward the door.

Jason and Christopher entered the library, armed with mugs of coffee. Jason placed one in front of Jeremy, and Sabine sensed sadness about him. She had made sure to destroy Kenan's vampires who had killed Jason's colleague and secretary, but she, like everyone else, would not rest until Kenan was dead. Gabriel had insisted that Jason stay at Casa della Pietra until he deemed it safe for him to return to his home in DC.

"I'm sorry about what happened to your secretary, Jason."

Jason nodded and sat down at the next desk. "Yeah, she was a good person. Looked after me more than I deserved."

"Why do you say that?"

Jason took a sip of coffee and signed in to his computer. "I'm a pain in the ass to work for. She told me so on numerous occasions."

In a rare show of emotion, Sabine momentarily placed a hand on his shoulder. "We'll find Kenan and kill him, I promise. And be assured that we're looking after your secretary's grieving family."

Jason nodded and handed her a folder. "Here's the information you requested regarding states where marriage under the age of eighteen is legal. There's also a list showing the highest number of such marriages—year and quantity—in the top three states."

"Jeez, is that even legal?" Jeremy asked. "To get married at sixteen?"

"Apparently it is in Florida," Sabine said.

"With parental consent," Jason cut in, staring at his computer screen. "For a country that prides itself on forward thinking, we apparently don't give a rat's ass about ending child marriage."

"There are some senators and representatives introducing bills to change current marriage laws in their states," Christopher said.

Sabine respected Christopher's input. As a lawyer, specifically for the Allegiance, he made a point of maintaining up-to-date statistics regarding policies and laws. And when the subject matter was out of his arena, he relied on lawyers such as Sam to keep him informed.

"The issue is in the wording 'to end child marriage, without exceptions,'" he continued. "Meaning both parties would need to be eighteen years of age."

"Are you serious?" Jeremy asked.

"Absolutely," Christopher replied. "There's one state where a governor vetoed the bill to end child marriage in his state, even though it had passed in both houses."

"Who in their right mind would do that?" Jeremy asked. "And why?"

Jason leaned back in his chair. "I'll take a stab at that question; teen pregnancy, abortion, and religious freedom. As long as the girls are married, the word *rape* doesn't enter the picture, even though in certain places, if a man is eighteen or older and has sexual relations with a child under sixteen, he's charged with a felony and imprisoned for up to twenty-five years."

Sabine stared at the statistics. "But that's ridiculous. It makes no sense."

"You're right about that," Jason said. "However, people are working to make changes. But the changes are half-assed."

"Meaning?" Sabine asked.

"In some states, the wording of bills to end child marriage still carries the wording 'except for emancipated minors.' I'd have to do some research, but in looking at this data, I'm going to step out on a limb here and suggest that religion and party politics are involved."

Sabine crossed her arms. "No matter how many millennia pass, it's still the same old story." She turned to leave. "See you soon."

"Where are you headed?" he asked.

"Boston."

CHAPTER 13

Boston, Massachusetts

SABINE KNELT AT the first pew in a small church located on the outskirts of the city. She wore a floor-length crimson crushed velvet cloak that flowed over her body like a river of blood. Her fierce gray eyes and merlot lips were framed by her pale face and dappled with the glow of candlelight. She heard the door open and close behind her and the falter of the priest's footsteps as he approached her.

"The church is closed," he said. "You're welcome to return to God's house tomorrow."

Sabine rose like a flame, moved into the aisle, and turned toward him, her head raised slightly but still in the shadows. "Would you turn Mary away from God's house?"

He took a step back. "No, of course not," he replied, his voice skittish. "Take your time in prayer, and I'll return shortly."

The priest backed up until he reached the entrance. The click of the lock echoed in the chamber. He tugged at the handle, desperate to pull it open.

"The doors are locked, Father," Sabine said. "Come forward—I wish to speak with you."

The priest's hand dropped from the door handle as Sabine's thrall ensnared him. He turned to her and walked up the aisle to the altar and the nave, stopping when he stood in front of Sabine.

"There was a young girl in your congregation in Florida; her name is Helen," Sabine said. "Do you remember her?"

The priest shook his head. "Many children pass through the house of God. I don't remember a child with that name."

"Allow me to nudge your memory, Father."

The priest reached for his throat and gagged.

"Helen was ten when you stole her virginity. Tell me what happened that evening." Sabine reached across to the pulpit, lowered her hand, and stepped back into the shadows.

The priest fell to his knees. "Helen was young—I couldn't resist her sweet flesh. God sent her to me, just like the others, as gifts for my loyalty to Him." His eyes bulged, and he tilted his head. "And the girl who jumped—what a fool—she carried my seed. My seed! What greater gift could a young girl receive other than the gift of life through a man of God?" He grabbed at his chest, tearing away his robe until he stood naked. "I am the keeper of God's children, the boys and the girls."

He fell to his knees. "I beg your forgiveness, Mary, for any wrongdoing. So that God will grant me entrance to heaven."

Sabine stared at him, raised a hand, and focused on the rapidly pounding pulse raging within his body. That body convulsed, and spittle flew from his mouth as he fell forward. Sabine walked over to the pulpit, retrieved a thumb drive, and laid it on the ground by the priest's head. She picked up her phone, pressed Pause, and sent the video of the priest's confession along with a text to Christopher and Sam. Then she strode down the aisle, her long robe flaring around her body. The double doors flew open, and Sabine raced into the dark night.

CHAPTER 14

ILLONA STARED OUT the window of her office at the adoption agency and watched the slew of peak-hour traffic crawling along Wilshire Boulevard fifteen stories below. Her secretary and assistants had left the office for the day, and now in silence and solitude she dropped the glamour of her identity and stared at the reflection of her true self in the window. Unlike the dark-eyed persona of Sylvia, the caseworker at the private adoption agency whose round face remained framed by a short, dark brown bob, the image looking back at her showed a woman in her midthirties with long white hair, full lips, and deep-set cerulean-blue eyes. She looked much like her brother, Elion, Arianna and Jeremy's father.

Months had passed since she first called Arianna and explained her birth mother's wishes. That was followed by the news that the young woman also had a twin brother. She thought of the moment she had handed Arianna a large manila envelope—right here in her office—and of the sense of endearment that seeped from her niece the moment she had seen the photograph of her birth mother, Katja, holding two newborn babies. Illona had kept the promise she made with her brother, Elion, to protect the identity of the twins.

Looking past her reflection to the expanse of high-rise buildings that encompassed Westwood Village, she thought of the nearby coastline that had first lured settlers to this area. Over the years, rugged trails had become sealed roads where palm trees dotted sidewalks, and shiny new soft-top sedans puttered along wide streets. Their passengers, dressed in glittering gowns and black tuxedos, clinked crystal champagne glasses on their way to movie premiers during Hollywood's Golden Age.

She had grown to love this city of angels, albeit a far cry from her birthplace where life had been much simpler and slower. Most of her childhood memories had long since faded, but the tangy scent of freshly cut fields and the sound of her mother's sweet voice as she taught her the songs of the fae were often shadowed by the frightened expression on the face of her little brother when she had said goodbye almost seven centuries ago. The terror in Elion's eyes remained etched on her heart like a piece of scar tissue; his screams of resistance still haunted her, but at that time he was barely five years old, too young to know that there were mortals fearful of the fae in his blood. If they knew of his talents, his death would have been imminent.

She had not seen Elion again until centuries later during the heat of a New York summer. He had immediately sensed her essence behind the façade of an older lady she sometimes wore at that time, and when he approached her and offered his arm, she had clutched his hand and leaned into his body just as a grandmother might do. She led him to the apartment where she lived, and once behind the closed door, she dropped her glamour and brother and sister embraced.

They had sat side by side on a sofa, absorbing the history of time between them until Elion spoke. "Father and I searched for you for years. We found the cave where Mother had taken her final breath, but there was no hint of you anywhere. After Father's passing, I never gave up hope that I would find you."

Illona squeezed her brother's hand. "I couldn't risk being seen, let alone with you. I'd heard whispers that you were searching for me, and as much as my heart yearned for family, your safety meant more, and always will."

"I understand your reasoning," he said. "However, please promise me that you'll not hide from me again."

Illona shook her head. "Our lives are not that simple, Elion. You know that."

"Then why now?" he asked. "Why have you decided to return to me at this time? And how long have you been here in the United States?"

Illona rose, walked into the small kitchen area, and poured two glasses of water. She placed the glasses on the kitchen table, and Elion joined her. When they were both seated, she looked up and began her story. "We both have much to share, but for now I believe this particular part of my life—here in the United States—is perhaps the most relevant, and there is much planning for us to do. You see, Mother also shared many visions with me." She reached across the table and held his hands. "Your beloved is destined to give birth to a boy and a girl—twins."

The edges of Elion's mouth lifted to a smile. "Yes," he said. "And the babies will be born April twenty-second."

Illona squeezed his hands. "The first day of *Walpurgis Thrimilei*. We'll need to protect the children. Does Katja know of your bloodline?"

Elion nodded. "Yes, and you'll understand why I told her when you meet her." He started to pull his hands away, but Illona's grip tightened.

She closed her eyes and immediately felt his essence reaching out to her. His memories flooded into her mind and flashed before her eyes like a fast-moving film; distinct moments and pivotal life choices: the moment Elion and their father first met the great seer, Prudence, and the multiple times he had witnessed the destruction done by Domenico and, later, Kenan. Illona saw the moment when Elion had first seen Katja… a woman in her late twenties. Her strawberry blonde hair, tinged with strands of purple and pink, was held together in an unruly bun on top of her head by a ribbon. Even from a distance, her light blue eyes twinkled in the late afternoon light. She stood curbside on a Brooklyn street, hailing a cab with a mismatched pair of garden gnomes at her feet.

Behind her, an elderly man pulled a grate across the windows of an antique store, and as he walked away, he turned and waved at her. "I'll call you when I find more."

"Thank you!" Katja said. She waved back at him just as a cab pulled up.

Elion rushed to open the car door, and when Katja turned to him, her breath caught for a moment and she smiled.

The image faded into another of Elion and Katja sharing marriage vows, running together in Central Park, planting flowers in a garden, and searching through antique stores for garden statuary, Elion presenting her with the Callot fairy statue, and more recently, the moment when Katja told him she was pregnant. But then Illona saw death—two deaths…

She opened her eyes, released his hands, and looked at him through tear-blurred eyes. "No." She shook her head. "Perhaps there's another way… It's a vision, Elion. They can change."

Elion laid his hands on the table, stretched out his fingers, and stared at them. "I've also seen the alternate ending and believe me, the death you saw is preferable. Fate has brought us together at this time so that we can plan for the twins and Katja's safety. Will you help me?"

Illona nodded. "Of course I'll help you."

Elion sat back in his chair. "Do you have children of your own?"

"No." She clutched her hands together. "Mother and I were raped countless times during the first months of our captivity. The beatings that followed, along with the spells Mother cast, prevented us from becoming pregnant. After my escape, I chose a life in midwifery. Perhaps it is not my fate to give birth."

He gave her a quizzical look. "And yet I sense children around you."

Illona took a sip of water and smiled at her brother. "Yes. Since my arrival in this city, my life has been centered around children."

"Please," Elion urged her to continue. "I want to hear everything."

She placed the glass on the table. "Most of my years in Europe were spent in hiding, and I will not lie—they were lonely times. But there was one man who gave me shelter whenever I was in need, but that story is one I will save for a later time. For now I'll share relevant pieces of my life since arriving here. When I came to this country, it was divided and in the midst of civil war. I couldn't stand by and do nothing, so I followed the brave women who walked across blood-soaked battlefields, hoping to find life among the barrage of death. What we found were men still clinging to life—young men, some barely in their teens—with bodies so broken that they begged for death.

"Years later, on the evening of May 9, 1865, I looked up at the stars and thought of you. In my heart, I knew you were still safe and with the Allegiance, but I missed you. Perhaps it was seeing so many men struck down by the horrors of war that made me hope you were making the most of your life.

"As it happened that night, I attended a young soldier in a tent that was part of a makeshift hospital. I was with him when he died. He implored me to tell his wife and his son that he loved them… He made me promise, in fact. He was clutching a letter in his hand, which I read after staying with him till the very end. The next day, I headed to New York."

"And did you find his family?"

She nodded and placed her hands, palms facing up, on the table. "Allow me to show you the story."

Elion settled his hands in hers…

New York, 1865

ILLONA ARRIVED IN New York amid a cholera epidemic. Signs were posted, warning people to "attend immediately to all disorders of the bowels" and that "medicine could be had for the poor by applying to station houses in each ward." Seeing that, Illona immediately made her way to the address the young soldier had given her. A gust of wind whistled past, guiding her, and with the chilled air came music, the eerie sound of a bow seamlessly sliding across the strings of a cello. Illona recognized the music as Bach's Suite no. 1 in G Major, sounding both prophetic and ominous.

The particular area she had entered was known as seventh ward and was unlike anything she had seen in any other great city. Even the squalor of London did not compare to the sheer poverty and wretchedness of this place. But Illona had made a promise to find the soldier's wife and child. She headed forward, lifting her dress so as not to drag the hem in the pools of slimy water mixed with waste matter, grateful for the wooden boards that had been set up so one could cross the deeper puddles.

The address the Union soldier had given her dictated that she turn from the main street and down the next alley, which she did, and immediately the façade of brick buildings dropped away, and Illona entered a world of impoverishment that she'd not thought possible. The stench in the air alerted her to a nearby privy, and her stomach roiled as the smell of boiled fish drifted down from an upper window. Clotheslines zigzagged across the alley, and barefooted children with dirty faces and close-cropped hair stood on a stoop while women washed clothes in steel tubs of coffee-colored water, their smocks stained and threadbare. Farther along, a group of men huddled together and looked up as she passed by. During her long life, Illona had never seen such despair as on the faces of the men—hope was but a distant memory.

She clutched the paper to her chest and kept walking, stopping once to ask for directions. When she reached the soldier's address, she walked up the steps, turning to look along the narrow verandah bordered by loose wooden rails. A young girl approached—her arms were covered in bites, and the dress she wore hung loosely over her frail body.

"I'm looking for a young woman who recently gave birth to a son," Illona said.

The young girl stared at her with faraway eyes.

"Her husband was in the army," Illona continued.

A look of recognition passed over the young girl's face, and she led Illona to an inner room. "She lived 'ere till a few days ago."

Illona's heart sank at that news.

"She took ill," the girl said. "Moved 'er to the battery army barracks. It's an 'ospital."

"And the baby?"

"They took 'im with 'er." The girl tugged at Illona's arm and whispered, "Cholera… Guess they dun thought the baby'd die too."

Illona took her shawl and placed it around the young girl's shoulders. "Thank you."

The young girl ran a hand over the soft wool and looked up at Illona with tears in her eyes. Illona squeezed the girl's bony shoulders, knowing that the poverty she had witnessed that day would change her life forever.

At the army barracks, a nurse guided Illona to the soldier's wife. She sat beside the woman who was sick with fever and wiped her brow while she told her the news of her husband's death.

"You and your child were whom he spoke of as he took his last breath," Illona said.

The woman reached for Illona's hand. "Please, take little Thomas away from this place… away from this city… Where he might have a chance of surviving. Please, we have no family left. Do this for my husband and me."

Illona knew from the woman's aura that she did not have long for this life. She nodded. "You need not worry. And yes, I shall take Thomas and raise him as if he were my own. He will be loved, I promise you this." Illona stayed with the woman until she passed into the next life.

A nurse guided Illona to a nursery area where the baby was being held. Thomas would be the first of her children…

Illona released Elion's hands.

"They just let you take the baby?"

She nodded. "At that time the streets of New York were home to thousands of children living as orphans, sharing the city with the destitute, ill and homeless adults, many of whom were soldiers. The orphanages were filled to the brim, and children were being moved from the city by way of the Orphan Trains. So yes, I took Thomas with me…"

෮

A sudden shift in the atmosphere brought Illona out of her past and back to her office in Westwood.

"It's time," she whispered. A recurring vision of this moment had aided her with the preparation of leaving Los Angeles for an unknown period of time. Her workers had been in agreement that she take time off and enjoy a well-earned vacation, and Illona felt confident leaving her adoption agency in their capable hands. However, although she had seen this moment many times before, the reality of coming face-to-face with the ancient seer who had known her mother so well brought with it a wave of sadness and anticipation.

She turned around just as a tall man dressed in the armor of a fae warrior stepped out from a cloud of mist. He was followed by the seer she knew to be Prudence and the ancient vampire Nikandros.

Illona stepped forward, and Nikandros embraced her. "My dearest friend," she said in perfect Greek. "How I have missed your company."

With his hands on her shoulders, Nikandros stared into her eyes and smiled. "You've always spoken the language of my heritage better than I, and yes, I have missed you too." He stepped aside and introduced her to Prudence and Hakon.

Illona placed a hand over her heart and held the other toward Hakon. He mirrored her gesture, and when their palms touched, sparks of light framed their hands. They stared into one another's eyes, searching deep into the essence of each other's souls. Moments later they lowered their arms, and Hakon brought her into an embrace.

"Have you seen the twins?" She switched to the language of the fae.

Hakon nodded. "Yes. Their unique strengths are about to unfold, and I would appreciate your help with their lessons. They have many questions about their family, especially Elion."

Upon hearing her brother's name, Illona turned to Prudence. "My brother told me of your friendship with him and our dear mother. How you were so kind to him, and many other creatures like us." She lowered her head. "There was nothing I could do… Elion sought revenge for what Domenico and Kenan had done to our family. I think there was a part of him that hoped he could change his own fate." She fell into Prudence's waiting arms and savored the caring embrace of the seer.

"Birgit taught you well," Prudence said. She cupped Illona's chin. "Perhaps too well, for there have been many times I've wanted to bring you to the safety of our fortress, but I could not find you."

Illona shook her head. "The timing needed to be such that it culminated with Katja's death and the twins coming of age. The risk of anyone discovering Arianna's connection to Elion was too great. And her destiny is linked to another whose story is yet to unfold."

She turned to Nikandros. "For so long I've wanted to share this part of my journey with you."

"We are creatures of secrecy," Nikandros said. "Those who share too much risk death to themselves and also their loved ones." He looked at a bag on the floor. "Do you have everything you need for this journey?"

"Yes," she said, walking over to her desk. She grabbed her computer bag and purse.

Nikandros hoisted her duffel bag over his shoulder. He turned and looked out of the window. "You'll miss this weather."

She smiled. "How can I, when I still miss the green hills of my youth?"

Nikandros raised an eyebrow. "I see your wit has not left you." He caught her elbow and guided her to Prudence and Hakon. Moments later, the lamp on Illona's desk flickered and the room fell into darkness.

CHAPTER 15

Casa della Pietra

COCO LOOKED UP as Chantal entered the studio. She was always bemused at the fluidity of her mother's movements and how her beauty was now frozen in her immortality. A smile caught the edges of her mouth as the scent of the lavender and rosemary that infused her mother's presence drifted throughout the room, reminding her of her childhood.

"Why do I feel like we're about to chat about the birds and the bees?" Coco asked.

"I think I'm a bit late for that." Chantal grinned. "But I do want to discuss something similar, a way to deepen your connection with Gabriel."

Coco's cheeks blushed. "Oddly enough, that's kind of what I'm trying to figure out before he returns."

"Maybe I can help," Chantal said. "Ask me anything."

"Grandpa told me that you never wanted to become an immortal," Coco blurted out.

Chantal sank into a chair and sighed. "Yes, I did say that. But now that idea—of not sharing the deep connection your father and I have—seems ridiculous. You see, in some ways, Kenan making me immortal proved to be a gift." She leaned forward and pushed her dark hair behind her ears. "Before that day, I thought I knew love, but that wasn't true. Perhaps if Alessandro and I had both been human when we met, then yes, we would know love as humans do, but since I became immortal and acknowledged what I am, I've realized what Alessandro gave up when he accepted my decision to stay human. The pain he must have felt when I was taken—the pain I felt—was unbearable. Now our blood runs through each other's veins, and as such, we share one another's thoughts and traits."

"When I saw Gabriel with Marguerite it broke my heart," Coco said. "I had no control over the situation, and that made me so damn angry. I think it's impossible to love him any more than I already do."

Chantal chuckled. "Oh, trust me, Colombina, if you were to honor your father's bloodline, your love for Gabriel would be infinite."

"How do I do that?"

"Drink from him."

"What?" she asked. "You can't be serious!"

"To share blood with each other will unite you for eternity." Chantal's eyes sparkled, and her whole face lit up. "You will never question each other's love again, and you will find one another if you are ever torn apart."

"So that part is true? Gabriel told me that exact same thing when we first met," Coco said. "But—"

Chantal held up a hand. "No, Colombina, there are no ifs or buts to speak of here. You either love him for who and what he is and want to spend the rest of eternity with him, or you don't. And if you feel the latter, then I suggest you get on with your life rather than waste precious time. That's not fair to either of you. Honor your immortal heritage, become the woman you were born to be. What are you scared of, little one?"

Coco's bottom lip quivered, and she shook her head. "I don't know."

"Perhaps you need to let go of the façade you've had to carry all these years and allow Gabriel to care for you the way he wants to. Don't throw away this chance for true happiness, but understand that there's no turning back once you've made the leap into your new life. Nothing will ever be the same, and you will kill anyone who tries to hurt your beloved. Can you imagine feeling so much love?"

"No," Coco said. "Perhaps that's what frightens me."

Chantal rose. "I know you've been hurt, I know you miss your old life, but time is running out, and we—the Allegiance—need to destroy Kenan. Alessandro, Christopher, and I, have made our choice—it's time for you to make yours." She hugged Coco before exiting the room.

Staring at nothing in particular, Coco sorted through memories—her childhood, teen years, college, and work. For the first time, she clearly saw the painstaking efforts the Allegiance had made to keep her safe. And oh, how she'd balked at Christopher every time he had stood firm with her. She walked out of the studio and returned to Gabriel's empty apartment.

Coco sat on the sofa and opened her laptop. The light from the screen cast an eerie glow over her face as she clicked on her email and stared at the screen for twenty minutes. After addressing a letter to the head of her department at UCLA, Coco sat back and began writing. Oddly enough, she found the words flowed effortlessly onto the screen, and she wrote as if she were in conversation with the woman who had been her mentor during her undergrad and graduate years, and later, her boss.

Layla's words from early November glittered like gold dust in the back of her mind. "Think carefully before you ignore a closed door merely because you're too afraid to see what's behind it." *Was it really just a few months ago we drove together from Florence to San Gimignano?* The corners of her mouth turned upward as she remembered Layla's snarky comment when Coco had asked about the tall man who was adjusting a set of stirrups in a Polaroid photograph on the wall in Christopher's childhood bedroom. "You might want to ask Christopher" had been Layla's answer.

The man in the photo turned out to be Gabriel.

Coco thought of the many times that, while lost in the zone of creativity, she had looked up at a finished painting and all she could see were Gabriel's eyes. It didn't matter if she worked on landscapes, portraits, or something abstract, she always saw his eyes staring back at her. It seemed the magic Gabriel had used when she was a little girl had not taken the memory of his eyes from her psyche. The headaches were nothing compared to the anxiety that phenomenon caused her, but she kept it to herself for fear that others might think her crazy.

Her fingers were on the keyboard, typing the letter she'd never envisioned herself writing. When she was done, she hit Send and closed the computer.

C HAPTER 16

Casa della Pietra

W HEN ILLONA APPEARED in the main library with Prudence, Hakon, and Nikandros, an air of familiarity swirled around her. The cool touch of Nikandros's hand on her elbow calmed her somewhat as he guided her. But there was another essence in the room, tugging at her heart, one she had not experienced before. Wanting to understand more, Illona opened her heart, just for a split second, and pocketed the new sensation. She halted in her steps, knowing no one but Nikandros would have noticed her hesitation, and he most likely would have attributed it to her excitement and anxiety.

The expanse of the library filled her with delight, but her eyes glistened as she caught the essence of her brother, Elion, floating in the room. She felt comforted knowing he had also been welcome here. She sought out Hakon, who stood beside a young woman with the azure eyes of the fae and the maternal glow of pregnancy.

"This is Layla," Hakon said. "Daughter of Antonia."

In a gesture of friendship, the two women held each other's hands.

"I'm Illona. I knew your ancestors from the north." She placed her hands over the small bump of Layla's pregnant belly and grinned as she felt the baby move. She looked into Layla's eyes. "Your secret's safe with me."

Layla smiled and nodded.

"Illona's a midwife," Nikandros said. "She guided Flora into this world."

"Then I hope you will attend the birth of our child too." Layla turned toward Christopher, and he stepped forward. "My fiancé, Christopher."

"Welcome to Casa della Pietra, Illona," he said. "And I'd definitely feel comforted having you alongside Sabine during our baby's delivery."

"That would bring me great joy," Illona said. She made her way over to the twins. "I was at your birth too, although not in this persona."

Jeremy pushed back his chair and walked around his desk to where she stood. "You knew our mom and dad."

The words in their past tense brought tears to Illona's eyes. "Yes. I'm Elion's sister. You look so much like my brother."

"Mom's dead."

"I know, Jeremy." Illona stepped forward and embraced him. "I'm saddened Katja's no longer with us." She closed her eyes and breathed in Jeremy's essence: gentle, caring, possessive, and protective. Qualities that had also made her brother so strong and easy to love. She eased herself back and stared into his eyes. "I'm happy you found your sister and the Allegiance; that is what Elion wanted." Her gaze found Arianna. "And you were never alone, Arianna." She brought the glamour of Sylvia forward.

Arianna gasped. "You're Sylvia, the woman from the adoption agency? Why did my parents send me away?" she blurted out. "Wasn't there another way to protect me?"

Illona dropped Sylvia's glamour and shook her head. "No, the risks were too high. We knew that Steven and Isabel would always protect you and love you. I'm so sorry, Arianna, but we did what we had to do to secure both your and Jeremy's safety."

"Did Isabel and Steven know the truth?" Arianna asked.

"No," Illona replied. "We would never have placed them in such a position. They fell in love with you at first sight, and they loved you as their daughter." She watched as Arianna pulled at the sleeves of her sweater and her lips tightened. Illona stepped forward and hugged her. Like her twin, Arianna's essence stemmed from her protective instincts, but there was more—where she sensed Jeremy's ingenuity for diplomacy and the awakening skill of clairvoyance, his sister had the element of empathy, a trait that would eventually steer her toward her destiny: a life of leadership and great love, with a man of equal stature by her side. She kissed Arianna's forehead and turned to Jeremy. "I met Pelayo once," she said. "Steven introduced us. He was helping him on a case that involved a family I had worked with. He has a good heart."

Jeremy nodded. "Yes, he does."

Illona became aware of the earlier presence she had perceived. She looked up and came face-to-face with a mortal. He stepped forward and held out a hand to her.

"I'm Jason."

"Illona," she said, accepting his hand. She forced back an urge to gently push the disorganized curls away from his black-rimmed glasses so she could see his eyes, but as if reading her mind, he ran his other hand through his hair, revealing the mirrors of his soul. *A man of numbers, a thinker, honorable, and passionate.* "It is impossible to be a mathematician without being a poet in soul."

Jason's mouth curved into a smile. "Quoting Sofia Vasilyevna Kovalevskaya gets you points with me," he said. "The woman was a mathematical genius."

"Yes, indeed," Illona said. "Imagine the possibilities if the universities had welcomed her for her brilliant mind rather than turning her away because she was not a man."

Jason nodded and released her hand, but not before Illona had memorized the characteristics of his fingers and palm. The art of palmistry had been taught to her by her mother and had proven to be an added bonus when understanding human nature. Jason's spatula-shaped hand told her, among many things, that he liked to be active—mentally and physically—and excelled at his work. The firmness of his hand was that of a determined person, rational and hardworking. As he let go of her hand, Illona glanced briefly at his palm, noticing the extended length of his head line; Jason had a natural draw toward intellectual concerns. *No wonder he thrives here with the Allegiance.*

Prudence approached. "Layla, would you show Illona her rooms?"

"Of course," Layla replied.

"I'll come too," Arianna said. "I'm sure Isabel would like to meet you."

"I'll follow shortly as we have a matter of importance to discuss. Layla and Arianna will introduce you to other members of the household," Prudence said and exited the room.

Illona glanced back at the twins. "There's something in the fairy statue that you both need to see. Perhaps later today we can meet, and I'll show you and the others connected to our world."

Jeremy nodded. "Sure, just let me know when and where and I'll be there."

From the corner of her eye, Illona saw her old friend, Nikandros, chuckle as he guided her toward the door and whispered, "Love finds us when we least expect it, my dear friend."

CHAPTER 17

ILLONA SETTLED HERSELF in a comfortable chair and admired the view of the mountains in the distance through a series of windows framed by medieval scalloped stone capitals.

Prudence poured two glasses of brandy before taking a seat opposite Illona and raising her crystal glass. "To you, my dear, and your sweet mother, Birgit."

The two women tapped their glasses, took a sip, and sat back in their chairs. Regardless of the austere stone walls and Gothic architecture, the study in Prudence and Stefan's private quarters radiated warmth, and Illona relaxed and opened up about her past.

"After Mother and I were stolen from our family home, the soldiers tied our hands together, gagged our mouths, and covered our eyes. We were like that for days. They raped us. Laughed at us. Beat us. They were monsters." Her voice caught. She twirled the glass in her hand. "When we arrived at the cave, we were weak and hungry… I wanted to die, but Mother refused to allow me to give up. We were thrown into a cell, and they removed the ties from our wrists, uncovered our mouths and eyes."

A flood of tears escaped her eyes. She placed her glass on the table and knelt in front of Prudence. The ethereal head of the Allegiance embraced her and ran a hand over Illona's hair.

"Even after our eyes grew accustomed to the darkness, it was difficult to recognize each other. We were bruised women—inside and out—barely holding on to our humanity. But Mother had devised a plan. She had learned the art of mesmerizing, and although it would take time, she intended to weave a spell so that we would be unseen to others. We were fed broth, that was all, until the day the devil arrived."

She clenched her eyes closed as if to clear away an unwanted vision. "The soldiers opened the door, and he entered. I knew the man was Domenico. He took me first, made Mother watch… I remember her screams. How they intensified when he bit into my neck. It took five soldiers to hold her down. And when Domenico was finished with me, he did the same to her.

"As he left the cell, he turned back and questioned us. 'What do you know of Prudence and the Allegiance?' We were both so weak, but I remember clearly the words Mother spoke… *Sine virtue omnia sunt perdita.*' Without courage, all is lost.

"Her words infuriated Domenico, and he left us. But the sound of a bolt sliding across the door reminded us we were his prisoners. From then on we were given bread with our broth, and it seemed to us that we were being fattened for slaughter. To fill our time, Mother used the edge of a rock she found on the floor and carved figures and words onto the walls. One of the drawings was of two figures—a figure with two faces, one male and one female. She told me that my duty in this life was to protect these two children."

Illona looked up at Prudence, whose golden eyes brimmed with tears.

"Mother ran a hand over my matted hair, cupped my face in her hands, and then smiled. It was too late to object… the strands of her magic were quick to take hold. When I tried to speak, my lips were frozen. Mother's spell was upon me, and the mask of death fell over my body. 'I love you, and it is because of this love that I need to let you go. You must hide, even from those you love, and do not come back for me, and never lose sight of Elion, for he will be the father of the twins. And as fae, twins are rare and must be protected. This is what I ask of you, my darling child. Be brave, and know that you are loved. That creature that fed from us is evil incarnate, and he must be destroyed, but not today. Today I give you life. Take this gift and live to honor our heritage.'

"I remember the soldiers carrying me out of the cell and a journey in a wagon surrounded by death. They threw what they thought was my dead body into the air, and then I landed in ice-cold water. It was dark, but I remember the freezing temperature and choking on water. I was alive. In that instant, Mother's spell broke, and with all my strength I pushed my way up from the underwater grave until I burst through the surface and my lungs filled with air. I hid in shadows until the sound of the wagon disappeared into the darkness."

"Birgit would be proud of you," Prudence said. "And you have done everything she asked of you. Rest here, and know that for now, you are safe with us."

She gazed into Prudence's eyes. "Are any of us truly safe from the evil Kenan spreads?"

"No," Prudence said. "That is why he must be destroyed. When I consider the current state of humanity, I am not sure that certain men will ever see women as their equal. However, we must remember that those men—although powerful—are the exception, not the norm. We can never give up our dignity. We have hope and courage, and each other."

Illona rose and walked toward the window. "With all due respect, Prudence, we need more than hope and courage. We need a well-executed plan. This world is vastly different from the place of our youth. Wars no longer rely on swords but on technology, logic, and structure. Wars are won by men like your son."

Prudence turned away.

"It's Gabriel's time," Illona continued. "I only ask that you listen to him."

"How do you know such things?"

"I have not told you everything Mother said before I was taken away. She said, 'The one with the name of the angel will save us.'"

"And did she say he would survive?" Prudence asked, her voice a whisper.

"A storm is coming." Illona placed a hand on the window. "Mother used to say that while storms can cause havoc, they clear the way for new growth. Once, I asked her if she were a tree, which would she choose to be. 'A willow,' she said. 'It is important to bend when the wind blows.'"

A beat passed and Prudence nodded. "Birgit was wise."

"I'd like to work with the twins," Illona said. She turned around to face the matriarch. "There's so much for them to know about their father and our family."

"Go to them," Prudence said. "And thank you for sharing Birgit's words with me."

Chapter 18

Casa della Pietra

COCO THOUGHT ABOUT her past and the time and energy she had spent distancing herself from the Allegiance. She thought about all the relationships she'd had—none of them more than an escape from her loneliness. She thought about all the people who had protected her during her childhood, teen, and adult years, and she thought about Christopher and the times she had screamed at him for being an overprotective brother, fencing her in, and stealing her anonymity.

In six months, her life had taken a 360-degree turn, and her family, friends, and the Allegiance had all been there to guide her along this newfound existence. And Gabriel, who had known about her for centuries, had watched and waited until the time was right for him to introduce himself.

She remembered the effect his presence had first had on her. It was only a few months ago at Maria's café in San Gimignano when his essence had reached out to her from across the room the moment he opened the door and entered. She had sat there, unable to move, knowing that when she lifted her head and looked at him, her life's path would forever be changed. The draw to him had not diminished but had become infinitely stronger. The image of him as he lay near death at Houdini's abandoned gravesite in New York flashed before her. Her body had betrayed her as she stood, shocked at the sight of his burned skin and fragmented bones. The realization of life without him had sucked her dry and paralyzed her with fear.

The rapid thumping of her heart brought Coco back to the present. She lifted her head and found herself immediately drawn to Gabriel's intense stare. He leaned forward in the chair where he was seated across from her, elbows on his knees, and she sensed desperation and sorrow around him. But those emotions were immeasurable against the love that reached out to her.

A long minute passed, and as each second ticked by, the exterior shell Coco had kept around her began to crumble. She held a hand out to him, and as she did, she noticed a glimpse of hope in his eyes, but still he was cautious in his movement. He rose, never taking his gaze from hers, and walked over to her. He knelt on the floor, took her hand, and placed it over his heart. His eyes were closed now, his breathing deep, slow, and steady. She knelt before him and with her other hand, she traced the outline of his face, finally coming to rest over his lips.

"You told me once that there were two times when a vampire drinks from his beloved," she said. "Before entering a battle, and when proclaiming eternal love."

His eyes opened, and the sadness had melted away and specks of gold had appeared and swam in a sea of hope and lust. She held his gaze, and when she spoke, her own voice quivered, mirroring the fragility of her heart.

"I'm ready to bind myself to you for eternity. Are you?"

Gabriel brought his lips to hers. Heat coursed throughout her body as he placed his hands firmly on her shoulders, only breaking their kiss to run his lips along her neck. Coco caught her breath, and her head fell back—an invitation she hoped he would accept.

"Of course I'm ready. But there's no turning back, Colombina. Once we've shared our blood, the union is eternal. We'll experience each other's emotions—good, bad, pain, sorrow, joy—no matter where we are, even when we're apart."

Coco rested her forehead against his. "I need you, Gabriel. We need each other." She undid the buttons of his shirt and pushed it over his shoulders. The subdued light of winter faded as the sun crept behind the mountains, leaving the room awash in the warmth of firelight. "Is it painful?"

"I don't know," he said. She drew her eyebrows together, and he smiled. "This is a first for me too. You are my only love."

He pulled her sweatshirt over her head and laid her down as if she were a delicate crystal glass, onto a nest of pillows and blankets that had magically appeared. They were both naked, and Coco trembled as his gaze slowly raked over her body, leaving a trail of goose bumps on her skin. An image emerged, of the first time his essence had touched her. This thought brought forth a deep, throaty groan from him.

His thumb circled over the bump of her clitoris as his fingers slid inside her wetness. He swirled his tongue over her nipples, nipping and sucking, until her muscles clenched and spasmed around his fingers. He rolled her onto her stomach, and his lips grazed her ear. "That day I saw you posing naked in front of Eduardo's drawing class was the closest I've ever come to losing my self-control. So now, I intend to explore every dip and rise of your body, *mi amore.*"

She could feel his lips before they touched her skin, and she shuddered as he lifted her hair and kissed the nape of her neck, the slope of her shoulders, and returned to her spine.

Coco sighed, clutching the blanket beneath her, aware of the wet heat pulsing at the junction of her thighs. "I love you," she said. She turned over and playfully pushed him onto the blanket and straddled him. Leaning forward, Coco gripped his biceps and claimed his mouth with hers. She broke the kiss but continued to nuzzle and nip at his skin—across his chest and defined abdomen, slowing down only when her hunger craved his length. She brought him into her mouth and moaned as she tasted him.

His hands ran over her shoulders to her breasts, and her body flushed with heat as her nipples hardened and stood erect with pleasure. She sensed his muscles tense, and in one swift movement he pinned her beneath him and entered her. She wrapped her legs around his hips, and he pulled her to his body as their rhythm increased. He kissed her with hunger, possessed her, explored her mouth with his tongue. At the apex of their climax together, he pushed back her hair and placed his mouth over the vein that pumped in her neck.

He sucked on her skin until the blood in her veins gathered in that place and his sharp fangs extended. Coco was aware of a prickling sensation. Intense heat flooded her body, bringing her to a plane of euphoria she had never experienced. Primal instinct took over, and she screamed. When Gabriel withdrew his fangs and turned his neck toward her, she latched onto the skin above his jugular vein, enjoying the new sensation as small, sharp fangs descended from her canines. She sank them into his skin and drew in his blood. Waves of electrifying passion crashed over her, sending her mind into a rich palette of reds and emotions brushed with words of love.

Absolute peace followed as she found Gabriel's pure essence in her blood, her thoughts, her core. Their lives entwined and floated through the universe—void of time—in a stream of endless love. She stared into his eyes but dared not speak. The silence swirled around them, drowning out reality and caressing their bodies with elation. Teardrops escaped her eyes and fell onto her cheeks, and Gabriel's golden-hued eyes also glistened. He lowered her onto the bed of pillows, cradled her in his arms, and covered their bodies with a blanket. She did not hold back her tears, or think about time, but held him tightly while he ran his fingers through her hair.

"There's no flower on this earth that compares to your beauty, no sonnet yet written to express the way my heart feels. You are all that is good in my world, Colombina. There's nothing more I'll ever need."

She kissed his neck and rested her head over his heart.

"So tell me," he asked. "Did I hurt you?"

"Yes." She smiled. "But it hurt so good."

"I'll take that as a compliment."

She snuggled into his body. They lay together in silence, enjoying the ecstasy of fulfillment and the commitment they had made to each other. After a while, Coco eased herself up and leaned on an elbow.

"I know this has nothing to do with what we've just experienced, but now that we share a blood bond, is there a way you can show me Isabella's story? I'm drawn to her, and I'm wondering if there's something that we're missing… something that maybe I can pick up on."

"You really want to do this now?"

Coco nodded.

"If it's important to you, then yes, I can show you. However, hearing only my interpretation would not do Isabella's story justice, and I would rather you understand it from her point of view."

She frowned. "Is that possible?"

"Yes." He ran a hand over her bare shoulder. "She kept a journal during the last month of her life and asked that I keep it safe for her. It was delivered to my lodgings in Florence."

Coco pushed herself into a sitting position and stared at Gabriel. "You have a journal written by Isabella de' Medici?"

In answer to her question, a rune magically appeared in the air before his face. He muttered a Nordic phrase and the rune disappeared. Moments later, Isabella's book safe hovered in the air before him. He reached forward and placed it on a blanket that fell over his naked body. He opened the lid and removed the letters written by Isabella and Troilo and handed them to Coco. She peered into the empty compartment and noticed an indentation. Gabriel placed a finger against the space, and a drawer popped open to reveal a small journal tied with a piece of blue ribbon.

"I'm happy to fill you in on the parts of her story that relate to me and the Allegiance." He handed the journal to her. "This tells Isabella's story after the birth of her son—her son with Troilo."

"Did he ever get to read it?"

A satisfied smile lit up his face. "Yes, and she would have been proud of him, for he was a kind and gentle man—one who chose to live a life away from the world of dukes and duchesses—and who, like his mother, was a skilled rider, but an even better equine breeder. Many of his horses led men across new lands and onto battlefields."

She placed the letters inside the book safe and ran a hand over the journal. "He didn't want to keep this… to show to his children?"

"No." Gabriel shook his head. "He said that it would be safer kept with me, and that one day, hopefully, an heir with his mother's lineage would show the courage and passion of Lorenzo de' Medici, and that he or she should be the one to inherit the journal."

Coco raised an eyebrow, and the corners of Gabriel's mouth turned upward.

"Yes," he said, "Prudence and I believe that such an heir has arrived."

"You're not going to tell me any more, are you?"

He covered her mouth with his, and when they parted, Coco looked up at him and placed a hand on the side of his face.

"I love you." She picked up the journal and silently read through to the final entry.

From the diary of Isabella Romola de' Medici
Florence, Italy, summer, 1576

It was twilight when I once again entered Kenan's villa and shared with him the news that I was to meet with Gabriel later that evening for dinner. His response was not something I had expected. He stepped toward me and ran a cold finger along the side of my face, to the opening of my dress. I stood still.

"You have done well, Isabella," he said. "And for your loyalty, I am happy to offer you a gift. A few drops of my blood… enough to take away the ailment of gout that has caused your family members so much suffering."

My stomach recoiled at the thought of drinking blood, but I kept my composure. "An idea to ponder, but that would not take care of what ails me."

"And what is it that ails you, my dear?"

"My husband," I replied.

Kenan waved a hand in front of his face as if flicking at an insect. "Then perhaps to seal our relationship, I can offer you my assistance in that area."

I cannot say that the idea did not interest me, for I sensed Paolo and Francesco played a game of cat and mouse, and I was not the cat. I made to leave, and once again the front door opened on its own. I turned to him. "And so, sir, when will you make good on your part of our deal?"

Kenan's lips curled into a sadistic grin, sending a cold shiver over my body. "Soon, my dear, and I look forward to giving you an end to your suffering."

I exited the villa and the door closed behind me. As I stepped into his carriage, I pondered his words. "Eternal health in exchange for information regarding my indiscretions with Gabriel…"

That evening, I dined with Marguerite, Gabriel, and Alessandro; however, they did not sense Kenan in the vicinity. Later, after taking me to visit my dear son, Gabriel returned me to Baroncelli, and I could tell that he sensed the sadness in my demeanor.

"What is it that troubles you this evening, Duchess?" he asked.

"Two matters cause me distress," I said. "That awful being offered me his blood in exchange for my loyalty and said he would 'take care' of my husband. It is my husband who is the reason for my sadness, Gabriel, for I have news that he is on his way to Florence. This is earlier than expected, and I fear that he will force me to return with him to Rome. I could not live there."

"Then come with us this evening," Gabriel said. "We will protect both you and your son."

I shook my head. "I cannot run from him, nor that awful being Kenan, nor will I run from my responsibilities as the lady of Florence. But there is something I would like you to keep safe for me." I asked him to wait and returned momentarily with what Gabriel thought at first to be a thick book, but when I handed it to him and he opened the cover, he saw it was a book safe and inside were letters. "These are letters written by two people who are deeply in love with one another. Some are from me to Troilo, others are written in his hand to me. The last time we were together, we decided to keep the story of our love in this way. Perhaps in time our son will read these and know that his parents were deeply in love. Will you keep them safe for us, please?"

"Of course, Duchess," he said. "It will be an honor."

Then I asked him to hold the letters while I showed him the secret drawer that will forever hold this journal.

A lightness caressed my being, knowing that one day my son would know the truth about the love shared between his mother and father. I looked up at Gabriel. "Thank you for all you and Alessandro have done to help me in my time of need. And know that no matter what happens to me, I love this city, as did my father. As I see her unraveling in the greedy hands of my brother, I pray that her people will find strength in their hearts and rescue her from those who do not see the value in the humanities, as Lorenzo did, for that is what gives this great city her splendor. Florence is the nest where art is nurtured." I stood on my toes, placed my hands on Gabriel's shoulders, and kissed his cheeks.

"Your legacy of love and devotion will carry on through your son, this I promise, Isabella." He stepped back, tossed a rune before him, and in a flash, he disappeared.

I could no longer hold on to my tears. I fell to the floor and sobbed.

Coco sniffed and did her best to hold back the tears that brimmed in her eyes. "You're not to blame for what happened." She stared at Gabriel. "I think Isabella knew that she was going to die, but she had no control over the situation. Perhaps she sensed her own demise, and in her heart, she knew that if she wanted her son to live, then she would have to make a sacrifice."

Gabriel kissed her. "Over the years I've thought of every scenario, but now I see that like so many other humans, she was another tool to Kenan. Sleep, *mi amore.*"

Coco closed the journal and rested her head on his chest. She fell into a deep sleep and dreamed.

Coco stands at the end of a wide hallway. Piano music is playing, and she runs toward the source. She looks up and notices the curve of the ceiling and the windows where streams of light flood the entire area. A little girl with long blond hair and a full-length dress is dancing around a grand piano. Coco smiles when she sees that it's Alessandro playing the piano. He looks up at her.

"This is one of my favorite pieces of music," he says. "There's magic in each and every note…"

Coco woke abruptly, surrounded by candlelight and Gabriel's arms. "Did you see into my dream?"

"Only for a moment," he said.

"Did you recognize the location?"

Gabriel nodded, and as he sat up, a book flew from a nearby bookcase and into his hands. He flipped through the pages until he found what he was looking for, and then he turned the book toward Coco. "I'm fairly sure this is where you were—Museo del Prado."

"Yes, that's the place," Coco said. She stared at the page, deep in thought. "And there was a little girl—I've seen her somewhere before—and Dad was playing the piano."

"Did you recognize the music—a name, composer, anything?" Gabriel asked.

"Dad told me that the piece he was playing was one of his favorites, and the little girl… she was dressed in period clothes and was dancing to the music."

Gabriel turned to the next page and pointed to a painting. "Is this her?"

Coco drew in a breath and nodded. "Yeah, that's her."

"We'd best find Alessandro." He kissed her forehead. "The piece he was playing is Ravel's *Pavane pour une infante défunte*."

"Pavane for a dead princess," Coco whispered.

"Yes, but, Ravel's intention with the naming of the piece was more in line with something lighter," Gabriel said. "He saw the music as something the little princess might have danced to."

"And what was her name?" Coco asked.

"Margarita."

"Margarita and Marguerite. I don't think that's a coincidence. Anything else about her that holds relevance for us?" Coco peered over Gabriel's shoulder and saw he was reading a short biography of the artist, Velázquez.

"This." He pointed to a section of the page. "Ravel's mother was Spanish. Velázquez was Spanish, so was Princess Margarita, and Isabella's mother—Eleonora di Toledo."

Coco's skin prickled. "As much as I want to stay here with you and indulge my inner vampire, I think we need to find Dad and go to the Prado. The painting by Velázquez—*Las Meninas*—has always seemed ghostlike to me. Now I know why." She jumped up and began throwing on clothes.

Gabriel looked over toward the door. "We have visitors."

Coco pulled on her running shoes. "What?"

He dressed quickly, then embraced her and whispered. "I called to Prudence and Alessandro—"

"Please don't tell me my parents are outside the door," Coco cut in.

"Okay, but my parents are."

Coco rolled her eyes. "How long have they been there? Do you think they heard—"

His lips met hers, and Coco's body responded by pulling him closer. Gabriel broke their kiss. "No, they just arrived. We have a museum to visit and two sets of parents waiting outside the door."

Gabriel waved a hand and the door to his apartment opened. He caught Coco's hand and they met Stefan, Prudence, Alessandro, and Chantal in the hallway.

"Dad," Coco said, "I had a dream, and you were in it. We were at the Prado, and you were playing the piano. You said to me, 'This is one of my favorite pieces of music; there's magic in each and every note...'"

Alessandro smiled. "That would be Ravel's *Pavane pour une infante défunte*," he said. "For little Margarita."

"Come with us, Dad. I need to see behind *Las Meninas*, and I think you're supposed to be there with me."

Alessandro turned to Chantal.

"Go," Chantal said. "I'm safe here, and our daughter needs you."

"Chantal will be safe," Stefan said. "Hakon, Nikandros, and I shall guard the fortress."

Gabriel tucked knives into his boot sheaths and handed a couple to Alessandro. "Tell Christopher where we are," he said to Chantal. "We shouldn't be gone more than an hour."

"I'll let him know," she replied.

Alessandro kissed her and then let go of her hand.

Gabriel turned to his mother. "Are you ready?"

"Of course," Prudence replied as a cloud of white mist rose from the floor.

CHAPTER 19

Madrid, Spain—Prado Museum

COCO WAS AWARE of Gabriel's thumb caressing her hand, massaging her palm and along the sensitive skin on her wrist. She looked at him, but this time she did not only see his golden eyes but also strands of his love reaching out to her. Finding it difficult to contain her emotions and knowing she had work to do, she lifted his hand to her lips and kissed the inside of his wrist, then they released their hold on one another.

Directly in front of her, displayed on a sage-green wall, hung *Las Meninas*.

"Velázquez is known as the painter of the truth," she said.

Alessandro nodded. "Yes—*el pintor de la verdad*—but even as the court painter under King Philip IV, Velázquez played many different roles. And now it seems that his paintings don't only hold truths but also secrets."

"I've not been here for many years," Prudence said. "When this is all over, perhaps we need to venture into art museums across the world to discover what other secrets are hidden beneath artists' works."

"Count me in," Coco said. She listened as the humming sound of a vacuum cleaner drifted in from another room, and the hushed voices of two men speaking Spanish caught her attention. Strangely, she understood what they were saying. She turned to Gabriel, who smiled and spoke silently to her.

"This is part of our new connection with each other, a side effect of ingesting my blood. We now share each other's knowledge. I'm fluent in many languages, one of which is Spanish. I'm currently seeing these paintings through your eyes—it's quite remarkable."

Coco blushed. *"I thought I knew a little Spanish, but obviously I was fooling myself. Ordering an enchilada at El Sombrero hardly counts—talk about ignorant."* She took in her surroundings: a rose-colored marble floor, doorways to her left and right. Above her, white skirting trimmed a series of square inlays that framed a skylight running the full length of the room.

"Are you ready, Dad?"

Alessandro nodded.

Coco returned her gaze to the painting and held out a hand. As if awakened from a deep slumber, the pigments of paint lifted from the canvas and hovered at her fingertips, bringing to life a new image.

A tall woman with pale skin, amethyst-colored eyes, and long silver hair twisted in matching braids wraps a piece of twine around a bunch of dried flowers. She pulls up her full, floor-length skirt, tucks it into her boots, and climbs a ladder that takes her from a stone-walled room with a large fireplace and living area up to a loft bedroom overcrowded with an assortment of flora and fauna. She hangs the flowers next to others that look similar.

As she makes her way back down the ladder, she stops on a rung, tilts her head, and listens. The creak of a gate, footsteps on overgrowth, a muffled tap on her front door. She steps onto the floor, walks across the room, and after sliding a bolt, she opens the front door. A hooded woman stands before her, then enters. The door closes.

"No one hides from me in my own home." The silver-haired woman speaks in Latin.

Her guest pushes back the hood with her small gloved hands and unfastens a cord attached either side of her cloak. A white wimple and black veil frame a young woman's flushed face and tearstained eyes. The hem of her woolen frock is muddied. The older woman guides the young nun to a seat by the fireplace.

"I am in need of your services once more."

The older woman nods. She busies herself, pulling dried flowers and leaves from stalks and crushing them with a pestle in a mortar made of stone. When the mixture is ground to resemble dried tea leaves, she pours the contents into a small linen bag, secures the opening with a leather cord, and hands it over to the young nun.

"Steep this in boiling water and drink the entire cup." She places a finger under the young woman's chin and stares directly into her eyes. "Is this the life you expected when you answered your god's calling? Rape is not something you must endure, my dear."

The nun shook her head. "Where would I go? I have only ever known this life of piety. This must be God's will for me."

"No," the older woman said. "This is the will of one man who uses the name of your god as an excuse to have his way with your body." She drops her hand and walks over to the door. "I may not always be here to prepare this tea, and then your fertility will be in the hands of the man who steals your femininity when he pleases."

The nun tucks the linen bag inside her sleeve, pulls up her hood, and approaches the door. "Thank you."

The scene melded into another.

A room lit with candles. Stone floor and walls. A fire burns and the sound of wind and rain are barely audible through the guttural screams of a woman in labor. The woman with long silver hair leans over a bed, gently wiping the forehead of the mother-to-be.

"'Tis not long now, my dear child. I know you are sapped of your will, but you must push with all your strength." She helps her daughter into a sitting position, then offers her a tincture. "This will help with the pain."

The young woman opens her mouth, and her mother places a few drops onto her tongue. After a few moments, the daughter's cries cease. A tall man stands in the doorway. The older woman gives him a nod, and he enters the room. They lift the pregnant woman to her feet and encourage her to walk. After a few steps, she folds over in pain. The man carries her to a birthing chair where he holds her shoulders while she bears down.

The older woman crouches in front of her daughter. "Your child's head is visible. The next time the spasms arrive, push down with all your might."

The young woman grimaces and falls back against her husband's chest. He kisses her forehead and whispers tenderly, "Our child is almost here, my love."

She pushes again, longer this time, and collapses back into her husband as a baby's scream fills the room. Her husband wraps his arms around her naked body, and the older woman cuts the umbilical cord and ties it close to the baby's skin. She brings the baby to her daughter, who sobs with joy at the sight of the healthy baby boy.

"Our sweet Alessandro. He has your eyes, Mother."

The older woman nods. "Yes, and I feel the magic around him too."

The scene faded. Coco caught Alessandro's hand. "There's more, Dad."

The woman with the silver hair lies sleeping in a low bed surrounded by linen curtains and an overhead canopy. Her eyes spring open, and she sits up, alert. "What do you want?" she asks. The curtains flutter. She clutches a medallion that hangs from a leather string around her neck and rubs it while muttering words of protection.

Suddenly the curtains are torn open. A pale man with dark eyes and garnet-red lips drawn into a hard, thin line stares at her. "I want you, witch," he says. His voice void of life and color. "Or would you rather I take your daughter and grandson?"

The woman throws back the covers and glares at him. "There are witches far stronger than I whom you would find more beneficial, vampir.*"*

The pale man grins. "But their Creative bloodline is not as strong as yours."

At these words, the woman lifts a hand, and a log from the fire hurtles toward the immortal. He moves quickly, and the log falls onto the bed, catching the curtains on fire. She leaps from the loft onto the floor below and grabs a dagger from the mantel. When the vampire appears before her, she aims for his heart and throws the weapon. But before the blade meets his body, he catches it. He throws it back at her and hits his target. She screams and falls to the floor in pain. She grabs the dagger, desperate to remove the blade from her right midfoot. She stares through tears of agony and anger at the vampire's stern face. In one quick movement, she pulls the dagger from her foot and plunges it into her heart.

"Fool!" The vampire spits his words. He rips out the dagger, slices open a vein at his wrist and forces his blood into the woman's mouth. She gags. The vampire tosses her over his shoulder, the door opens, and he flees into the darkness as flames engulf the cottage.

The woman stands before a wall of solid rock. Her dress is stained with blood and grime, her silver hair unkempt and her eyes dull and sad.

Kenan questions her. "When will Prudenza's son return to Florence?"

The silver-haired seer shakes her head. "Do you think I trust that you will not kill my grandson?"

"Tell me!" Kenan yells. "Or Alessandro is as good as dead."

When she refuses, he wrenches her arms behind her back.

"Kill me!" she screams. "I will NEVER utter another word!"

Kenan grabs her hair, yanks back her head, and sinks his fangs into her vein. He drinks from her until the last drop of her lifeblood is gone and then tosses her limp body to the ground.

Coco turned to her father and hugged him. "I'm so sorry, Dad."

Alessandro held on to her. "Don't be, Coco... I finally know what happened to my grandmother. She did her best to weave a path of half-truths to protect our family. And seeing how Kenan tortured her has given me even more of an incentive to kill him. Let's return to the fortress and get to work."

Gabriel had an arm around his mother and her cheeks were wet with tears.

"We must stop him," Prudence said. "We'll find him, Alessandro, and make him pay for what he has done."

Alessandro looked across at Gabriel and gave him a quick nod.

Gabriel tossed a rune into the air, and gradually the gallery fell empty.

CHAPTER 20

Casa della Pietra

ILLONA ENCOURAGED THE twins to place the key into the fairy statue. She hoped that this time—because of her presence—new information might come to life. She watched closely as Arianna turned the key and the figure of the fairy became animated. The fairy stretched her wings, and as she did, a small crystalline ball appeared in her cupped hands. Her arms stretched upward until they were parallel to her mouth, at which time a puff of air burst from her mouth, causing the sphere to rise and hang midair.

"What's that?" Jeremy asked.

"A chronicle crystal," Hakon answered. "It stores information."

"So it's a fairy thumb drive." Jeremy stepped forward and, without touching the object, had a closer look. "There's a cloud moving around inside. Any ideas on how this thing works?"

Layla sat forward and tilted her head. "I've seen one of these before—my grandmother has one. She said that when she passes, I'm to see what it holds. I believe the cloud is a collection of memories. Am I correct, Illona?"

"Yes, my brother has left the twins his story. Perhaps we should leave you both to view this on your own."

Arianna shook her head. "No, everyone here is part of the fae community, and in many ways, Elion's story belongs to all of us." She looked to Illona. "Can you open it?"

"I can show you how," she replied. "However, your father left this for you and Jeremy. In order for it to open, one of you must place your palm under the crystal, whisper your name, and the stories will appear."

"Kind of like a movie?" Jeremy asked.

"A little like that, yes." Illona waved a hand, and the lights dimmed.

"You do it." Jeremy nodded reassuringly at Arianna.

She stepped forward and followed Illona's instructions. When the crystalline ball reached the end of her fingertips, a crack appeared, and the cloud seeped out and grew until it reached the size of a double bed-sheet. Arianna stepped back and sat between Illona and Jeremy. Slowly an image appeared on the cloud and gradually formed a series of scenes.

A teenage girl gathers a small white-haired boy into her arms and hides him in a secret place under the floorboards in a cottage. She sobs as she kisses him. His bright cerulean-blue eyes stare back at her in terror.

"Don't leave me, Illona, please…"

"I have to, little brother. But I will find you again, I promise."

Illona replaces the floorboards over her brother and then lifts her arms above her and utters a ward of protection. "Detrinus-e-nish-ure-shan-ti-pac-e." The boy's cries are immediately silenced. The door bursts open, and intruders wearing leather and chain mail storm into the room. They grab Illona and drag her away.

Another scene emerged.

Two men walk slowly through a dark cave, carrying torches. The flames bring to life images of frescoes depicting people being tortured. They step inside a stone cell, and the younger of the two—a handsome man with blue eyes and white hair—stares at a wall where images have been carved to tell a story. He runs a finger over the figure with two faces, one male and one female. A woman's voice whispers, "Sine virtute omnia sunt perdita." The older man weeps.

The young man holds out a hand, and a crystalline ball appears in his palm. He watches as a cloud forms inside the ball.

As the two men leave the cave, they are greeted at the entrance by a woman whose eyes sparkle with gold, and white hair flows down her back. Tears shine in her eyes and send frac-tured rays of light into the lulling twilight. "I knew your dear mother Birgit. I am Prudence, of the Allegiance."

The scene dissipated and images of how their parents met, and other shadows of their lives together appeared.

Elion gazes at Katja's face while she sleeps; her head resting in his lap. He smiles as her impish nose crinkles while she dreams. He speaks to her softly. "When the time comes for my departure, I will count on memories such as this to get me through the loneliness and anguish of being without you. Car-rying the twins has not been easy on you, my love, and as your delivery date comes closer, I am concerned for your well-being. In essence, the reality of what we must do to protect both our children looms like an approaching storm before us."

He places a hand on her rounded belly, and the edges of his mouth curve upward. "Ah, there you are, Arianna. You have sensory abilities—the peacemaker—that is how I shall remember you, and your life partner will be from a legacy. And Jeremy… clairvoyance will be your strength, and you shall know great love, my dear son. When the time is safe, you will both remember your connection to my world, I promise."

Katja's eyes flutter open, and she reaches for her belly, easing herself into a sitting position. "Were you speaking to the twins?"

Elion smiles and nods. "Did we wake you?"

"Let's just say they tend to get excited when they sense you near." She leans into his embrace. "Are you sure that separating the twins is the only way to keep them safe?"

Elion kisses her forehead. "Unfortunately, yes. I've no way of knowing if other seers saw Mother's drawing on the cave wall, but I do know that in the world of fae, twins are rare and always gifted. Illona will keep watch over them and has asked Arianna's adoptive parents to send photos of our daughter to you regularly."

"Will Arianna find us?" Katja asks, her voice catching in her throat.

Elion holds her close. "Yes, my love, she will find us."

The front door opens and an elderly woman enters. The door closes and a veil of magic dissipates as Illona appears. She steps forward and reaches out to Elion, and they clasp hands.

"It's good to see you again," he says.

"Likewise." Illona leans forward and kisses Katja's forehead. "How are you?"

Katja's lips tremble. "In all honesty, the closer the date of delivery, the more anxious I become. The pain of letting go of my daughter... Elion's departure..."

Illona reaches for Katja. "I'll be there for you. You have my word."

"What can you tell us about her adoptive parents?" Elion asks.

Illona relaxes into a chair. "I've known Steven for many years. He's an immigration lawyer—one of the best in LA, actually—and he truly cares about his clients. He works pro bono for a nonprofit that protects the rights of immigrants and their children. His wife—Mexican by descent—teaches dance and also works part-time in the office for her husband. Their time together has been spent in service to others. Now they've made the choice to adopt. The timing is perfect. I swear on my life that Arianna will be unconditionally loved. Steven and Isabel are good people."

"And Steven is aware of our kind?" Elion asks.

"Yes." Illona nods. "In fact, a vampire connected with the Allegiance works with him."

Elion leans back in his chair, and the edges of his mouth curve upward. "I've seen him in a vision… Yes, he's a good man."

"And Steven's wife?" Katja asks.

"She has the heart of a Creative, albeit without the amethyst eyes," Illona says. "Isabel is a gentle soul, and if you lived closer, you might well be good friends."

Katja nods and leans forward. "Promise that you will not leave my side during the birth. I'm frightened."

"You have my word."

"How long will we have with our daughter before she leaves us?"

"A few days. I've arranged for certain paperwork to disappear so no one can trace Arianna or Jeremy back to you and Elion. When I leave the hospital, she'll be in my arms."

"The thought of losing two of my family in one night breaks my heart." Katja looks at Elion with pleading eyes. "Is killing Kenan so important? I need you to return to us, Elion."

Elion holds her as she sobs. He looks up at his sister's eyes awash with tears.

The screen dissolved along with the image of Katja, Elion, and Illona. The crystalline ball reappeared in the fairy's palms, her wings retracted, and she settled back inside the statue.

Illona spoke quietly. "Your parents wanted you both to be safe.

Please try to understand the importance your lives hold in the wider collective. Elion gave up his life to protect you both. He had seen your alternative fates and decided that keeping you together was not an option."

Jeremy placed an arm around Arianna's shoulders. "They sacrificed their happiness so that we could live. We had great parents."

"Yeah, we sure did, and I'm also in awe of Isabel," Arianna said. "I think in her heart she knew that sooner or later I'd want to know more about my birth mother."

"Isabel is a remarkable woman," Hakon said. "And I see her strength within you, Arianna. Our adoptive family and friends are as important as the blood relatives in our lives. Perhaps you and Jeremy should consider sharing what you have seen today with her. Let her know the importance of the role that she and Steven played in your destiny."

Arianna nodded, and her eyes glowed with love.

"I've got a question." Jeremy's gaze met Illona's. "Dad spoke of certain traits that Arianna and I would both develop. Can you explain more about that, please?"

A sense of calm settled somewhere deep within Illona's soul. She knew her cheeks glowed with pride for her niece and nephew. "Your clairvoyant abilities will come through shortly, Jeremy. In fact, I think these traits have begun to surface." She looked at Arianna. "Your sensory abilities have already become a part of your life, through your dreams. But you must both remember that perfecting these skills takes practice. The more you practice, the easier it is for your mind to access the path to clairvoyance."

"*Ancora imparo,*" Jeremy said.

Arianna frowned.

"I'm, still learning," Jeremy said. "A Michelangelo quote."

Illona smiled. "Yes, and a good one."

CHAPTER 21

COCO STOOD IN hanmi position, one foot in front of the other, knees bent. She focused on the fingers of her right hand stretched out in front of her body. Every time her mind drifted, she refocused. *Fingernails, fingers, skin.* For a split second, she allowed her eyes to wander from her hand to the man she sensed standing beside her. A razor-sharp jolt of pain squeezed her brain, bringing her to her knees.

"Damn it!" she looked up at her assailant, but he was no longer there. She sought him out and found him sitting in a chair at the edge of the room, reading a book.

"The lure of distraction is stronger than your focus," Kishu said, his gaze never leaving a much-loved copy of a collection of Rumi poems.

"No kidding." Coco staggered to her feet. "So how do I stop it?"

Kishu placed the book on his knees. "Distraction cannot be stopped. It must be tamed and trained."

In a flash he was standing before her, the surprise sending Coco once again onto her backside. "How did you do that?"

He grinned, offered her his hands, and pulled her to her feet. "You were distracted by the book. I merely used that opportunity to catch you off guard."

"If that had been Kenan, he'd be in my head right now," Coco said. "I can't allow that to happen."

"It's all right for you to address the distraction, but don't ever allow your focus to wander," Kishu said. "The human brain is alert. It works continuously and instinctively, searching the environment around you. Your intuition told you someone was approaching, but you chose not to trust that thought. Instead of protecting yourself, you wasted valuable time to confirm what you already knew to be true. You have an overflow of physical energy."

Coco gave an audible sigh. "That's an understatement."

Kishu continued. "When you find your mind wandering, return immediately to the flow of moving meditation—divert the distraction and deter your mind from aimless travels."

"Let's do it again."

"What is it that you need to do?"

She stared at the sage-colored tatami mats, then looked up at Kishu. "Stay centered."

Kishu nodded, turned away from her, and began a series of tai chi movements familiar to Coco. As her body moved in harmony to the ancient patterns, cell memory kicked in, and her body and mind converged. The invisible ball that she pushed and pulled with her hands vanished, and in its place appeared an invisible coruscating vortex of energy sending tingles into her fingertips as it skimmed across the pores of her skin.

Whenever a thought popped into Coco's mind, she acknowledged it and placed it on an imaginary to-do list, never allowing it to interrupt the flow of her movement. A high-pitched buzzing sound began to grow in volume; Coco acknowledged it, not allowing her mind to lose focus. After the buzzing sound had disappeared, she found herself in a place of complete silence. Away from the corporal ties of her body, she drifted to the ceiling in the corner of the room. From that viewpoint, she watched in awe as she practiced with her grandfather. She witnessed the beauty of his movements—a dance of sorts, smooth, organized, fluid. A sense of stillness fell over her and seeped into her body.

Her grandfather stopped dancing and moved so that he stood beside her. A sudden throbbing pressure pounded at her head.

Stay centered.

Breathe.

The pressure stopped, and she was back in her body again, face-to-face with Kishu.

He grinned at her.

"What was that?"

"History!" He walked toward the door.

She ran after him. "Wait a minute, Grandpa! What just happened?"

"You emptied the trash can."

"The trash can?"

Kishu tapped the top of Coco's head. "You empty the trash on your computer right?"

Coco shrugged. "Yes."

"Why?" Kishu asked.

"Because I don't need it, and because too much crap on my computer slows it down."

"Exactly!" Kishu opened the door and walked through. "I'm hungry, and Maria has dinner waiting."

"It's that late?" Coco asked. "How long have we been practicing?"

"Five hours, forty-five seconds." He looked back at her and winked. "You had a shitload of trash to discard."

"Jeez," Coco said, grinning. "I guess so."

CHAPTER 22

Coast of Lazio, Italy

SITUATED BELOW KENAN'S hillside property lay the ruins of Domenico's villa. The edges of the steps leading to the beach were dimpled from use, and for a moment a distant memory tugged at Kenan's conscious thoughts. The gruff and cruel voice of Domenico yelling orders as he readied to enter one of many battles. The musky smell of overworked and fear-filled men permeated the air. Even now, centuries later, such images taunted him. He shook his head briskly and walked with deliberation down the steep and broken path to the ruin that bore witness to his corrupt life.

He climbed over what was left of a crumbling staircase and ran a finger along part of a wall that had once been his quarters. Memories of the many brutal physical assaults he had suffered under Domenico played in his mind; the torturous beatings and rapes had left not one scar on his body, but the pain was etched deep within and acted as a constant reminder to always be the hunter, not the hunted.

The gardens that surrounded the villa had long since been swept away by ocean winds and storms. Kenan had heard that when rumors spread of Domenico's death, villagers had come brandishing flaming torches and destroyed the dwelling. They sensed the evil it held and wanted their lands cleansed of the cloud of debauchery the *vampir* had cast upon the area. Kenan had been told that the flames from the fires rose into the sky in the shape of a gnarled hand reaching up to the heavens and that screams of the dead echoed across the land and were heard all the way to the outskirts of Rome.

But Kenan had not heard the cries or seen the flames, for he was deep in the tunnels below Domenico's villa in Rome, experiencing the excruciating changes in his body as it morphed into that of the devil. Once the transformation was complete, he had called upon Domenico's immortal followers to bring him live humans to feed on. He ordered them to continue to run his businesses while he remained underground, reading the journals left by Vinicio and Domenico, in an effort to understand the legacy he had inherited.

Tossing his clothing aside, Kenan walked across the sand, stepped into the water, and exhaled as it washed over his feet. He swam through the breaking waves and out to the open sea. Dark clouds shaded the moon and stars, and the ink-colored water answered the call of the approaching storm. Lace-trimmed peaks rose and fell around him as he floated on the surface, listening to the crashing of the waves as they pounded the shore, growing in intensity like the strange hunger that lurked beneath the surface of his cruel demeanor. Something brushed against his skin, and he thought of the bodies that lay buried in centuries of sand beneath him, and that sent a chill through his blood.

Kenan looked toward the shore and to the north. He remembered this area in centuries past before tourists flocked to see ruins and bathe in waters of this forsaken place. And yet there was one area of land that he had purchased many years ago. He had fenced it off and let nature have her way with the land. Over the years, many had offered him a fortune for his piece of paradise, but no amount of money tempted him. He knew the property held a secret—one that he hoped to unlock.

He let the waves carry him onto the shore where he dressed and then made his way up the hill to his sanctuary. By the time he climbed onto the patio, the sky was tinged with indigo and hunger dulled his mind. He walked across the cold gray polished cement floor to the kitchen and grabbed two bags of blood from a refrigerator. As the thick crimson liquid curbed his hunger, Kenan fell onto a chair and stared at the large ring on his right middle finger.

The ring, made from bronze, bore the shape of a cross set in front of a pair of wings carved into the metal. Kenan held his right hand over his left palm, turned it over, and tapped one side of the ring. A lock of gray hair fell into his palm along with a tiny, stained remnant of fabric.

"The assassin did well to gather a lock of your hair before his unfortunate death," he said. "And although you slipped through my fingers in the cave, your blood fell onto my hand, and I have one drop to savor."

His eyes darkened as he inhaled the scent of the hair and bloodstained fabric. He placed his booted feet on the coffee table, leaned back his head, and unzipped his pants. "Gotcha! Dear, dear, Colombina…"

CHAPTER 23

Casa della Pietra

COCO STEPPED INTO a steaming shower. The hot water stung her skin, but she welcomed the momentary pain as it dragged her attention away from a nagging thought that had suddenly resurfaced, of Gabriel with Marguerite. As steam filled the bathroom, Coco heard the shower door open.

"I'm glad you're here," she said. "I don't want the shadows of our past to ruin what we have." She relaxed into his body and enjoyed the sensual touch of his lips moving over her shoulders while his hands explored the rest of her. His fingers traced over her mound, teasing and touching.

"Mmm," she moaned. "I need you." She stroked his erection and rested her head against his hard chest. Coco turned to face him. She opened her eyes and screamed.

The door to the bathroom burst open, and Chantal was beside her. Coco sat huddled on the tile floor in the corner of the shower recess, unable to control the shaking of her body. She wrapped her arms around her knees.

"Colombina," Chantal said. "What happened?"

The water had stopped. Chantal placed a towel around Coco's shoulders, coaxing her up from the floor and onto a chair in the bathroom. Coco stared back at the glass walls of the shower.

"Kenan was here. He touched me." She looked up at Chantal. "I touched him. I thought he was Gabriel. I had no idea it was—" She broke down sobbing.

Chantal sniffed the air. "Kenan was not here in the physical sense, Colombina—I would have been pulled to him. Whatever you saw and experienced was dark magic, but I've no idea how he could do such a thing."

For a second Chantal disappeared but then returned with a glass of brandy. "Drink this, little one. It will warm you and ease your shock."

Coco accepted the glass, drank the liquid, and then gasped when Gabriel knelt in front of her. Tears spilled down her cheeks as he pulled her into his arms.

"I'm sorry," she whispered.

She felt Gabriel's body tense. "Did he—"

"No! But I touched him. I thought it was you." She clung to Gabriel as he lifted her off the chair.

He pushed her wet hair away from her face and kissed her. "You're safe now, *mi amore*, but I need to speak with Prudence and Kishu immediately. Chantal will not leave you alone." He strode into the bedroom, lowered her onto the sofa in front of the fire, kissed her again, and turned to Chantal. "When she's ready, come to my study."

From the corner of her eye, Coco saw Chantal place a hand on Gabriel's arm. "How did you know this had happened?" she asked. "I thought you were in Rome with Alessandro."

"Colombina and I are blood-bound."

Chantal smiled and then leaned forward and kissed Gabriel's forehead. "You're family now, Gabriel. Treasure my daughter always."

"*Sempre*," Gabriel said. In a flash he disappeared.

"I'm sorry, Mom—I wanted to tell you, but there's been no time."

"It's okay," Chantal said. "In retrospect, I sensed a shift in your love for each other. Now I understand why, and I know that if you're ever lost, Gabriel will find you. We'd best get you dressed and downstairs. Hopefully Prudence will shed light on what's happened."

CHAPTER 24

DOWNSTAIRS IN HIS study, Gabriel shared Kenan's intrusion into Coco's reality with Prudence and Kishu.

"How the hell is that possible?" he asked.

Prudence took a sip from the wineglass in her hand and then placed it on the mantel. "You're forgetting that up until recently, Kenan had access to an immense source of power and dark magic: Beatrice. The only way for him to be able to enter Coco's mind would be through a spell, and you and I know what is needed for that to work."

A chill ran over Gabriel's body as his mother's words pulled at a memory; the words from the assassin he had confronted in the stairwell months ago echoed in his head. Goose bumps forming over his skin confirmed his thoughts. "He has a lock of Colombina's hair. The assassin Kenan hired to kill her attended one of her art classes disguised as a homeless man. It was there that he stole a lock of her hair. He told me that Kenan used it to test her DNA, to see if it matched Chantal's."

"Her hair would be adequate," Prudence said. "But not enough for him to appear in a physical form. We both know what that entails. When has Kenan been in close enough contact with Colombina to take her blood?"

Gabriel closed his eyes and replayed a recent scene in the cave below the Island of the Crescent Moon…

A gust of wind rushes at him and throws him to the ground. He looks up and sees Kenan bent over Coco, weaving his fingers around her hair as he pulls back her head. A knife is buried deep in her chest. Kenan dips a finger in the blood that is pooling on her shirt. He falls forward and then staggers back, blood seeping from his mouth. He wipes his bloodstained finger on his shirt…

Gabriel opened his eyes and stared at Prudence. "In the tunnel underneath the Island of the Crescent Moon," he said. "I saw him put his finger in the blood pouring from the wound he inflicted on Colombina, then he wiped it on his shirt."

Prudence sighed and shook her head. "Then he can taunt her. Our best bet is you, dear Kishu. You must continue to train Colombina to resist Kenan."

"I'm not sure resisting him is what she should do," Kishu said. "But rather pretend she's under his control. Resistance is not always the best form of defense."

Gabriel inhaled. "And what if he drags her into his world using his wicked illusions? How will we get her back?"

"We make sure that doesn't happen," Kishu replied.

The door opened and Coco and Chantal entered. Coco walked over to Gabriel, and he embraced her. Now that their blood ran through each other's veins, there was no hiding the fact that she was drenched in shame from touching Kenan. Although the image made Gabriel seethe with anger, he needed to know Coco understood that dark magic had played into the scenario.

She looked into his eyes. "Now I know how you felt when you knew I'd seen you with Marguerite. I'm sorry."

He kissed her and tucked her under his arm. "Kenan's doing his best to destroy us by toying with our relationship. To him, we're chess pieces on a board. Right now he has no idea we've bonded our love with blood; otherwise he'd realize his stupid games are useless."

Coco leaned into him, and her body relaxed. "He invaded my privacy—our privacy."

"Kenan wants to destroy your relationship—our family—and ultimately the Allegiance," Chantal said. "That would give him absolute power."

"Power to destroy all that is good," Prudence said.

"Grandpa, do you think it's possible, through your training, for me to learn to contain my reactions to Kenan?"

Chantal cut in. "I know this to be true, Coco. I've experienced it. But more importantly, through Kishu's work, you'll be able to pick and choose what messages to reply to."

"But won't that just piss him off?"

"He's only in control of what images he sends you," Chantal replied. "It's more complicated for him to see your reactions, and I'm not sure he's capable of doing so."

"Then I want to train harder."

"My blood will strengthen your abilities," Gabriel said. "The more you drink, the stronger you'll be. And the stronger you are, the easier it will be for me to connect with you wherever you are."

"You mean if this whole thing goes belly-up?" Coco asked.

"We can't allow that to happen," Prudence said.

Gabriel stepped away from Coco when her body suddenly tensed. She whipped around to face Kishu. He was testing her, slamming into her head when she least expected it, hoping she would use the techniques he had taught her to deflect him mentally. As much as Gabriel wanted to protect her, he understood that this mental training was imperative to Coco's safety.

Coco's arms dropped to her sides. She squared her shoulders and then lowered her eyes as if in submission. But in the next moment, she lifted her head and glared at her grandfather. For a split second,

Kishu faltered, but he suddenly took a step forward. Coco gasped, and both her hands went over her ears. Kishu stepped back.

"Not bad, little dove," Kishu said. "The only reason I stopped was that I sensed Gabriel's protective instincts kick in, and I never want to be at the other end of his anger."

"Thanks for your mercy, Grandpa." Coco sighed. "Now, will someone please tell me how the hell Kenan appeared in the flesh, and here, at the fortress."

Prudence rose and made her way to where the others were standing. "Kenan used dark magic, most likely learned from one of the seers he tortured."

"While you were in the hospital—after the hit and run—I confronted the assassin," Gabriel said. "I asked him how he'd found you. He told me that the person who hired him requested a sample of your DNA. The assassin attended one of your Saturday community classes, and it was there that he managed to get a few strands of your hair. But the dark magic Kenan used also needs the blood of the person one is targeting, and it wasn't until a few minutes ago that I realized how that happened."

Coco frowned.

He continued. "I remembered when Kenan stabbed you in the cave. He leaned in and whispered something to you right before Flora threw a knife in his back. I saw him place a finger into the blood pooling where the knife entered your chest. He must have saved it, although I don't know why he didn't ingest it—"

"Because he realized that if he couldn't take her, then he would at least take some of her blood," Prudence cut in. "We can be thankful that he did not have time to drink from her or we would not be having this conversation. He knew that one drop of Colombina's blood was more use to him as a specimen than it would be on his lips."

Coco's mouth went dry. "So what does that mean, and is there a way to shield me from his intrusions?"

"It means that Kenan will use this to lure you away from us," Gabriel replied. "But he has no idea of Kishu's talents."

"Then I need to train harder." Coco looked at Kishu. "Is there a way that I can mentally lie to him?"

Kishu nodded. "Yes, but to learn this practice takes time, and that is something we don't have."

"Gabriel's blood has already made me stronger. What if I drank more? Surely the magic that runs through him would make me mentally more astute."

Kishu looked at Gabriel. "Would it be safe for her?"

"Yes," he replied. "I already sense my magic in her blood."

"Then why are we standing here?" Coco turned to Kishu. "Let's go train."

CHAPTER 25

FOR THE NEXT few days, Coco focused on her classes with Kishu. She had come to a point where she could block him from entering her mind and had also discovered that since ingesting more of Gabriel's blood, her body had become infinitely stronger. Seeing that, Kishu began to integrate aikido into her daily workout. He stressed the importance of using her assailant's energy rather than trying to block it, emphasizing that the latter took away her power. Everything Kishu taught her came back to strengthening her mind.

They had been practicing a simple move that involved Coco running toward Kishu, but as she went to tackle him, she found herself on the ground with one arm bent back and Kishu's knee holding her on the ground. A sudden thrust of energy clamped down on her mind, the pain more intense than anything Kishu had served her. She pulled her focus away from the bodily pain Kishu was inflicting on her arm and instead directed her energy to keeping the force pulsing in her brain at bay.

When the pain subsided, Coco slowly let down her guard, only to be bombarded once more with shards of agony. She screamed, but the torment only intensified. When at last it subsided, she opened her eyes and found herself spread-eagle, staring up at Ignacio.

"You put up a bloody good fight, luv," Ignacio said, his slight cockney accent and mischievous grin hiding his lethal ability to kill. He offered her a hand and pulled her to her feet.

She rubbed her temples. "Was that you in my head?"

Ignacio nodded. "Yeah, sorry 'bout that, but Kishu requested that I partake in your training."

Coco looked over at Kishu, who was once again sitting in a chair at the edge of the dojo, reading a well-worn paperback. He raised a hand. "Guilty as charged," he said. "Because of Ignacio's shady past, I thought him the best warrior to teach you the next step of your training. Good luck!"

Coco stared at Ignacio, whose glare had returned to what she called his "you're totally fucked" look. His fierce eyes bored into her, and he struck out. Coco leaped back and then realized her mistake. Seconds later, Ignacio had her arm twisted behind her back and slammed down on her mind.

"Shit!" Coco said through clenched teeth.

Ignacio released his mental and physical hold on Coco and then turned her to face him. "Let's slow this down. Watch my moves, how I approach you."

He moved toward her in slow motion, and this time she sensed his energy. Instead of running away, she mentally beckoned his power to her.

"That's it," Ignacio said. "Now what you gonna do?" He froze, waiting for her answer.

She placed a hand on his wrist and guided him in a circle. When he broke the flow, she went in the direction he led rather than against him.

Ignacio froze once more. "Now what?" He chuckled. "I mean, we can't go on like this forever, luv!"

Coco changed direction and twisted Ignacio's arm behind his back as he fell to the floor.

"Not bad," he said. "Again, only faster." He sprang up and immediately attacked her.

She embraced his forward movement and went with it, but this time he did the same to her. Before she had time to react, she found herself flat on the floor.

Coco heard a familiar chuckle and glared at Kishu hiding behind his book. A sudden urge to punch him crossed her mind, and he lowered the paperback and winked at her. His reaction reminded her of his lessons. The next time Ignacio charged at her, Coco not only used his physical energy to her advantage, but as she connected with him, she slammed into his mind with her mental strength.

Ignacio fell to the ground. "Fuckin' 'ell," he said, looking across to Kishu. "What you been teaching this woman?"

"She taught herself that one," Kishu said. "It's uncanny what she can do when she's angry."

Coco walked back a few steps and beckoned to Ignacio. "Again!" In a flash, she was sprawled out on the ground. "Jeez, I'm not ready for vampire speed."

"That's why I'm here," Ignacio said. He pulled her off the floor and beckoned her to him. "C'mon, luv, give me your fastest speed."

"Speaking of speed, where's Louisa?"

Coco charged at him. She landed on the floor with Ignacio's foot planted firmly on her back.

"You tryin' to distract me?" He removed his foot, and Coco sprang up.

"Actually, yes," she said. "But in retrospect, I haven't seen her for a while. Since you rescued her from Freyja's hold. She's had a lot to deal with… The news of her mother's death, becoming immortal… Is she okay?"

"My beloved's doing remarkably well," Ignacio said. "She's ravenous, but that's to be expected. I left her in a deep sleep, kind of synonymous with newborn vampires. Hopefully, when she wakes up, she'll notice the liquid refreshment I left on the bedside table for her."

"And if she doesn't?" Coco asked.

Ignacio shrugged and beckoned her to attack him. "Let's just say

I wouldn't want to be in your shoes. Now come on, luv, charge me like you mean it!"

Suddenly the door flew open, and Louisa had Coco pinned to the ground.

Ignacio knelt beside her, easing her fingers away from Coco's throat. "I'm okay, luv. You need to let Coco go. She's your friend."

Louisa drew her gaze from the bulging vein on Coco's neck to Ignacio's dark eyes. She jumped up and clung to him while simultaneously staring at Coco. "I could have killed you!"

"Shit," Coco said. "You're lightning fast!"

"I'm so sorry," Louisa said. "I thought you were hurting Ignacio."

Coco's eyes lit up and she burst out laughing. "Yeah, right, like that's ever going to happen!"

Ignacio kissed Louisa and draped an arm around her shoulders. "Nice to know you've got my back, luv. Don't think that's ever happened."

Louisa leaned into him. "I'll always protect you, *tesoro*. But this is a strong emotion and difficult to control."

"Learning to control all emotions is difficult for newly turned vampires," Kishu said. "And in the short time you've been in your immortal body, you've shown great restraint under difficult circumstances. Perhaps it would be good for you to train alongside Coco, as she too is learning to control her emotions."

"I think that's a great idea, Grandpa." She smirked at Ignacio. "Maybe we can have a group physical training session, and I'll get Gabriel in here to kick your ass."

Ignacio grinned. "Sounds like fun!"

"I'll speak with Prudence," Kishu said. "Jokes aside, it would be good for Jason, Arianna, and Jeremy to learn some defensive skills. The sooner, the better."

CHAPTER 26

HOURS LATER, AS Kishu, Ignacio, and Louisa exited the dojo, Gabriel arrived. His gaze moved possessively over Coco's body, making her skin tingle. She gasped when he suddenly appeared behind her and moved her hair away from her neck before kissing the skin below her ear. She leaned into his soft lips but faltered when she realized he was no longer behind her. Instead, he stood across the room, arms crossed, staring at her like she was prey.

"Gabriel." She took a step toward him, but instantly he was behind her. "What are you doing?" He stood in front of her now. "Stop it, you're making me dizzy."

"That's the idea. Kenan will play these games with you, Colombina. He enjoys the hunt as much as he enjoys the kill, and he's fast—he'll treat you like a toy. He'll touch you, whisper words that will make you want to surrender to his every whim. Your love for me will be second to appeasing him."

"Never! I'd never do that!"

He circled her, inhaling her scent. "You may not want to, but you're being foolish if you think Kenan will not have such power over you."

She turned around, but he was gone. Her eyes darted around the room, searching for him. She spun around and crashed into his chest.

"Then teach me how to resist his power." The tingling in her body that she felt when Gabriel had first entered the room had intensified and showed no sign of weakening.

"Yes," he said. "That's my energy coming alive in your body." He stood in front of her, still as the dead and barely touching her. "You need to learn to control it."

"What if I can't?"

"That's not an option." He placed a hand over her heart, and warmth spread over her skin. "I want you to recall the night you dove into the lake in Tuscany when you wanted to get to your mother standing on the shore."

"I remember," Coco said. "Prudence was there, and she… she placed an amethyst stone against my heart." The tingling in her body had grown into a pulse that now beat in syncopated rhythm to her heart.

"Yes, that was the moment you accepted the call to your destiny," Gabriel said. "And taking my blood took you to another level—a love that no one can tear apart. Our love for each other is the key to breaking Kenan."

"Does Kenan know that?"

Gabriel's eyes were dark and serious. "I've no doubt he has wondered, and that's why he wanted you dead. But when his attempt to have you killed failed, he realized that you were worth more alive. Now he wants to draw you to him using the skills he learned from your own great-grandmother."

"Dark magic," Coco whispered.

"Yes," Gabriel said. "But I believe your great-grandmother saw your strength and hid that secret from Kenan. No doubt he figured out she was hiding something from him, and sadly that led to her death. I think she saw our blood bond, and that allowed her to let go." He ran his thumbs down Coco's neck. "With my blood running through your veins, you can fight back. You can beat Kenan at his own game."

"Why didn't you just tell me this earlier?"

"You know the answer," he said. "Prudence has always stressed that your journey must be one of free will. If I had told you earlier, you would have drunk from me to protect the Allegiance and all we stand for—and that decision would not have been based on love. And when all is done, love is the true motto of the Allegiance."

"Without love, all is lost," Coco whispered.

He was behind her now, one hand firmly holding her head against his body, a leg twisted around one of hers, an arm across her waist, his lips on her throat.

"How will you get out of this hold, Colombina?" His voice seeped with erotic connotations.

"Don't," Coco snapped.

Gabriel pulled down her tank top, caught a nipple between his fingers, and squeezed. "Kenan will do this to you, and you may want him to continue."

"No!" Coco breathed in short gasps. "Never!" She wondered if she could reach for the stiletto dagger sheathed at her ankle.

The dagger went flying across the room.

"Nice try," Gabriel said.

Coco cursed through pursed lips.

"How will you fight back?" His hand left her breast and rested over her mound. "Or will you give in to him?"

Coco imagined Kenan's hand in place of Gabriel's. She fought against her lover, using every cell in her body to escape his clutches.

"Physical strength will not work against him," Gabriel whispered. "Use your mind."

Gabriel's words hit like a tornado. She pictured them drinking each other's blood and the sheer bliss the act had given her. But something niggled at her mind, something her mother had said. *"Our blood runs through each other's veins, and as such we share each other's traits."* Coco drew her focus to Gabriel's energy, which now flowed within her. She silently called to his blood pulsing in her veins, and as she did, something shifted within. A feral scream rang from her throat, and then her world turned black.

He called to her, his velvety, deep voice reminding her of chocolate melting against her skin, thick and sweet.

"Mi amore." He held a glass of water to her lips. "Drink."

Coco opened her eyes and sipped the water he offered. Without missing a beat, she shoved him backward, rolled him over, and yanked one of his arms up behind his neck. In an instant she found herself flat on her back with him straddling her.

"Damn," she said. "I thought I had you!"

Gabriel raised an eyebrow. "Do you remember blacking out?"

"Kind of," she said. "But then someone flicked a switch and all hell broke loose! What was that?"

"Things falling into place," he said. "Think of it as your body, mind, and spirit all connecting at the same time. That's what you want to happen."

"How long will it last?"

"As long as you want," he said. "It's up to you to learn to plug into that energy whenever you need it."

"I feel like I'm full of electricity… How do I turn it off?"

He leaned in and kissed her.

When he broke away, she murmured, "I don't think that's helping."

He picked her up and fled the room.

CHAPTER 27

SNUGGLED IN A nest of blankets and pillows, Coco leaned against the window seat in Gabriel's bedroom where for the past few hours she had been recovering from the immediate connection to Gabriel's power. After she'd promised him that she would rest, Gabriel had left her while he met with Alessandro. She watched the moon ascend above the mountains, allowing her thoughts to sift through everything she had learned while training with Kishu and Ignacio, and later, Gabriel.

The hot bath she had taken had done little to ease her tired and bruised body, and likewise her mind still lingered over the subtler elements of the plan to corner Kenan, those that were specific to her. Tomorrow morning she would train again and in the afternoon would work alongside Luciana, Flora, and her mother, finalizing the details of the paintings that were imperative to the success of the plan.

She ran a hand along Thalia's body, and the cat purred in response. That prompted Coco to think back to last year and the moment she had seen the mountain lion jump in front of the car near the Temescal Canyon trailhead. The large feline had sheltered her from the full impact of the collision. Coco realized that as her guardian, Thalia had most likely accompanied her on all her runs and she had never been entirely alone in the oak woodland around Los Angeles. She thought of her time in the hospital, the sprigs of lavender that appeared beside her pillow each morning and the voices she would hear during the night. She had yet to remember to ask her father who it was he had been in conversation with.

Coco deepened her concentration and focused on the woman's voice. Another image crossed her mind, a dream she'd had where she entered a house painted entirely in a shade of light blue. A staircase stood directly opposite the front door, and there were spirits of the dead around her.

"It's her," a voice whispered. "Yes—finally, Colombina's here!" said an old lady as she drifted by, trailing the scent of roses.

Coco blinked. "My grandmother." She leaned into Gabriel's hand now resting upon her shoulder. "I didn't hear you enter."

"You seemed lost in thought."

"My grandmother's been waiting for me," she said. "I saw her once, in a dream soon after I arrived in Tuscany with Layla."

"Do you remember what she looked like?"

Coco nodded. "Like a younger version of the woman held prisoner by Kenan; perhaps in her seventies, but her face wasn't wrinkled, and her eyes were light with a hint of amethyst. She was my height, and her face seemed triangular in shape, high cheekbones and a strong nose like Dad's. But mostly I remember her scent; she smelled like roses."

"The scent of roses is not surprising," Gabriel said. "A sign that she's been in contact with the Lady and the Rose—goddess and protector of the Allegiance. Remembering that encounter now is confirmation that our plan is aligned with our spirit friends."

Coco stood and kissed him.

He lifted her into his arms and carried her across the room to the bed. His blood called to her, bringing heat to every part of her body. They tore at each other's clothing until they lay naked together.

Coco straddled Gabriel, claimed his mouth with hers, and trailed a path of kisses down his neck and chest to the taut muscles that defined his abdomen. His body moved in ecstasy as she took him into her mouth, and his fingers ran through her hair as he groaned in pleasure. The taste of him made her shudder. He placed his hands under her arms and lifted her up, then thrust his tongue into the wetness of her femininity. Moments before she climaxed, he flipped her over and lost himself inside her.

As waves of bliss rocked their bodies, she recognized the two small fangs that emerged from her canine teeth. She sank them into his jugular and savored the sweet and sensuous taste of her beloved's blood as it spilled over her tongue and slid down her throat. When she was done, she licked the blood from his neck and waited in anticipation for his bite. When it came, it took her to another level of orgasmic bliss, making her body shudder and her skin glisten in the afterglow. Their spirits soared into the night sky, their minds reeling in the passion of sharing each other's blood. In time, they drifted back into their bodies, gratified and wrapped in the glow of love. Coco drifted off to sleep, breathing in Gabriel's scent of sandalwood and berries.

CHAPTER 28

WHILE COCO RESTED, Gabriel worked in his study, reviewing the plans to eliminate Kenan. He looked up from his work as the door to his study opened and Alessandro and Prudence entered. He stood in his mother's presence out of respect and waited until she was seated before returning to his chair.

"Stefan tells me the journals you retrieved from Kenan's underground hideout are proving to be both invaluable and disturbing," Prudence said. "There is no limit to the atrocities the three incarnations of evil have thrown upon humanity."

Alessandro pulled up a chair. "This is not news, Prudence. The pressing issue is where Kenan is now and what he's planning next. With the dreams and images he's feeding Colombina, I guess now that holding her hostage is no longer a viable option, he wants her dead. He knows her death would destroy Gabriel and my family. Kenan sees Colombina's death as payback—to you, Gabriel, and my grandmother."

"I understand your reasoning in the past for the Allegiance maintaining a rule of nonconfrontation," Gabriel said. "But the new information we've gained makes it imperative for us to use every resource available to track Kenan and end this. You and I have the power to awaken a force of spirits to help find him, to drag him out of hiding. But we must act now, while Colombina is strong—and before Kenan realizes the magnitude of her abilities."

Prudence rose, walked over to the window, and gazed out at the dark clouds gathering over the surrounding mountain peaks. "It is you who holds the power of the past, Gabriel," she said. "The spirits will heed your call, not mine."

Alessandro leaned forward in his chair. "Does your answer mean we're in agreement?"

Prudence nodded. "Our timing must be perfect. I can hold the space for the souls who wish to enter our fold, but we will need a conduit—someone to act as a funnel between the past and present."

Gabriel opened a drawer, retrieved a roll of papers, and laid them out on his desk. "Here's what Alessandro and I have planned." In a flash, Prudence stood at the desk beside Alessandro and contemplated the paper. "The conduit must be Alessandro," Gabriel said. "For this plan to work, we will need to awaken the strongest seers; it must be Alessandro's grandmother and the twin's grandmother, Birgit."

"How does Chantal feel about this?" Prudence asked. "You must understand that as a conduit, there are risks. If our time runs over, any one of us could be drawn into the realm between the living and the dead."

"We're aware of the risks, and we've discussed everything with Christopher and Coco," Alessandro said. "Kishu assures us that Coco has exceeded his expectations regarding the mindful training. In fact, he brought Ignacio in and began basic physical defensive tactics. We'll all be taking risks, Prudence, but the alternative is getting us nowhere fast."

"My mother will help us," Prudence said, "but as there must be three of us to hold the space open for the spirits to enter, I will ask my father to suggest another female. The pyramid must be strong." She pointed to a specific location on one of the papers. "Why here?"

Gabriel's gaze lifted from the map to Prudence's eyes. "I'm hoping Caprecia will hear my call in the world of spirit, and she knows this place well. What better strength to have on our side than the protective essence of a mother for her child?"

Prudence steepled her fingers and rested the tips against her chin, then closed her eyes in concentration, and when they opened, the specks of gold in her irises sparkled. "Contact every member of the Allegiance here in Italy and tell them of our plan. We have much to do. We'll meet again soon."

CHAPTER 29

COCO AWAKENED SHORTLY after Gabriel left to work in his study. While she knew he was meeting with her father and Prudence, she sought out Hakon and found him on the *terrazza* off the main library where Christopher, Jason, and Jeremy were working.

"You are in need of something, Colombina?"

She hoped they were far enough away from Christopher's keen sense of hearing. "I have a request."

"One that you wish to be kept secret," Hakon said, and as he looked at her, the corners of his eyes crinkled.

"Yes, that would be best." She pushed a stray piece of hair behind her ear. "My request is regarding Gabriel's plan to lure Kenan into our world. I see a fault, one that has the potential to spoil the outcome. Once Kenan is through the painting, I can't stay at the fortress as Gabriel wishes—I must be at the site of Kenan's death so that you have bargaining power with Freyja."

Hakon furrowed his brow. "How so?"

"When Freyja saved my life, I caught a quick glimpse of an image in her mind—perhaps it was not her wish—but I saw it nonetheless."

"What did you see?"

"I saw a woman—someone familiar, but I can't place where I've seen her. There was a man beside her, dying. She fell across his body.

Everywhere around her was white with snow and ice, but as the woman cried, the ice began to melt, and it seemed life in every form was dying. I thought of the story of Persephone. Does any of this make sense to you?"

Hakon's somber expression veiled his customarily contained demeanor. "Yes; however, while I am grateful for your courage, I'm concerned that seeing you there will distract my grandson, and that would not be wise while he has one foot in the other world."

"Is there anything you can do to help hold his focus?"

"No," he said, and the corner of his eyes crinkled. "You must tell him what you have told me. He will understand."

"What makes you so sure?"

The fae prince placed his hands on her shoulders. "As you have entrusted me with this knowledge, I must also share what Freyja's kiss means to you."

"No," Coco said, shaking her head. "Some secrets are best kept as such. However, if you think it is best, then I'll speak to him."

"To speak the truth is always best."

"The truth's not always easy." Coco turned to leave but halted. "Who were the couple I saw in the snow?"

"My parents," Hakon said. "But that story is not for today."

"I understand." She made her way across the *terrazza* and into the library, stopping momentarily to speak with Christopher.

He leaned back in his chair and looked up at her. "What are you up to, Coco?"

"I had a question for Hakon, that's all." She knew damn well he wasn't buying her answer.

He walked with her. "Ignacio tells me you're an awesome student, which comes as no surprise."

"Word travels fast around here."

"Stay aware and never let down your guard," he said. "My child will need you around."

"Your child is why we need to end this. None of us can exist at our full potential while a blanket of fear hangs over us," she said. They had reached the door, and she turned to him. "Thanks for putting up with me for all these years. Knowing what I know now, I understand your protectiveness with me, and I appreciate everything you've done to keep me safe. I'm just sorry that I've been a complete bitch of a little sister. I love you."

"I love you too." Christopher opened the door for her. "See you soon."

Coco called to him over her shoulder. "Be careful—I might just kick your ass next time you're in the dojo!"

CHAPTER 30

IN THE DARKNESS of night, while the mortals of Casa della Pietra were sleeping, Gabriel slid into the main living room, closed the door, and cast a web of magic around the entrances to secure his privacy. Dressed in dark jeans and a faded black T-shirt, his feet bare, he crossed the room, aware of the slick texture of the worn threads of the antique Persian rug.

Alessandro stood by the mantel, dressed similarly to Gabriel, and also without shoes. Both men were solemn. "Where do you want me?"

With a wave of his hand, Gabriel created a circle marked in white chalk measuring ten feet in diameter directly in front of the fireplace. "As we're calling the feminine, you must be on my left side," he said. "Between me and the edge of the circle. When you see me rise, do the same; however, no matter what happens, please stay in the same position. You're needed to hold the space. You're the conduit between the spirit world and ours. Frankly, this is the first time I've conjured up this spell… I'm unsure how the spirits will react. They may come forward quickly, or not."

"In all honesty, I think I'd be concerned if it *wasn't* your first time," Alessandro mumbled. He made his way to his designated spot and settled himself into a kneeling position. "I'm ready."

"Good." Gabriel sighed. "What's your grandmother's name?"

"Leonie."

A smile tugged at the edges of Gabriel's mouth. "The lion," he whispered. He knelt inside the circle in front of the portrait of Prudence. He stared up at the image and remembered the city of Florence in 1497 and the insidious Bonfire of the Vanities spearheaded by the fanatical Dominican friar Girolamo Savonarola. He thought of Alessandro and the fierceness of his sword as together they had fought to save treasures born of artists of the Renaissance. This was their mission, to protect art, artists, and the Creatives born among them. Gabriel considered that as he reached into a pocket and brought out a small mother-of-pearl-inlaid pocketknife. The last time he had used this blade was to give blood to Colombina in the hospital when she lay near death. Had that moment been only months ago, or years? For an immortal, time was the trickster, the imp, and sometimes the traitor.

Gabriel swiped the blade across his right wrist and then placed the implement back in his pocket. His runes whispered to him as they gathered like soldiers before him. His breathing deepened as he mentally reached out to the souls of women who had suffered at the hands of Vinicio, Domenico, and Kenan. The runes began to move clockwise in a circle, rising above Gabriel until they were positioned between him and the portrait.

As he stood, he held the small bag of ashes Prudence had given him and emptied the contents over his left hand. He dipped his fingers in the blood seeping from the cut on his wrist and then placed his left hand through the ring of runes. He smeared the blood around the inside of the frame of the portrait, repeating a string of words in a strange language—a mix of Latin, Italian, and French—the language of the Allegiance.

"I call upon the strength of the feminine.

To all who have suffered at the hands of brutal men,

Evil men,

Vinicio, Domenico, and Kenan.

I call upon the strength of the feminine,

To gather your courage and aid us in fighting this madness,
To expel evil's lust for hideous acts
That has invaded these three men for centuries.
I call upon the strength of the feminine
To join those of us who have fought to protect the beauty of this world,
To protect others from the wrath of this being.
I call upon the strength of the feminine,
So the women of our future can rise without fear.
I call upon Isabella, Birgit, Caprecia, and Leonie to guide others forward.
Take this offering of my blood,
May it give you the power to answer the call of your sisters.
Awaken.
For we are here to carry you upon our shoulders."

A woman's hand burst through the painting and grabbed Gabriel's wrist, smearing his blood over her fingers and palm. The fire flared, and a crash of thunder rocked the fortress. Gabriel perceived the vibrations of approaching spirits, their memories, their pain and anguish. The furniture in the room began to move, but he remained perfectly still, his stern gaze focused on the portrait. He heard their muffled voices now, first anger and then acceptance as Gabriel silently revealed his plan.

When he had finished, the woman's hand slowly slid away from his grip and receded back into the painting, leaving the image as if it were untouched. Gabriel pulled his hand through the circle of runes and dropped to his knees in exhaustion. In the palm of his hand, covered in his blood, sat a gold ring bearing the Marzocco and the lily, the symbol of Florence, made famous in the early fifteenth century by Donatello. Gabriel's plea had been heard. His runes fell from the air into his waiting palm. He gazed up at the portrait, then to Alessandro, who lay on the floor beside him.

"Are you all right?" he asked.

Alessandro rolled over onto his back and stared up at the ceiling. "Yeah, thanks. How about you?"

"I'm glad they're on our side," Gabriel said. "They're a force of women to behold."

"No wonder men like Kenan want to see them suppressed," Alessandro said. "They're an army of hope and courage."

"Did Leonie speak with you?"

"Not in words. But with images, similar to when you reveal what lies behind a painting. I guess that's the Creative in her."

"And you, my friend," Gabriel said. "One day, maybe you'll pick up a paintbrush."

CHAPTER 31

A SILKY MIST CREPT toward the fortress, bringing with it a host of wounded souls. Prudence heard their whispers, their pleas for release from the permanence of the horrific deaths they had suffered at the hands of brutal men. She considered the mental pain her son had endured to cast such a spell, to awaken such misery, such unfinished trauma. She understood that emotion well; it had called to her deep in the bowels of Freyja's realm, when she journeyed there with her parents and Ignacio and Caprecia to rescue Louisa. *Ah yes, I know you well… your dense, empty darkness and how it pulls at one's soul in an effort to find understanding and acceptance for how their lives ended.*

Another memory fluttered by, and Prudence pulled it close to her heart. With slight hesitation she allowed the scene to open, knowing that it would cause her sadness. She had often wondered if by chance her beloved friend, Sandro, had known while painting her portrait centuries ago of the magic she had wound over the image. That night she had entered Sandro's rooms while he slept, watched him breathe, not daring to enter his dreams, for she had already foreseen his fate— the death of his beloved Colombina, the pull of the church, and the twisted mental torture Savonarola would bring to the exceptional artist's mind. But who was Prudence to tempt fate? On that day she had witnessed the joy on Sandro's face as he had looked up and seen his Colombina dancing in the Medici garden.

No, love was the one thing worth dying and living for, and to play with such fate when she had seen Sandro's alternate scenario would have dragged the world of art back toward the darkest ages, and that was not the purpose of life. She thought of the time long ago when she had first met the artist who would later become known as Botticelli…

Florence 1461

A FRESH BREEZE caught leaves on the path and lifted them into the air, carrying them across the grounds of the church where tools used by builders lay on makeshift worktables. Prudence and Stefan were there on the pretense of meeting with the artist Filippo Lippi, but it was one of his pupils who had attracted the attention of Prudence.

The young man's essence crept toward her the moment she entered the church, and her gaze sought him out. He stood before a series of frescoes; his light brown hair, thick and flowing, ignited an image in Prudence's mind—a godlike creature, destined to reveal himself in more than one of the artist's future paintings. In her mind, Prudence whispered his name, *"Sandro."* The artist turned and stared at her. She approached him, and he smiled, his deep-set, velvety brown eyes alight with childlike enthusiasm.

Artist and sage lost within the realm of the unknown, of senses tugging at something unfamiliar yet familiar. Prudence stepped closer to him, and a joy deep within told her she was in the presence of greatness, of someone whose talents would not be appreciated for many years. She vowed to protect this man's legacy and his work.

"My name is Prudence."

"The wise one," Sandro said.

Her mouth lifted into a smile. "So I have been told, and that is what has brought me here today."

Sandro tilted his head, and she knew his eyes searched her face.

Prudence wandered closer to the series of frescoes Sandro had been admiring, but it was the figure of Salome in *The Feast of Herod* that called to her. "She stands out from the others. You have captured her dancing with her spirit rather than her humanity."

"Ah, but you see I did not say I painted her."

This time it was Prudence who smiled. "Your secret is safe with me."

Stefan approached, and Prudence reached for his hand. "My dearest, this is Sandro."

Stefan bowed his head to the young man. "I am Stefan Lazarevic, also an admirer of your work."

Sandro's forehead creased. "I was not aware my work is known by others."

"In time your art will inspire great love," Prudence said. "I have seen this, Sandro."

"Then I can only believe they will have seen a portrait that I will paint of you," he said. "For your ethereal beauty inspires me to return to Florence and paint the images that seep into my dreams."

"And I shall treasure forever the portrait you paint of me."

A year later, Sandro had asked to paint her portrait. Of course she had agreed eagerly, and she arrived at his studio the following day. He requested that she pose in a gown of white, and a smile lit up her face when she saw the dress he had chosen. It was not unlike the chiton she had worn when she first left the Island of the Crescent Moon centuries ago. As if reading her mind, he placed flowers in her hair and pulled it back from her face so he could see her "eyes of starlight."

During the sittings, Sandro spoke of his want to express himself through his paintings, to bring to life the true Florence of the people, the joy in their hearts and the passion in their souls.

"One day," he had said, "I will portray women as the seasons of this earth, in all their beauty and sensuality, their heartache and sadness. But most of all I want to paint emotion… something not previously captured in art."

That moment, and Sandro's words, had become etched in Prudence's memory, for she knew that while it might take centuries after Sandro's death for people to appreciate the importance of his work, once they saw it, there would be no returning to a world of painting where emotion was not encouraged. That, in truth, would be Sandro Botticelli's legacy.

Florence 1497

WHEN PRUDENCE, STEFAN, Alessandro, and Gabriel appeared in an alley behind the Piazza della Signoria, the pungent smell of fire permeated the air. They emerged onto a street where they found children crying while women clutched rings, necklaces, and simple toys only to have them snatched out of their hands by soldiers caught in the mania of the mad friar, Savonarola, and his want to destroy art and culture.

"Gabriel and Alessandro," Prudence said. "Go to the gallery— protect what you can!"

With swords drawn, the two immortals took off at lightning speed, disappearing in a sea of people who lined the streets, many hysterical as soldiers dragged books and paintings out of houses and toward the piazza.

Prudence and Stefan sprinted in the opposite direction, down an alley that led to a dead end where more soldiers poured out of a nondescript stone building. Pushing past the line of men carrying statues, artwork, jewelry, stylish clothing, and books, Prudence raced into the villa and immediately forced her way into the main living room. Her eyes sought out a familiar portrait that hung above the mantel, and in its absence she turned to Stefan, her eyes awash with tears. "I must find it! Search here, my love, and I shall go to the piazza."

As she ran along the streets and into the piazza, Prudence eyed every article the soldiers carried. As much as she wanted to save what she could, she knew she must find the portrait, for its actual value lay in what could not be seen. She stood at the edge of the fire, her eyes darting over the artwork piled high like pieces of unwanted trash. She watched as burning flames licked upward toward the sky, her golden eyes sparkling in the orange glow and her white hair blowing across her face.

Like the tongue of a serpent, two flames parted, and she saw the image of herself not yet touched by fire. But there was something else, a sense of foreboding itching at her skin. From the corner of her eyes, she saw a group of men approach with their swords pointed at her. She fell to her knees and screamed as everything slipped out of her control.

Familiar, strong hands lifted her into a protective embrace. She reached out toward the fire, and through the flames she saw a young man staring at her.

"We need to get out of here, *tesoro*! The entire city has erupted into chaos," Stefan said. "Your safety is all that matters to me."

Prudence knew by the tone of his voice that it would be useless to argue with her beloved's protective instincts.

Casa della Pietra, Present Day

PRUDENCE SENSED HER father's presence. "You told me long ago, when we stood on the Island of the Crescent Moon and said our goodbyes, that my journey would not be an easy one—that is the way of gods and heroes. I am neither, Father. There have been times when the loss of friends has taken me to dark places, and all I have wanted to do is beg you to lift this burden from my soul. And there have also been times when I have wanted to scream at you for giving me this position." She turned to face him. "Why did you do this to me?"

Hakon looked heavenward, and then his golden eyes met Prudence's. "Because humanity needs hope, and it is up to immortals like you and me to give them that. And giving hope and comfort to others is the food that feeds our souls, for ours is a life of sacrifice."

He gazed toward the mountains. "At times I wondered if you would be able to cope with the utter sadness and loneliness of losing loved ones, and that is why the Lady and the Rose watches over you. I told you once that there is no other being like you, but in fact, there is another."

Prudence placed a hand over her heart. "You kept this secret from me? Why?"

He shook his head. "Because of a promise."

"Another of your deals, Father? How could you lie to me?"

"A parent will go to great lengths to protect their child," he said. "Am I not correct?"

Prudence was well aware that her father knew she had asked the Lady and the Rose to watch over Gabriel while she answered her mother's call. She nodded. "I was torn between heeding Mother's summons and protecting Gabriel. I needed to know he would be safe… When the bomb exploded and Gabriel was caught in the flames, his pain erupted in me. I was comforted only by knowing that the Lady held him in her arms so he would not die."

"I do not judge your actions, for I know how strong the roots of love can be," he said. "But I am not here to speak of such things, for I came to ask if you are ready to meet your grandmother?"

Prudence's eyes lit up.

"She is asking for you." With a wave of his hand, Hakon beckoned forth the mist, and when it surrounded father and daughter, their images dissipated.

Chapter 32

FROM WHERE PRUDENCE stood, the world looked to be a magical place, serene and peaceful. A blue tinge caressed the snow-covered landscape where time seemed irrelevant as light and shadow morphed into one another in a string of endless magnificence. And the quiet of this place, it lingered, never faltered, the magnificent mountains holding secrets of time hidden forever under layers of ice and snow.

This place awakened Prudence's spirit and made her smile, and when she gazed upon her father's face, she also recognized the lifting of his spirits, how it is when the vibrancy of life connects with one's deepest roots. In the distance, a figure emerged, and the closer she came, Prudence saw that it was a woman dressed in a full-length cloak of pearl-colored velvet, but she also wore an air of familiarity, and it was not until the woman stood before her and raised her head that Prudence recognized her.

Swirling pools of blue water made up the woman's otherworldly eyes, and the scent of roses emanating around her whispered a sense of family. The woman reached out to Prudence and framed her face with her hands. "Yes, dear Astridr, I am your grandmother."

Prudence stepped forward and embraced the woman whom for centuries she had thought of as a goddess and the protector of the Allegiance—the Lady and the Rose. "How could I not have sensed your blood running through my veins?"

The Lady chuckled. "In our world, it is best to hold some secrets close to our hearts."

"But had I known that you were my grandmother, that I was not alone—"

"You would have doubted your decisions. By being your protector, I allowed you to search within yourself for answers. I was always beside you." She stroked Prudence's hair. "Who do you think it was that guided you back on the road the day you wandered off alone into the forests of Serbia?"

Prudence lifted her head and met her grandmother's gaze. "You guided me to Stefan?"

"With the help of Juno, yes," she said, her gaze momentarily catching Hakon's. "On the day that your father and Juno wrote the accords of the Allegiance, Hakon insisted that Juno give you a husband and child. It was part of the deal, for he has witnessed firsthand the emptiness of life without one's beloved. He did not want that for you."

Prudence closed her eyes and shook her head, and when she opened them, she looked to Hakon. "All this time, I didn't think you cared about me. I thought you created me to do the work in the human realm so that you could return to your homeland."

"No, Astridr, or perhaps we should call you Prudence, as you wear the name well," he said. "My heart broke the day I left you and your mother on the island, but I had to keep you both safe from the wars that raged upon the earth at that time. And although I wanted to bring you both here, Mother reminded me of the pact I had made with Juno; to break it would bring chaos to the world of mortals."

"You see," the Lady confessed, "humanity cannot live without hope, and it is through the beauty of the visual and performing arts that hope can be found. Music, art, dance, the written word, these are the elements that spark curiosity. You have witnessed the truth in my words—think of the day when your portrait lay among the burning pile in the city of Florence and of the madman responsible for lighting the flame. Humanity wails at the loss of art because it is through it that our imagination thrives. Hakon and I ask for your forgiveness, Prudence; however, we would do the same again if needed."

Prudence nodded. "I do understand, but now I am sad that I have missed so much time without you in my life. Are there others in our family?"

A glimmer of sadness washed over her grandmother's eyes, and Hakon reached out and placed a hand on her shoulder. The Lady sighed and tenderly tapped his hand with hers. "Walk with me, and I shall share the story of my beloved, and also how your magic and mine are connected."

The Lady and the Rose, Hakon, and Prudence walked together along a path at the foot of tall mountains while the story of Prudence's family unfolded.

"I once lived below the limbs of the great ash tree known as Yggdrasil, with my two sisters. As seers, we were the guardians of the Well of Urd, and it was our task to write the destinies of all children." The Lady halted for a moment but Prudence understood her repose. Often when the memory of sadness surfaces, the moment tends to trip one's consciousness. The Lady continued, "When Ragnarok came to be, the great tree fell, killing my sisters. Had it not been for my brave Gunwald, king of the fae, I too would have perished. He lifted me from the depths of the earth, out of the world I had known for eons, and brought me into the world of mortals, the world of light.

"The truth is that Gunwald and I had been in love for centuries, but in my world, our love was forbidden. But, as fate unfolded, we were free together, and our love bore us our son, Hakon. Time passed, and all seemed well until tragedy struck our family." The Lady looked around and pointed to a spot across the tundra. "My beloved and I were walking together when suddenly an arrow pierced his heart." She took in a deep breath and shook her head. "The tip of the arrow was made from Charon's obol and had been dipped in pure silver—a deadly mix for a fae king.

"Gunwald fell to the ground, and I knew he was dying. Freyja appeared, and I screamed to her that she could not take him, and as my heart broke, so did nature's. The glaciers began to melt, and that would mean death to the fauna of this place. I called for Hakon, and upon seeing the extent of my sadness, Freyja promised that Gunwald would not die. She bade me give him three drops of my blood, but the silver had already done its damage. Freyja took my beloved to a place below this tundra, a place known as Sanctuary, a place where he lives as a scribe and where he has documented your life since before your birth."

"Have you not seen him in all these years?" Prudence asked.

"Each year on the eve of the equinox, Gunwald ascends to this world." The Lady's eyes glistened. "We are together for twenty-four hours."

"Why can't he stay?"

A sad smile crossed the Lady's face. "His death was imminent. Freyja gave us this time, but he will die if he stays in this world."

"Is there a way for me to see him?"

"Only on the equinox," the Lady said.

"Then I will be here," Prudence said. "And I will bring a healer with me, one who has skills born of science. Maybe she can save him."

"Perhaps there is also another way," Hakon said. "All this time I've thought it was Freyja who shot the arrow into Father's heart. Her jealousy is renowned. What if what she saw at first as a gamble to experience love turned into something that she later realized was a grave mistake? Since gaining the memories of her time as Ravinka, she has had to live with the pain of loss, and each passing day drives her closer to insanity. Gabriel is correct. This is a time when we must use every skill available to win this war against evil."

CHAPTER 33

Lazio, Italy

FROM A SAFE distance, Prudence watched Freyja as she stood atop a cliff, staring out across the ocean. She knew the area held a special connection to the goddess, for she had seen a vision of the moment when she fell and tumbled into the sea below. That particular moment had been prompted by a bribe Freyja had made with Hakon centuries ago: she had allowed the great Nordic seer, Sonja, to live, but in exchange she'd asked that he enable her to experience love as a human female.

Centuries later, when the time came for Hakon to fulfill his promise, Freyja had awakened and found herself standing at the edge of the cliff. That is where she stood when she first saw Kenan and fell in love, and where the sea below had called to her when it was time for her to return to her true home. During her time as a human, the only information she could remember of her family was that they lived in the north, somewhere cold.

The constant roar of waves crashing below nudged Prudence back to the present time, and a ripple in the ether told her Freyja's torment was edging her toward destruction. She called to the mist, and moments later she stood beside the goddess.

"What you are feeling is grief," she said. "It pertains to a feeling of loss, of losing someone you loved."

Freyja stared out to sea. "I understand now Hakon's reasoning and why the wind pushed me off this cliff so many years ago. The waters of the Great Mother needed to wash over my body—to take away my pain and return me to the place of my birth, my home." She opened her arms wide, and the wind embraced her. Tears welled in her eyes. She fell to her knees and sobbed. "I cannot bear this pain, Prudence," she cried. "My soul is dying."

Prudence knelt beside Freyja and embraced her, stroking her hair as if she were a child. "My father only wanted to protect you—he would never harm you."

"I know. But I have lost my will to go on… The light in my soul is dying. More than once, I have found myself at the end of the pier and contemplated throwing myself into the River Styx. I imagine myself sinking until I reach the depths of nonexistence." Her shoulders sagged. "How does mankind endure such torture?"

"They do so for many reasons." A look of sadness mixed with pride spread across Prudence's face. "When a loved one passes, mortals are often left with family members to look after, work to attend to… for by their very existence, they need to continue to earn money to survive in the modern world. We have much to learn from the endurance of the human spirit. Surely you have sensed the pain of souls who pass on to death too early, perhaps after experiencing an unexpected or violent death. Consider the lives of parents who have had to watch a child die or a man or woman after they have witnessed their beloved take a final breath. I've heard it said the pain softens after a while, but I know it lingers… It is always there, haunting, wanting so desperately to feel that love again."

Freyja clung to Prudence. "I know he loved me."

"Yes," Prudence said. "I believe he did. He killed Domenico in the hope that it would set him free to be with you."

Freyja rested her head against Prudence's breast and gazed out at the whitecaps. "Is there a way to bring the man who loved me back?"

Thunder rolled in the distance.

"I am not sure it is possible," Prudence said. "The devil has resided within Kenan for centuries and now grows exponentially stronger with each full moon. That is not a decision I can make."

Freyja nodded. "I know… But after the dark deeds Kenan has done, Hakon may not grant him back his earlier life."

"And would you love him in his human form, if he were no longer an immortal?"

"He was not always bad. He was once a little boy who had the only person who ever loved him murdered before his eyes. Even I save children from the darkness of my world. They go to a special place of light and love."

"As they should," whispered Prudence. "Speak with Hakon, but Kenan must die, or this world will fall into darkness."

"I do not want the darkness on this earth again," Freyja said. "I have begun to find peace in the light. But I sense you have a question—what is it that you need from me?"

Prudence shook her head. "I would not dare to ask more of you than you have given. It is my father who wishes to confer with you."

Hakon appeared.

"What do you want?" Freyja asked.

Prudence rose, and Hakon stood tall beside her, ready for the consequences of his question.

"We are calling on the spirits of the dead to help us capture Kenan," he said.

Freyja leaped up, and as she did, her persona changed to something much darker. A gust of wind caught her long ebony hair, and her eyes set in a piercing stare as they burned deep into Prudence's soul.

"You come here to console me, and then you turn on me, saying you plan to kill the man I love?"

Hakon held a hand out, and the wind subsided. "How can you

love the creature Kenan has become? He is not the immortal you fell in love with, Freyja. Surely you see that! The reason I am here is that I feel your pain and your love for who Kenan once was. You are a woman of strategy, and I am here to present a deal."

Freyja's hair fell gently over her shoulders, and the atmosphere around her calmed. "Then I am listening."

CHAPTER 34

Florence, Italy—Laurentian Library

THE SHADES WERE drawn across the windows in Marilyn's office, and the interior lighting now resembled that of an archival room. Four large wooden tables took up the center area, each set with a tabletop book lectern, gloves, magnifiers, polyester sheets, and other archival supplies. Directly off the office was a bathroom that led to a small interior room that up until recently had been used for storage. However, with the urgent need to research Vinicio, Domenico, and Kenan's journals, the boxes had been removed and replaced with a pullout sofa bed since Marco and Marilyn had chosen to live at the premises while studying the journals Gabriel and Nikandros had delivered.

Bach's *St Matthew Passion* drifted in quiet tones throughout the room while Marco translated the text to Marilyn, who then transcribed each page onto a document on her desktop computer. As she listened to Marco, she rolled back in her chair.

"What is it, *tesoro*?"

"Repeat that last paragraph, please," she said. "Something about the wording is ringing a bell."

"Of course. 'There are evenings when the spark of something

familiar digs at my soul, and the only place I am able to find solace is on the beaches of Lazio. When I can no longer bear the emptiness, I go to the ruins near Domenico's villa. Even when I am atop the cliff face, the ocean calls to me, just as it has for centuries.'"

Marilyn punched keywords into her browser and then navigated her way through layers of information until she found what she was looking for. "Got it!" She walked over to one of many bookshelf-lined walls and pulled out a small book, then flipped through it with the skill of the literary historian that she was. A smile tugged at her mouth.

"Listen to this… 'One particular ghost story derives from Lazio, Italy. This story tells of a madman who has appeared over the years at the ruins on the cliff at what is now known as Circeo National Park. It is said the man stares out across the ocean and then dives into the water. For centuries, inhabitants from nearby villages have said the man haunts the dreams of young men and that some have fallen victim to him, only to be found the following evening… dead, on the rocks below the ruins.'" She glanced at Marco. "I'll search through the documents using the word *Lazio*. Any other keywords you think might be relevant?"

Marco removed his gloves, then walked over to a table where a large, detailed map of Italy lay spread out. He placed a finger on the area known as Circeo Parco Nazionale. He picked up an iPad, typed in a link, and scanned the information. "Write these down. Circeo's Acropolis, Villa Grotta della Sibilla, Necropolis of Selva Piana, Villa dei Quattro Venti, Fountain of Mezzomonte, and let's also use Papal State, Roman Coast, and Villa di Domiziano. The latter is not on the coast, but who knows how these men thought? They were obviously drawn to history, and as previous incarnations have lived in certain centuries, I believe that gives cause for exploration into historical monuments within the area."

Marilyn nodded. "Agreed, and I think I'll ask Gabriel for some help with this—time is of the essence."

"You're a genius," Marco said. He walked over and kissed the top of her head.

➋

Gabriel arrived at Marilyn's office with Stefan, Nikandros, and Jason, the latter carrying two laptops, various cords, and adapters. After introductions, Marilyn asked for a table to be set up next to hers for Jason. Fifteen minutes later, he had downloaded Marilyn's translated documents into his computers and had begun searching for alternate keywords.

He handed printouts to everyone in the room, showing the journal and page numbers and where geographical descriptions and similar phrasing had been replicated. "Great work with the translations and documentation, you two," Jason said. "I can't believe how quickly you were able to get all this work done."

Marco raised an eyebrow. "It helps to have immortals with quick-reading abilities."

"No doubt," Jason said. He scanned the printout. "Marilyn's correct—multiple sightings of the supposed madman, or pale man as he's also been cited, seem to coincide with Kenan's behavior and Circeo National Park. Also, earlier phrases used by both Vinicio and Domenico allude to a similar geographical area." He looked at Gabriel. "We've found him!"

CHAPTER 35

Arianna looks at her reflection in the window, but the face staring back is not her own. She spins around, hoping to see Coco, but she isn't there. Myriad bookshelves are lined up like dominoes and run perpendicular in rows ending in an area decorated with modular-style sofas and conference tables. Turning back to the window, Arianna contemplates the view. It looks familiar, especially the building opposite with its charcoal windows jutting out from a cement structure, tall cement pillars, and a nearby rectangular pool of water. She walks quickly down an aisle walled on both sides by books. She's aware of the absence of people—just a few here and there sorting books, and none seem to notice her.

At the front door she exits and runs down a few steps. When she reaches the sidewalk, she turns around, looks up, and finds what she needs. A sign tells her she's at the Charles E. Young Research Library at UCLA. She walks to the side of the building and gazes out across the sculpture garden. In the faintly lit grounds, she sees a familiar figure standing near the statue of Freya by Gerhard Marcks. Arianna walks toward her friend and mentor, and when she finds herself a few feet away,

Coco removes a mask from her face. She appears as a woman with long dark hair and even darker eyes.

Arianna lurched out of bed, ran into the bathroom, and stared at her reflection in the mirror. When her breathing calmed, she ran the dream over again in her mind. A firm knock at her door brought her focus back to the present. She walked through the living area and opened the door to Jeremy and Pelayo.

"You okay?" Jeremy asked.

"Yeah, why?"

"Got any coffee?"

"Sure. Come in—it's brewing, I'll get you some."

"Allow me," Pelayo said. "Jeremy needs to speak with you."

Jeremy followed Arianna into her apartment while Pelayo disappeared into her small kitchen.

"What's up?" she asked. "Did I scream in my dream? Is that why you're here?"

"No, but I sensed you'd had a nightmare."

Arianna tilted her head and her brows knitted in a frown. "You sensed it?"

As he eased onto the sofa Jeremy gave a quick glance to Pelayo, who entered the room carrying two mugs of coffee.

"It's just a feeling I get."

"Get?" Arianna asked. "So this has happened before?"

Jeremy accepted a mug from Pelayo and placed it on a side table. He drummed his fingers on his jeans and nodded.

"Just with me," she asked, "or do you get these feelings about other people too?"

This time Jeremy looked up at Pelayo, then back to Arianna. "You and Pelayo, mostly, and sometimes I hear words, but—"

"But what?" Arianna cut in. She placed a hand on his shoulder.

"I saw an image of you and Coco. But it was strange because she was wearing a mask to make her look like someone else, a woman with long black hair and sad eyes." He looked up at her and grinned. "Oh, and you're hungry."

Arianna's eyes widened and she dropped her hand from Jeremy's shoulder. "Jeez, you know when I'm hungry? Prudence and Hakon said we'd both inherit fae traits from Dad. I guess yours is connecting with people you're close to."

She saw Pelayo take out his cell and send a text. A few moments later, Layla walked into the room, flanked by Christopher.

"Did you dream about a mask?" Layla asked.

Arianna nodded, and her skin tingled.

"So did I," Layla said. "You were at UCLA, in a library. Then you walked out to the sculpture garden and saw Coco. Both of you wore masks."

"That's exactly the dream I had," Arianna said. "How's this possible?"

Gabriel and Alessandro arrived.

"I thought you'd want to know about this, *amigo*," Pelayo said. "Layla and Arianna shared the same dream. It has to do with masks."

Gabriel's eyes darkened. "Tell me in your own words about your dreams. Arianna, you first."

Arianna took her time, replaying her dream in as much detail as she could remember. When she finished, Layla did the same.

"Any ideas as to the identity of the dark-haired woman?" Arianna asked.

"Perhaps," Gabriel said.

His poker-faced expression didn't fool Arianna, and she realized then that he knew precisely the identity of the woman.

"Does Coco know about this?" Alessandro asked.

Arianna shook her head. "It just happened. Should I text her?"

"No," Gabriel said. "She's resting. I'll tell her shortly. Alessandro and I need to speak with Prudence." He turned to Christopher. "Are you available?"

Christopher caught Layla's hand.

"I'm fine, Chris," she said. "I'll stay with Arianna and Jeremy."

Gabriel turned to leave, but Arianna placed a hand on his arm. "I want to help find Kenan," she said. "If this dream is a roadmap as to how that might happen, then promise that you won't discount my ability to help or my commitment to the Allegiance. I have no interest in returning to my life as it was before I found Jeremy."

"I understand," Gabriel said. "And if I'm reading your dream correctly, then you're already involved. We'll speak again shortly." He turned to leave.

Arianna continued. "And you should know that Jeremy's fae side has surfaced."

Gabriel halted midstep and turned toward Jeremy. "I'm listening."

A flush of color crept over Jeremy's face. He cleared his throat and looked up at Gabriel. "I pick up stuff about people, kind of sense what they're feeling."

"All people?" Gabriel asked.

Jeremy shook his head. "No, so far just Arianna and Pelayo. But a few moments ago, Arianna touched my shoulder and two things happened: one, I was suddenly hungry; two, I saw an image of her standing with Coco, and they both wore masks."

"See what happens when you hang out with us for too long?" Gabriel said. "You need a teacher, Jeremy, and lucky for you, you're in the best place to find one. I'll let Hakon and Illona know."

"I can still go to law school, right?"

Pelayo chuckled. "With a gift like that, you'll make one hell of a lawyer."

"I'm glad he's on our side," Christopher said.

CHAPTER 36

AFTER DESCRIBING TO Prudence the twin dream Arianna and Layla had shared, Gabriel waited while she considered the hidden meaning.

"Arianna's subconscious is calling out for her to help her mentor, Coco," Prudence said. "In fact, she's screaming to get out." She stroked the smooth, velvety coat of her black jaguar, Algiz. "And the masks they both wore… It would not be the first time you would be called upon to use your talent with such things, Gabriel."

He ran his hands through his hair. "And what good did that talent do then, Mother? Isabella died."

"Her son lived," Prudence said. "You would do well to remember that rather than the darkness surrounding her murder. For without the mask, Isabella would not have been able to hold her son one last time before her death."

Gabriel crossed his arms. "And without the mask, Colombina would not be dragged into this mess!"

Prudence rose from where she was sitting and walked over to the bookcase in Gabriel's office. Her gaze lingered on the book safe Coco had discovered. "What the dream tells me is that there is no doubting Arianna's commitment to the Allegiance, and for Layla to receive the twin dream is serendipitous. We must listen and take heed." She turned and looked directly into Gabriel's eyes. "Please ask Colombina and Arianna to join us."

"No," he said. "I won't allow either of them to be bait."

The door opened, and Coco, Arianna, and Jeremy entered.

"This is not your choice to make, my love," Coco said. She walked toward him. "Arianna and I want to do this. From what I've been able to learn, Isabella made her own choice. She decided to stay in Florence… perhaps she was also intuitive. And perhaps, like her father and Lorenzo, Florence was her great love, not a man or a woman. Prudence is right about this. Isabella made her choice, and now Arianna and I are making ours."

The golden hue of Gabriel's eyes had dissolved into pools of obsidian. Using a carefully controlled tone, he chose his next words wisely. "What you're asking is for me to agree to put you in danger. I'm not sure I can do that."

"Gabriel," she said. "I had the same dream. We can't ignore this."

His posture stiffened. "You dreamed the same dream?"

"Yes. You told me once that there are no coincidences, that every-thing we do has a purpose." She brought one of his hands to her mouth and kissed it. "I trust you with all my heart. Together, you and I can do this."

He was caught between wanting to keep her safe and knowing that if the situation were reversed, he would want to do the same. He also knew better than to ignore multiple signs from the psyche. He ran a hand over her hair, cupped her chin, and kissed her. "What have I done?"

She smiled softly. "You've given me strength."

He was suddenly aware that the entire household of family and guests had entered the room. No doubt Prudence had requested their presence.

"They need you too," Coco whispered and stepped aside.

Gabriel considered his thoughts carefully before addressing his fellow members of the Allegiance. "Prudence has agreed to a plan that Alessandro and I have devised to capture Kenan. But it's compli-cated. It involves calling upon elements that we've not used before. To win this battle, we must plan accordingly."

He looked around, taking the time to look others directly in the eye. "The locations, timing, everything must be precise. There's no room for failure. As such, we'll divide into teams, focusing on our individual strengths. I consider each one of you a link in a chain of events that needs to be completed in order so that we can move forward with our lives."

"Allow me to work with Arianna and Coco," Kishu said. "There's much they need to learn."

Gabriel gave a quick nod of approval. "Agreed; however, I'll need Arianna tomorrow morning. We have a job for her."

Arianna's brows knitted together, and she placed her hands on her hips. "What kind of job?"

"House hunting," Gabriel said. "Marilyn and Marco found matching geographical descriptions throughout the journals. We're fairly sure the area described is on the coast of Lazio, and Frederico and Jason have narrowed it down to one particular location. There are a few villas for sale close by, and we need some reconnaissance done. Preferably by someone not easily traced back to the Allegiance."

"Then I'm your girl," Arianna said.

"You're not going in alone," Gabriel said. "Jason's going with you. He'll be acting as your older brother."

"When do we leave?"

Jason glanced at his notebook. "The first appointment's at nine thirty in the morning."

Gabriel raised his eyebrows at Layla. "Can you handle this?"

Layla rubbed her hands together. "Of course." She smiled at Isabel, Arianna's adoptive mother. "This time, you and I get to dress two people to go incognito!"

"I look forward to helping," Isabel said.

"Kishu's raised an important issue," Alessandro said. "While we're aware of Kenan's fighting abilities and his planning ingenuity, we can't underestimate his psychic strengths, which he's forced others to empower him with. One of whom we recently discovered was my grandmother." A shadow of sadness crossed Alessandro's face.

"Like seers before her, she was imprisoned, forced to relay information about future events—events that included destroying Gabriel and Coco—but Kenan was not able to break my grandmother's love for her family." He looked around the room, meeting everyone's gaze. "We've discovered fragments of information she left for us, tools that we can use to end Kenan. It's been difficult to decipher fact from fiction, shadow from light, for a clever jester can make us believe vicious lies, and Kenan's persona is built on deception.

"This is the only chance we'll get to finish him. His madness must be stopped. The difference between Kenan's transformation as opposed to his predecessors'—Vinicio and Domenico—is that by killing Domenico, Kenan thought he would be a free man; free to love Ravinka. What he didn't know was that the devil's persona would transfer to him. And according to the Holy Father, the third incarnation of the devil will become the deadliest. He will do what he must to stay in this world."

Ignacio raised a hand. "How can we be sure that not one sliver of a memory of Ravinka isn't tucked away in Kenan's thoughts? And that he's not playing us?"

"We wondered the same thing," Gabriel said. "But Freyja swears she found nothing but darkness in his soul. That's why she turned against him."

"While I admire your ambition to always look for the good in people, Gabriel, I have known Freyja for eons," Hakon said. "I watch over the lives of the people in the far north, and it is Freyja who gathers their souls at death and takes them to her realm. And yet, I agree with Ignacio and would stress that we use caution where she is concerned. Long ago we struck a deal—the life of my beloved Sonja in exchange for Freyja to live as a mortal and experience love."

He inhaled and shook his head. "I did not see that her true love would be Kenan. This time I intend to strike the bargain, and it will be in our favor, not Freyja's. Do not turn your back on the goddess of the underworld, for a brokenhearted goddess is a rare and dangerous being."

"Perhaps it would benefit us to seek the wisdom of the Lady and the Rose," Prudence said. "We will need her foresight in this matter."

Hakon nodded. "Agreed."

Gabriel glanced at Nikandros, who stood with his shoulders back and chin high. He thought of the many battles his grandfather had fought, and how strange it must be to have known many in this room for millennia. "Nikandros," he said. "What can you share with us?"

"Make no mistake," Nikandros said. "We are dealing with pure evil. Kenan is physically powerful, devious, and cruel, and like all immortals, he's extremely protective of his privacy. Marilyn, Marco, Frederico, and Jason have done well in uncovering not only the underground tunnels in Rome but also other addresses attached to Kenan and his clan. But we would be naïve to think he does not have other bolt-holes here in Italy. After all, I trust that you all have one or more of your own, for as immortals we are often hunted."

The room was deathly quiet.

"I'm guessing our silence says you're correct." Ignacio chuckled. "And yes, some of us have needed more than one bolt-hole!"

Nikandros's mouth twitched before he continued. "Over the centuries, there've been stories told of a madman who appears at random times, standing on the remains of a dwelling destroyed by fire, on the coast of Lazio, before diving into the ocean. Local folklore states that images of this man taunt the dreams of young men, some of whom have later been found dead on the rocks where the ruins meet the sea.

"I know this villa. It was once owned by Domenico and destroyed shortly after he went missing. According to information Freyja has shared, this area is near where she first encountered Kenan during the time she lived as the mortal Ravinka—before he killed Domenico.

It could be that although he has no memory of Ravinka, he senses something… perhaps an energy that soothes his tormented soul. It's feasible he has a villa close to the area.

"Sabine and her warriors have uncovered another area of Kenan's depravity. For years he's encouraged men of the cloth to prey on the innocent. Girls were raped, many not yet in their teens, and if they became pregnant, they were married off to men in the priest's congregation. Let me be clear—these girls were children."

He flexed his fingers and narrowed his dark eyes. "One of these priests recently gave a full confession before he died. His words have been publicly aired. The Catholic Church is being scrutinized by journalists worldwide. From what Sabine tells me, all hell has broken loose, and many of the children who were raped and married off at a young age are coming forward to tell their stories."

A current of anger flooded the room.

"The devil within Kenan seeks to disrupt humanity. To bring us into chaos. We cannot allow that to happen," Nikandros said. "I've gone over Gabriel and Alessandro's plan, and I give it my full support. Yes, it will mean delving into new territories—a few of which I have steered away from for centuries—one being dark magic. But I have known Prudence and served her mother, Sonja, for over a thousand years, and I intend to serve them now. I am a warrior, and as such I'm prepared to train those who wish to stand by my side. We are headed into a deadly war, one which must be hidden from humanity. Sabine, Frederico, Pelayo, Ignacio, and I intend to weaken Kenan's army; our scouts have found many of his strongholds. Tomorrow evening the final battle begins. We will wipe the schadenfreude from Kenan's warped mind."

A cheer erupted.

Nikandros strode over to Jeremy. "I ask that in my absence, you comfort my beloved Luciana and our daughter, Flora. Will you do this for me?"

Jeremy glanced at Pelayo, who gave him a short nod of agreement.

"You have my word, Nikandros," Jeremy said. "I'll watch over Luciana and Flora until you and Pelayo return."

Nikandros and Jeremy clasped elbows. "I met Elion," Nikandros said. "And your aunt Illona is a close friend. You'll be a fine warrior."

Gabriel raised a hand, and the cheers subsided. "It's vitally important for everyone standing in this room to have a basic understanding of defensive fighting skills. We do not intend for the unspeakable to happen, but it would be irresponsible of us not to train our mortal comrades in basic defensive and offensive strategies. I ask that we all meet Kishu at the dojo directly after this meeting adjourns for a two-hour training session."

Prudence spoke up. "I have added another layer of protective shields around the fortress. Please know that I will do everything in my power to protect you all. I deplore violence and use it only when communication and other means fail. However, in this case, I've agreed to Gabriel and Alessandro's plan because fighting back is our only means of defense. Kenan must be stopped, no matter the cost. I need to leave with Hakon but shall return shortly."

"For those of you who are new to combat, I suggest you wear comfortable clothing," Gabriel said. "We'll adjourn to the dojo momentarily. But first, let's remember why we're here."

Everyone in the room placed their hands on their neighbor's shoulder and spoke in unison. "*Sine virtute omnia sunt perdita.*"

COCO WATCHED KISHU as he scanned the room, looking at the familiar immortals and mortals standing on the mats before him. His stare stopped momentarily on her, and he gave a quick nod. She jogged to where he stood at the front of the class, bowed her head, and stood to face her grandfather in hanmi position, one foot slightly in front of the other. In slow, exaggerated moves, Kishu struck out at her with his right arm, and she, in turn, placed her left arm out to meet him and then slid her whole body to her left. After they had repeated the motion a few times using both the left and right sides, they bowed to each other, and Coco returned to her place beside Gabriel.

Kishu faced the members of the Allegiance. "Partner up and practice this move. This is not so much about blocking the strike but more about accepting your attacker's energy."

He approached Isabel and Eduardo, who stood next to Coco.

"You go first," Isabel said. "Slowly, please."

Eduardo moved his arm as if to strike Isabel, and she mirrored the movement Coco had done, causing Eduardo to momentarily lose his balance. They repeated the move with their alternate sides.

"Your dancing experience will come in useful with aikido, Isabel," Kishu said, "for this form of defense is closely related to the art of dance. Do you feel it?"

She nodded. "Yes, I do."

Kishu grinned and clapped his hands twice. "Switch partners."

Everyone did as Kishu asked, and when he seemed happy with their movements, he jogged to the front of the class, and this time he requested Jeremy as his partner. Kishu kicked out with his right leg, and as he did, Jeremy stepped back and to the side. Kishu raised an eyebrow. He struck out at Jeremy with his left hand, and Jeremy lifted his right arm to the outside of Kishu's arm and slid to the side to avoid contact.

"Pelayo's a fine teacher," Kishu said.

They bowed to each other, and Jeremy jogged back to stand with Pelayo.

Over the next forty-five minutes, Kishu demonstrated a variety of beginner defensive moves. He had the group practice until he felt confident they had a basic understanding of the art of defensive action and then called Nikandros to partner with him.

"Make no mistake of the swiftness and cunning of a vampire," Kishu said. "I'm sure some of you are wondering how any of these moves will help when confronted with an immortal, whose natural instincts are to hunt and attack. We hope that none of you will ever be in the position of having to be face-to-face with one of Kenan's creatures, but it's possible. So, what can you do to protect yourself in such a situation?" He tapped his head. "Use this! The immortals among us are controlled, compassionate, intelligent, and do not need to kill to stay alive. Kenan's men are not trained in this way; they are trained to kill. From today, you will all carry one of these." He pulled out a switchblade knife and gave a quick nod to Nikandros.

In a flash, Nikandros had Kishu against a stone wall with his mouth at his neck, but then he stumbled back and grasped at the blade protruding from his throat. The door to the dojo slammed shut.

Moments later, Kishu walked back into the room. Luciana raced up to Nikandros, but she smiled when she realized the knife was a prop and that the blade had slid back into the handle upon contact.

"You see," Kishu said, "the knife gave me precious seconds to run away. Use your head. Focus. Stab. Your life depends on it. A few seconds is all you need to either get to safety or call for help. Partner up with an immortal, and I'll hand out the stunt knives. You'll all receive a real switchblade as you leave."

By the end of the session, the vampires among the Allegiance were teaching their fellow fae and mortal comrades other combat moves. They showed each other how to dive into a forward roll when thrown to the floor and where to stab a vampire in order to bring the most harm.

Coco walked with Gabriel as he approached Kishu.

"Jeremy shows talent as a warrior," Gabriel said.

"His sense of knowing is a worthy gift," Kishu said. "And if nothing else, this practice has given each of us hope."

"Agreed," Gabriel said. "Hope is a powerful weapon to carry into battle."

CHAPTER 38

AYLA OVERSAW THE dressing of Arianna and Jason as brother and sister, with help from Isabel. As per Arianna's previous incognito trip to the bank in Manhattan, the pantsuit she wore mirrored the same slick Italian style and fit like it had been tailored for her. The luxurious dark navy fabric intensified the cerulean blue of her eyes, so much so that both Isabel and Illona had insisted she wear contacts. She also wore a wig as no one wanted to take the chance of Arianna being recognized. And so it was that her disguise included hazel eyes and shoulder-length auburn hair with bangs.

Dressing Jason in a tailored suit had taken more effort, but Layla's persistence had paid off. A flush crept over Illona's face when Jason entered Christopher's living room, resembling a successful business entrepreneur. And she was fairly sure she wasn't the only one who caught the raised brow and the smile that dangled on the corner of Jason's lips as if asking for Illona's approval.

He adjusted his tie when he saw Christopher. "Jeez, is this what you go through every morning?"

"You get used to it," Christopher replied, circling his arms around Layla. "Although it helps that I have a stylish fiancée who dresses me."

"Yeah, I seem to remember your dressing habits resembled mine during our undergrad years," Jason said. He stood beside Arianna. "You ready, sis?"

"Thanks to Layla and Isabel, yes, I'm ready," Arianna replied. She walked toward the door. "Come on, we don't want to keep the wizard waiting. He might accidentally lose you in transit."

"Oh Christ," Jason said. "That freaking nano-travel thing slipped my mind. Isn't there an—"

"No!" Christopher cut in. "Trust me, you'll get used to it."

"Spoken like a fucking lawyer," Jason muttered as he followed Arianna into the hallway.

"So let me make sure I have our story right," Arianna said. "Our parents left us a heap of money, and we're in Italy buying a vacation property. Anything else I need to know?"

Jason shrugged. "That's it in a nutshell, although I think it might be a good idea if you stick to English and not let on that you speak Italian. That way you can listen to conversations… maybe pick up snippets of information that might be useful."

"Got it!"

They entered Gabriel's study and were greeted by Pelayo.

"Arianna," he said. "Remember this?" He handed her a necklace.

"My smart camera," she said. "I'll make sure to stand outside and get some good panoramic images for you."

Pelayo handed Jason a cell phone. "Frederico has placed a high-powered telescopic-lens camera inside this cell. When he calls, stand outside and hold the phone as you would normally, he'll get images remotely—you don't need to do anything—just answer the call and walk outside."

Jason placed the phone in his inside jacket pocket. "Anything else?"

Gabriel walked into the room. "We can go over the finer details with Marilyn and Marco. Ready, Pelayo?"

"Always." Pelayo hoisted an equipment bag over his shoulder, and Gabriel grabbed another.

"Then let's go." Gabriel looked at Jason from the corner of his eye. "Won't hurt a bit." He tossed a rune into the air, and the four members of the Allegiance dematerialized.

Moments later they arrived in Marilyn's office at the Laurentian Library. After introductions, Arianna listened while Marilyn and Marco read phrases from Vinicio's, Domenico's, and Kenan's journals pertaining to the area of Lazio where Jason and Arianna were scheduled to view properties.

Marco explained their findings like a true professor. "The keywords we've found vary slightly in description in all three voices. However, particular words insinuate the same area, albeit one that encompasses the introduction of the human element and therefore the growth of communities. Here are a few examples taken from each incarnation. Note the gradual increase of singular to plural: 'Light from a distant lantern, a sprinkling of lights, streetlights; solitary villa, neighbors scattered few and far between, and the coastal town.'

"In the final journal—second to last chapter—the author speaks of 'the view across the ocean toward Ventotene and the Island of the Crescent Moon.' With this information, we've chosen the coastal area of San Felice Circeo as the location. That particular area is close to a few ancient villas that were long ago destroyed, but because of the proximity to the national park, there are still areas where privacy can be bought."

"How many properties are we viewing?" Arianna asked.

"Three," Jason said. "But I think it's the last one on the list that will give us the best views across the area."

Marilyn pointed to the location on a map spread out on a table. "Here, Arianna. This will give you a better idea of the geographical layout of the area. Marco, Jason, and I believe that this particular spot is where Kenan is drawn."

Arianna pondered the map and then looked at Gabriel. "Do you think he's there now?"

"It's highly possible," Gabriel said. "That's why Pelayo and I need to keep our distance. Any hint of our scent, and our plan is doomed. He has no idea who you are, Arianna, and with Jason's makeover and the change in the scent Prudence cast over him, he won't be recognized. Kenan's too busy funneling his energy into distracting Colombina, and that's draining his power."

"I don't understand," Arianna said.

Gabriel explained, "He's used to someone else—an imprisoned seer—doing it for him."

Arianna nodded. "So, where do we go from here?"

"Borgo Grappa." Gabriel pointed to a place on the map.

"A driver's picking us up at a hotel and driving us to San Felice Circeo," Jason said. "It's about a thirty-minute drive. We'll meet the real estate agent at the first address."

"Is the driver one of us?" Arianna asked.

"Of course," Gabriel said. "She's one of our mortal friends." He checked the time on his cell. "We'd best leave."

The drive from Borgo Grappa to the first villa in San Felice Circeo went smoothly. The second villa had a terrace on the rooftop, and from there Jason took a call from Frederico and strolled around while Arianna explored the interior of the villa. But it was the third property where they spent the most time; its 360-degree views were perfect for what they needed. While Jason answered multiple calls, Arianna found herself intrigued by the villa. From every window and *terrazza*, views encapsulated the essence of freedom, and she understood the pull of this location. She gazed out across the ocean to the islands and then walked up to the highest point of the property. The landing captured the stunning view of the national park and the isolated villas dotted among the native flora.

"It's impressive, isn't it?" the realtor said.

"And private too," Arianna said. "Are the houses around here owned by families or corporations?"

The realtor thought for a moment and then pointed to a couple of nearby homes. "The two over there are owned by single families, and the only corporate properties I know of are the one up on the hill and another down by the beach." She turned to face the park. "Honestly, I can't tell you much about the villas up there, only that they've never come up for sale since I've lived here, and that's just on fifteen years. I have a feeling one's owned by an old local family, but as for the one hidden behind the rocks and trees, my guess is the owner's some kind of recluse. Maybe an artist or writer, someone who likes privacy."

"What makes you say that?"

"There's a chain-link fence around the entire acreage, and a few months ago, while I was up here checking on a property, a delivery truck driver showed up. The driver was lost. Turns out he had a delivery of art supplies he had to drop off at the gate. It's a pretty special place though, even has a private path down to the old ruin at the cove."

Arianna walked toward Jason. "You really need to go up there and have a look at the view. Apparently an artist lives in one of the properties. Not that you can see much of it, but I like the idea of living near an artist. Don't you?"

Jason shrugged. "Maybe, as long as they're quiet. I'll be right back—better check out the view."

The realtor smiled a white, toothy grin. "Is there anything else you'd like to see before we leave?"

Arianna narrowed her eyes and smiled. "Maybe one more look at that walk-in closet in the master bedroom."

"Isn't it superb? And by the way you're dressed, I'm sure you have a great wardrobe to fill it."

"Oh, you have no idea…"

An hour later, the driver pulled the car up to the hotel and opened the door for Jason and Arianna. On their way through the foyer, Arianna suddenly stopped midstep, and for a moment time seemed to stand still. An excited flutter in her belly caught her by surprise. She looked around the area and saw a young man about her own age playing chess with an elderly gentleman.

"Checkmate," the elderly man said in Italian.

In a show of defeat, the young man leaned back and hung his arms over the armrests; his dark hair fell across his forehead as he shook his head and grinned at the old man. He sat forward, turned, and stared directly at Arianna.

"What is it?" the old man said. "You look like you've seen a ghost."

Arianna felt a tug on her elbow.

"Come on, sis," Jason said. "We need to get moving."

With another quick glance at the dark-haired young man, Arianna followed Jason into the elevator.

"You okay?" Jason asked.

Arianna nodded.

"You sure?"

"Have you ever had that feeling that you've met someone before?"

"Yeah, actually, I have." Jason leaned against the mirrored wall of the elevator.

"Did you approach her, or him?"

"Her," he said. "And not yet." He pushed the button to take them up to the fifth floor. "But I'm thinking about it."

Upstairs in the suite, Pelayo and Gabriel monitored Arianna's movements via the laptop screen.

"Do you know him?" Pelayo asked.

Gabriel crossed his arms. "Yes. They are each other's destiny."

Pelayo pointed to two elegantly dressed women sitting a few tables away from the young man and the elderly gentleman. "Those two women seem familiar."

"Sabine's warriors," Gabriel said. "They watch over the two men and their family."

Pelayo raised his eyebrows in expectation of more information, but the door opened and Jason and Arianna entered.

"Well done, both of you," Gabriel said. "The information you gathered is invaluable."

"Thanks," Arianna said. "Um…"

Gabriel hoisted one of the equipment bags over his shoulder. "Yes, what's up?"

She shrugged. "Nothing, let's go."

"Maybe when this is over, we can all come here for a few days' break," Gabriel said. "We could visit the islands—they're quite stunning."

She nodded. "I'd like that."

CHAPTER 39

Casa della Pietra

GABRIEL MADE HIS way to the lower level of the fortress. The stone steps were just wide enough for two people to walk side by side, but the deeper you descended, the more extensive they became, with landings and archways leading off in alternate directions. His thoughts were lost to a time of chaos when men in armor tended to their horses in readiness for bloody battles.

He stopped beneath the keystone of the central arch, placed a hand to the dimpled rock wall, and for a moment he caught the sound of his father giving orders to the men and women who fought beside the Allegiance. Gabriel's thoughts were interrupted by a familiar chuckle. The corners of his mouth turned upward and formed a childlike grin. He pushed himself off the cold stone wall and quickened his pace.

As he walked along the curved tunnels, torches set into stone came to life and illuminated the deepening darkness with a fiery orange glow. He reached a set of five steps leading up to a landing and a thick wooden door inlaid with metal strips and sturdy pins. He pushed the door open, entered, and heard it close behind him.

The room was long, stone, and featured a tall, arched ceiling. The floor was lined with sage-colored grappling mats, and on the wall to Gabriel's right hung an assortment of traditional Japanese wooden bokken. He kicked off his boots, stepped up to the wooden entrance, and stared at the two men fighting in the center of the room.

Pelayo charged Kishu at full vampire speed, only to find himself flat on his stomach with an arm twisted up behind his back. He struggled, but Kishu tweaked the vampire's finger and Pelayo slapped the mat three times. When Kishu released his hold, Pelayo jumped up and the two men bowed to one another. Cheers went up from the small group of men lounging on chairs in the waiting area.

"Thank you for the use of your speed, Pelayo," Kishu said.

"*De nada.*"

Kishu glanced at Gabriel. "It's good you're here. Alessandro could do with getting his butt kicked."

Alessandro jumped over his chair and ripped off his jacket.

Kishu walked off the mat, bowed, and then shook his head at Alessandro. "My rules tonight. Change into the appropriate clothing and we'll begin."

"Are you joining us, Jeremy?" Gabriel asked.

Jeremy grinned. "One day, maybe."

"Might be sooner than you think," Kishu said.

Jeremy raised an eyebrow.

"Pelayo's lessons have paid off. You show promise."

"Thanks," he said. "Baby steps, I guess."

Kishu stared at him. "Before practice, men must remember three things: their strengths, their friends, and the transformational energy of laughter. Now, watch and learn."

Alessandro, Gabriel, Stefan, and Christopher headed into a nearby room to change. When they returned, each of them were wearing a gi, the traditional uniform of white pants, crossover jackets, and black belts. Alessandro cracked his knuckles. Gabriel clasped his hands together, brought them above his head, and swung his body from side to side.

"Remember," Kishu said. "No weapons, no magic."

"Understood," Alessandro and Gabriel said in unison.

The two men stood at the edge of the mats. They bowed and walked to the center of the dojo. After taking their second bow, their eyes held the stare of warriors.

Alessandro punched out with his right hand, followed by his left, then right again. Gabriel quickly deflected his opponent's next punch and left kick, grabbing his shin and bringing him to the ground. But Alessandro was known for his speed, and as he sprang up, he landed a solid kick to Gabriel's stomach. Gabriel sneered, launched himself into the air, and slammed his body into Alessandro's chest, forcing him down.

An audible flurry of foul curses escaped Alessandro's mouth. Gabriel landed a few feet away and stood ready. Something that sounded like a cheer erupted from the sidelines. He ignored it, focusing his mind on the commitment of practice.

Alessandro reared to his full height before settling his body into an attack position. As if mirroring a dance, the two men moved in a wide circle, gradually moving closer until they were within a few feet of each other. Alessandro faked a blow with his left arm, and as Gabriel reached to defend himself, he realized his drastic mistake. His body lurched forward as Alessandro used the momentum to throw Gabriel off his center, gripping his wrist and steering him in a circular motion. Alessandro's hand pushed against the base of Gabriel's skull, shoving him toward the ground where he fought uselessly to gain his equilibrium. Alessandro's other hand caught under Gabriel's chin and forced him to suddenly change the direction of his fall. Gabriel fell with a thundering thump onto the ground, followed by the sound of bones snapping in two.

Alessandro flipped Gabriel over, thrust a knee into his lower back, and pulled one of his arms into a precarious position. Any movement from Gabriel would mean a dislocated shoulder. Immobilization was immediate. He pounded his other hand on the mat. Alessandro released him and helped Gabriel back onto his feet.

The two men bowed to one another and jogged off the floor. The small crowd erupted into a bountiful chorus of acclamations. Gabriel made his way over to Kishu. The older man clasped a hand on his shoulder.

"To stand, one must first learn to fall," Kishu said.

"I've forgotten the basics," Gabriel said.

"You've forgotten how to get up." Kishu turned to the others. "Stefan, you and Gabriel are up next."

"I've been looking forward to this," Stefan said. "It's been too long since we practiced together."

Gabriel grabbed a towel, wiped his face and hands, and fought through the pain as his battered body quickly healed. A few minutes later, he joined his father at the edge of the mats. His mind flashed over the hundreds of times he had sparred with his father in this room. The tatami mats were a relatively new acquisition, as for centuries their bodies had smashed against the hard stone floor. But the main rule had not changed: the use of magic while sparring was not allowed. As a child, that had been a problematic rule for Gabriel to understand. After all, magic was his birthright, and wizardry was where his strength lay. To abandon it during a fight seemed somewhat unethical. But Stefan had insisted that his son learn to defend himself without conjuring up enchantments. In time, Gabriel had come to not only understand his father's reasoning but was grateful for it.

Despite the lapse in time since Gabriel had faced his father in one-on-one combat, the heightened sense of awe Stefan exuded was not quickly forgotten. Gabriel knew from experience that the only way to win a fight against him was to empty his mind completely.

Father and son jogged to the center of the mats and bowed to each other. Gabriel inhaled and welcomed the momentary familiar rush of air that crashed through his mind, sounding like a wave thundering into a cliff face followed by absolute silence. He lifted his head and met the determined stare of his *uke*, his father.

The two men circled each other like predators, each waiting for the perfect moment to attack. A ripple in the atmosphere alerted Gabriel to a vacant space, and he used the moment to punch out and then land a kick to the side of Stefan's head. He flipped into the air, landing in hanmi position behind Stefan. But his father was quick and used the momentum of the kick to his head to roll across the mats.

The two men stood face-to-face.

Stefan lunged at Gabriel, grabbing his wrist and forcing him into a spin, pushing him to his knees and immobilizing him with *kote gaeshi*. This quick wrist turnout sent a stream of agony to Gabriel's core. Instinct told him to breathe into the pain, to welcome it. He crumpled his body, and without hesitation flipped his father over him. Stefan landed on his back behind him.

Gabriel swung around just as Stefan jumped up. He immediately thrust a kick into his father's stomach and brought him to his knees, then pushed him to the floor and yanked his arms behind his back. Stefan kicked out at Gabriel, striking full force at a knee. The sound of bones snapping echoed through the room. Gabriel released his hold and used his other leg to launch himself into the air.

His shattered bones were in the process of healing, pumping a searing heat down his leg. When he landed, he stumbled. Stefan used the moment to ram into Gabriel with his whole body. Knowing that to fight that force would be useless, Gabriel chose to welcome the momentum.

The two men tumbled across the floor, gaining speed and getting precariously close to the stone wall. Gabriel found sanctuary in the silence. His father's attack triggered lessons from Kishu's training. The sound of air rushing by and drops of sweat bouncing in slow motion onto the sage-colored tatami mats, followed by the muscular frame of his father landing, ignited his cell memory.

He took hold of one of Stefan's arms just before they collided with a stone wall. The two men sprang up, and once again their feet moved together in the familiar dance, the only difference being that one man played the lead, and this time it was Gabriel.

As the moment peaked, Gabriel quickly changed direction and forced his father to the ground, twisting an arm unnaturally at the elbow while scissoring his legs around Stefan's torso.

He was pulled out of the silence by a tapping noise, followed by someone calling his name. Gabriel saw that he had Stefan pinned to the ground. He released his hold and helped his father to his feet, then pulled him into an embrace.

"Thanks for reminding me of what my spirit had forgotten."

Stefan clung to him. "You are my son, and you are a warrior."

The two men bowed to each other and rose just in time to see Pelayo, Christopher, and Alessandro step onto the mat.

"Well done!" Kishu chuckled. "That was a good warm-up."

Stefan rolled his shoulders and cracked his knuckles. "This will be fun!"

"Yeah," Gabriel said, wiping his brow. "Nothing like being attacked by multiple warriors to put a smile on your face."

CHAPTER 40

Casa della Pietra—Main Art Studio

THE PAINTING STARED back at Coco. Dark though it was, an element of lightness emoted from the field of gold where a woman stood in the distance. The foreground showed the edge of an aged stone building and a cobblestone road that wound past the area and vanished in the distance. The image had movement—the wheat leaned away from the onlooker, caught up in a breeze that swept locks of the woman's ebony hair across her face.

Coco was drawn to her, and yet she had painted her quickly, a few strokes that radiated intense love. At the forefront of the painting, near the edge of the field, sat a black cat, her dark eyes staring at the observer. A nudge at Coco's knees brought her out of the semi-dream state that overtook her while she painted. She looked from the canvas to find the long tail of a mountain lion passing by her knees.

"Thalia," Coco said. "Why all the drama?" She looked across the room at the Creative, Luciana, who was cleaning her brushes. She also seemed intrigued by Thalia's sudden change in personality and wandered over to Coco.

"May I take a look at your painting?" she asked. "Something seems to have brought out Thalia's protective instincts."

"Of course." Coco nodded. "Maybe you'll recognize the location. It's not familiar to me, and yet the woman reminds me of Freyja."

Luciana walked around the easel, stood next to Coco, and viewed the painting. She grabbed Coco's hand and pulled her back a few steps. Within seconds, Nikandros stood by Luciana's side. Thalia sat in front of the painting, blocking Coco.

"Do you know this place?" Nikandros asked.

Coco shook her head. "No. I don't think it's somewhere I've been, but the woman reminds me of Freyja."

Gabriel's pack of dogs ran into the studio with Max in the lead. The pack darted back and forth and circled Coco while Max sat next to Thalia. Nikandros took a photo of the painting with his cell, sent a text, and waited for a reply, which came in the physical form of Gabriel and Alessandro. When Gabriel saw the image, he tucked Coco protectively behind him.

"What's going on?" she asked. "Do you recognize the location?"

Gabriel turned to her. "Yes. Do you?"

Coco shook her head. "No. Where is it?"

"Near the coast of Lazio," Nikandros said. "Not far from one of Domenico's strongholds."

"Oddly enough, it was not the location that made me call for you but the cat," Luciana said. She turned to Coco. "Black cats are synonymous with Freyja. But this painting has a glimmer of darkness beyond the woman that seems to stem from the cat… I can feel it, reaching out beyond the canvas. Something evil lies behind the paint."

Coco stepped around Gabriel but held on to his hand. "Kenan," she said. "It's an invitation."

A gust of wind swirled around a far corner of the studio, and in its wake, Freyja stepped forward and drifted over to Coco. As she gazed at the painting, her demeanor softened. "I remember this day well," she said, her voice saturated with melancholy.

Coco noticed that the figure in the painting held two black kittens.

"Kenan followed me from the market to these fields," Freyja continued. "I placed a kitten in his hand. I believe it was the first time he had felt unconditional love since the death of his uncle. There was goodness in him then, buried deep under pain, violence, and abuse. I fell in love with him that day."

"He's calling to me," Coco said. Gabriel's hand tightened around hers and she silently spoke to him. *Don't be concerned, my love, I'm in control.*

Nikandros directed his next question to Freyja. "Do you know of any hideouts Kenan has near the location in this painting?"

"Domenico's stronghold fell centuries ago, and I've not sensed Kenan in the area."

"He's there somewhere," Gabriel said. "We just haven't found him yet."

Freyja's gaze left the painting and landed on Gabriel. "I swore to Prudence that I would let her know if I find him. My vow is true." She turned and walked away, her image fading with each step until she disappeared entirely.

"She speaks the truth," Luciana said. "Although her heart is in turmoil against her mind, she would not defy what she knows to be true. I believe a part of her yearns for the day when she carries Kenan's soul on Charon's boat across the River Styx and to her world. But for now, Colombina, you must decide if you have the strength to guard yourself against Kenan and see what lies beneath this painting."

Coco's gaze met Gabriel's. "Is there a way to create an escape for me—something like a safety net?"

Gabriel nodded. "Yes, I can provide that for you." He placed a hand above her heart and then stepped away until he was not in the periphery of the painting. He motioned for the others to stand with him.

"What about Thalia and Max?" Coco asked.

Gabriel gave a command, and both animals dropped to the floor. "They are out of eyeline, but in a position to attack if needed. Keep your mind focused as Kishu has taught you. Feel your feet rooted to the floor. Remember, *mi amore*, you have power over him."

Coco nodded and then raised a hand toward the painting. The pigments of paint lifted to reveal Kenan. He raised his head, and his dark eyes pinned hers.

"How good to see you, my dear," he said, his voice thick like molasses and tinged with evil.

"What do you want?" Coco asked.

A corner of his mouth lifted to a sneer. "Always the same question with you, Colombina. Surely you have others."

"No. That's the only question I have, and one you've not answered."

He paused, the silence around him dark and dismal. "I'll answer that question soon enough, but first I thought you might enjoy seeing where I've been spending my time."

A scene emerged. Coco recognized the studio where she taught art at UCLA. Kenan stood just outside the entrance to the Eli and Edythe Broad Art Center, eyeing students as they entered the building.

"Now I'll answer your question. I want you, Colombina… with me. How much are the lives of your students worth?" He ran his tongue over his lips, and she saw the tips of his sharp fangs. "I'll give you an hour to decide. Choose wisely, my dear. A few of these freshman boys look particularly mouthwatering." His image began to fade.

"Wait!" Coco said. "Where will I meet you?"

He raised an eyebrow. "If I'd known that getting you by my side would be so easy, I would have asked sooner. Wait for me inside that horrendous piece of metal just outside the entrance to this place." He gestured toward the art school. "Oh, and don't plan on bringing any of your Allegiance buddies along with you… I'm getting hungrier by the minute." His eyes drifted toward a young man carrying a large canvas up the stairs and into the building.

The scene disappeared, and the pigments of paint returned to the canvas. Coco stared at the painting of the lone woman standing in the field of gold. Gabriel's arms were around her, and she fell into his embrace, desperate for the moment to never end but knowing in her heart that this might possibly be their last hour together.

"Did you hear him?" she asked.

Gabriel cupped her chin, and she found herself lost in his gaze. "Yes. How long do you need to paint the image?"

"I've painted the sculpture garden multiple times since I've been here." She pointed to a stack of canvases leaning against the table that held her paints. "I guess my psyche is more in tune than I give it credit for." The smile she tried to give him failed dismally as she did her best to quell the fear in her belly.

Gabriel kissed her forehead and turned to Alessandro. "Gather the others and tell them what's happened. Alert every one of our mortal comrades in Westwood that Kenan's on the campus grounds and to safeguard themselves."

"But you heard him," Coco said. "He said no Allegiance members or—"

"Kenan has no idea of the mortal force of our family," Gabriel cut in. "This is war, Colombina! We must use every asset we have. If Kenan wants a student, he'll take him regardless. His promises are shallow—they mean nothing."

Coco knew he was correct, that Kenan's word meant nothing, and that if their places were flipped, she would do anything she could to protect Gabriel. "I understand."

Alessandro and Gabriel clutched each other's elbows. "We'll meet in the main living room in forty-five minutes," Gabriel said. He lifted Coco into his arms, and in a flash, he was kissing her in their bedroom.

The hunger of Gabriel's kiss lit a fire in Coco's soul. He pushed down her jeans, lifted her in his arms, and held her firmly against a wall. She wrapped her legs around his body as he entered her with ardent passion. Her body moved with his, and at the height of their climax, he bit her neck. Coco cried out in ecstasy. Gabriel kissed her and encouraged her to drink from him. She welcomed the odd sensation of her small fangs descending and bit into the skin above his jugular vein, drawing his blood into her body. When she went to release her mouth from his neck, she felt his hand gently stroke the back of her head. "Take more, *mi amore*," he whispered. "The more you take, the stronger our connection."

When Coco could drink no more, she kissed his lips, exploring his mouth as if for the first time. She looked into his eyes. "If—"

He placed a finger over her lips. "I'll find you, Colombina, *sempre*. I've watched you paint from a distance many times over the years. I've witnessed your concentration—your focus is powerful— use that asset tonight. Let's finish the evil that burns inside Kenan so that we can move forward with our lives, together."

Coco ran her fingers through his hair and leaned her forehead against his. "Thank you for believing in me and encouraging me to discover who I am and learn the truth about my family. I understand now that letting go of our loved ones gives them the freedom to grow into their true selves. That's what Mom had to do. I used to wonder why my world felt so empty, but since you've entered my life, I've not experienced that emptiness. Instead, I'm filled with an over-abundance of love and trust, an innate need to protect you and the Allegiance. Where these instincts come from, I don't know, but I'm forever grateful to you."

Gabriel smiled and embraced her. "When you return and this part of our adventure is over, I'll have Hakon explain everything to you—that's a promise. But for now I want to go over the plan with you once more." He handed her the discarded clothing from the floor.

"I'd suggest we shower together," she said. "But I want your scent all over me, just to remind Kenan who he's messing with." She headed into the bathroom. "I'll be right back."

Coco dressed quickly and stared at her reflection in the mirror; she looked alert and strong. The training with Kishu and Ignacio had strengthened her psychologically and physically. Her whole body had sprung to life, her muscles were defined, her mind was alert. She now welcomed the vampire genes given to her by Alessandro, thankful for the astute skills of his bloodline. But as she stared at her face, a rush of gratitude reminded her of the power behind the color of her eyes, the amethyst hue of Creatives.

"Who needs superpowers when we have art?" she said to her reflection. "Art can change the world."

CHAPTER 41

Kittery, Maine

SABINE RETURNED TO the bridge where the young girl had jumped into the icy waters of the river below. She knelt, placed a hand on the road where Frances's photos had shown the young girl standing, and inhaled deeply. The faint stench of sulfur lingered, but another scent caught Sabine's attention. She sneered, and her fangs lowered when she recognized the vampire's scent. She leaped over the bridge and flew along the river toward a derelict area on the outskirts of the city.

She landed outside a deserted warehouse. Wasting no time, she ripped the door off its hinges and stormed inside. A woman cried out in pain, a human, bound and lying naked on a bloodstained mattress. Sabine waved a hand, and the woman fell silent and closed her eyes. Standing over her was a vampire. Sabine knew instantly that he was the vampire Frances had seen on the bridge. He held a sword over the woman's heart.

"One move toward me and she's dead," he said.

"Always threats," Sabine said. "Is that all the fighting strategy Kenan has taught you?"

"It's all we need."

In a flash, Sabine had a knife in his heart and had sliced through his neck with his own sword. She tossed his body to the side, took out her cell, and sent a text. It was then that the hair on her nape and arms rose. She slipped her phone under the woman's body and turned around slowly. Twenty feet from her, Kenan stood on his own.

"Oh dear," he said. "Looks like you're in a spot of trouble. And without the Allegiance to protect you."

"Unlike you, Kenan, I do not ask others to protect me. I protect myself." She cleared her mind, ready for battle as her father had taught her, knowing that shortly he would sense her predicament.

Kenan now stood directly in front of her. She drew a knife, but it was too late. The jolt of pain to her torso made her double over. From her boot, she retrieved a stiletto dagger, but it was gone before she could use it.

"Oh my… Your friends had better hurry," Kenan said. "Or maybe I'll hold you as collateral."

In a flash, he had her over his shoulder, and everything in Sabine's world faded.

CHAPTER 42

WHILE GABRIEL WAITED for Coco, a vision flashed across his mind. *On a beach near Lazio, a dark-haired vampire fell to his knees, clutching his belly, while rose-colored tears fell over his cheeks. An earsplitting scream shot through the night as he rose and leaped into the air, bound for the Dolomite Mountains.* Gabriel also sensed his grandfather in pain.

Coco was by his side immediately. "What's happened?"

"It's Sabine." He picked up Coco, and in a flash they appeared in the studio.

Nikandros writhed in pain on the floor. He gazed up. "I need Prudence!"

She clutched his hand seconds later. "What is it?"

"Kenan has my daughter. She's dying."

"Do you see where she is?"

Nikandros closed his eyes, inhaled. "All I sense is—" He doubled over and clutched his stomach, and then his eyes sprang open.

Alessandro appeared with a distressed-looking Frederico.

"Kenan has Sabine," Frederico said. He stood with his feet planted wide and his fangs bared.

Nikandros rose from the ground and reached out to Frederico. "I know, and together, you and I will find her." He turned to Gabriel.

"There's a scent I'm familiar with around her. It's rampant around Parco Nazionale del Circeo."

"That's the area we've pinpointed," Gabriel said. He turned to Prudence. "It's now or never, Mother. Kenan's calling to Coco."

Prudence nodded. "Are you ready, Gabriel?"

"Yes."

"Then we begin." Prudence addressed Nikandros and Frederico. "The moment Kenan enters this place, you must both go to Sabine. From there, you know where to find us."

Gabriel looked around the studio, which was filled with members of the Allegiance. He nodded and bowed his head.

"*Sine virtute omnia sunt perdita.*" They spoke in unison.

Gabriel grabbed Coco's hand and headed for the main living area.

CHAPTER 43

GABRIEL TOSSED HIS runes into the air and muttered a spell in a language unfamiliar to Coco; moments later, she watched as Arianna's face, hair, and body slowly morphed into a replica of the dark-haired woman they now knew to be Ravinka. Earlier, Layla had dressed Arianna in a dress of the period when Ravinka and Kenan had been lovers. Coco wore jeans and a long-sleeved T-shirt. Now both women stood in the main library and stared at one another.

"How do you feel?" Coco asked.

Arianna shrugged. "At first I experienced a slight tingling sensation throughout my body, but it disappeared quickly, and now I feel normal. How do I look?"

"Like a woman from the sixteenth century." Coco glanced at the Botticelli portrait of Prudence that hung above the mantel in the main living room and then turned around and sought out the painting of the Tuscan landscape she had completed earlier: the willow tree that bore a scar where twenty-eight years ago Kenan had flung her mother against the trunk. In her mind, Coco heard Chantal's pleas for her to run away to safety, then came the screams, followed by the sound of her own heart thumping. The safe and secure touch of Gabriel's hand on her shoulder brought her out of her thoughts. She leaned into his chest as he placed his arms around her.

"Remember, you're stronger than you know," he said.

She nodded. "It's not only your blood that gives me strength but also your innate sense of doing what is right and your will to help others. How about you? Do you feel ready to enter the world of the dead?"

He smiled. "I'm ready, *mi amore,* because at the end of this darkness I envision us together. Besides, I owe you a first date, and I'm a man of my word."

"Then I'll see you soon." She kissed him and stepped back. "Please don't linger in the darkness… and don't allow anyone to talk you into staying there. I need you."

Gabriel squeezed her hands. He looked up and saw Jeremy and Isabel exit, leaving only Alessandro, Chantal, Prudence, and Hakon. Thalia nudged Coco's legs, and she leaned down and stroked her soft fur.

"I can't take you with me," she said. "You must stay here with Max and Algiz." The ragdoll cat gave a quiet meow and then padded over and sat next to the door.

"Are you quite sure all the paintings are in place, Prudence?" Chantal asked.

Prudence nodded. "Yes. Gabriel and I rechecked everything a few hours ago. All is ready. And should something go wrong, Colombina knows what to do."

"We'll see you soon, little dove," Chantal said.

Alessandro pulled in a deep breath and stood tall as he stared at Coco. A knowing grin caught at the edges of his mouth, and with a final nod to Coco, he guided Chantal toward the door, embraced her, and watched her leave with Thalia at her side.

"I must join the others," Prudence said to Hakon. "For it is not good to keep fate waiting. I shall see you soon, Father." She turned to Gabriel. "May the souls of those who have passed at the hands of Kenan lift you up, my dear son."

"And may the Well of Urd see fit to be kind to our destinies, Mother," Gabriel replied.

Flecks of gold formed an arc in the air connecting mother and son before dissipating. A swirl of mist gathered around Prudence and she faded.

"Let's proceed," Hakon said. He walked over to Arianna. "Are you ready?"

"Yes." She looked at Coco. "See you soon."

Hakon whispered a string of words, and a cloud of mist surrounded both him and Arianna; seconds later they disappeared.

Gabriel embraced Coco. "Remember the traits we share, and use them without question... I'll hear, I promise." He kissed her with such fervor that Coco's breath caught. *Mi bella musa.*

Coco turned toward the painting of the sculpture garden at UCLA, which leaned against a nearby chair. She held out a hand, and pigments of paint drifted from the canvas to her fingertips. "I love you, Gabriel."

She stepped forward and into the painting.

CHAPTER 44

FOR A MOMENT, Gabriel stared at the empty space where moments ago his beloved Colombina had stood. He turned to Alessandro. "Ready?"

Alessandro gave a quick nod and made his way into the circle that had magically reappeared and stood where he had when Gabriel first called to the spirits.

Gabriel waved a hand, and the lights faded. The dying embers in the fireplace gave a soft and eerie glow to the room. He knelt on the ground in the middle of the room, faced the portrait of Prudence, and removed an old letter from his jacket pocket. He placed the paper before himself and then tossed his runes into the air. The gray stones stopped midair, and once again he began speaking in the language of the Allegiance, which sounded like a mix of the romance languages. His words caused the embers to crackle and flames to flare.

"I call upon the strength of the feminine.

To all who have suffered at the hands of brutal men,

Men drenched with evil,

Vinicio, Domenico, and Kenan.

I call upon the strength of your joint femininity,

To gather your power and join us,

For today we fight this madness,

Women and men,

Mortal and immortal,
We ask for your strength in numbers to help us defeat this being,
To expel the lust for hideous acts
That has invaded these three men for centuries,
To protect others from the wrath of this being.
I call upon the strength of the feminine,
To join those of us who have fought to protect the beauty of this world.
I call upon the strength of the feminine,
To help us cull this evil.
Take this offering of my blood to give you the strength to rise."

Gabriel pulled his penknife from his pocket, cut his wrist, and held the wound above the letter. Drops of blood splattered onto the paper and spread out, drenching it in crimson. A sigh emanated from the document before it floated up from the ground, above the mantel, and hovered in front of the portrait. A pair of hands reached out from the canvas, and as the letter drifted upward, the hands caught it and then withdrew back into the canvas. A woman's voice echoed in the room as she read the letter aloud in Italian.

Isabella,

Does your husband know of the child you gave birth to last week? If you wish me to keep quiet about your indiscretion, then I suggest we meet and discuss a way to protect your… integrity. Tomorrow, at dusk, I shall send a coach for you.

A crackling noise, like static from an old radio, emanated throughout the room, and a tall woman with pale skin, amethyst-colored eyes, and long silver hair twisted in matching braids drifted from the painting to the outer boundary of the circle, close to Alessandro. Her mouth lifted into a soft smile.

"I delivered you into the world of light," she said, her voice sentimental and ethereal. "Such a beautiful spirit you hold within your soul, full of the joy of life, and yet for so long you had to bear the pain of loneliness brought to you by Kenan. Do not be afraid to use the gift the amethyst in your eyes has bestowed upon you." She reached out to him, and Alessandro's fingers closed around his grandmother's hand. "There is another here who has heard your call," Leonie said, and her gaze met Gabriel's. "She is Birgit, a seer and dear friend of Prudence. Together, with my grandson, we will hold the space while Isabella brings forth our sisters to assist you in ending the devil's presence."

A woman floated from the painting, and she resembled her granddaughter, Arianna, in appearance—white hair, cerulean-blue eyes, her perceptiveness apparent even before she spoke.

"My mother speaks of you with love and tender memories, Birgit," Gabriel said. "And your daughter and granddaughter are safe and with us now."

"Yes," Birgit said. "I have seen this, and I heard Prudence's call asking us for help."

The two women caught each other's hands and floated upward toward the painting. They gazed at Gabriel and nodded before dematerializing, leaving the Botticelli portrait of Prudence as it had previously appeared.

Gabriel leaned forward on his hands and looked to Alessandro. "After meeting your grandmother, I see where Colombina's sense of beauty and courage derive from." He rose from the floor, closed his eyes, and focused on an image of Coco in his mind. He sensed her control, her underlying fear, but mostly he sensed her courage. His eyes blinked open, and he spoke to Alessandro. "We must leave here now and place our trust in the otherworld."

With a final glance at the portrait of Prudence, Gabriel waved a hand, and the outline of the circle faded until it was only visible to those in the spirit world. "*Grazie per il tuo coraggio.*" He tossed a rune into the air, and the two men slowly disappeared.

C H A P T E R 45

COCO SENSED KENAN close to her, not that she could see him. It was more than that, something more profound and cognizant. Suddenly he pulled her to his body, an arm held tight around her waist as he leaped into the air while holding her captive. Had Coco been sharing this experience with anyone else but evil incarnate, she might have enjoyed the sensation of flying; however, the icy wind coming off the nearby ocean and the expanse of darkness around her made the experience terrifying.

The freezing air bit at her face and chilled her body to the core. She had no idea how fast they were going, for it seemed in some ways that one minute Kenan had grabbed her and the next her feet touched the ground. He let go of her waist but snatched her hand and yanked her forward in step with him. She looked around, hoping for a clue as to her whereabouts, but in the darkness of night, ominous shadows told her nothing. Kenan slid open a door and dragged her out of the cold and inside. He let go of her hand and shoved her backward. She barely had time to think about where she might be headed before her body landed in a heap on a hard floor.

Her heartbeat echoed in her ears, and she used the constant pulse as a focus point, calming herself and lowering her heart rate. *Show no fear*, Kishu had told her. She stood slowly. Since opening up the channels of the blood bond with Gabriel, Coco enjoyed the spike in her sensory perception.

"I did what you asked," she said. "Are the students all safe?"

Kenan stood in front of her now, his face close to hers, his nostrils flaring as he inhaled her scent. "You stink of the mutant."

Coco ignored his words.

He ran a hand over her hair and traced the outline of her ear before moving her hair away and baring her neck. Coco braced herself for the inevitable, clamping down her mind so that Kenan would not see the plans laid out by Gabriel and her father. He lowered his face to her neck, inhaled, and then ran his tongue over her throbbing jugular vein. She stayed still.

"You smell a little like your mother."

Coco refused to let him evoke a reaction from her. She remained focused. His words were bait, something she must not accept. Instead, she steered his attention away from her and back to his want of destroying the Allegiance.

"I'm here against the better judgment of Prudence."

"And how is Prudenza?" He hissed the name as if saying it aloud gave him pleasure.

"You said if I came to you, the students would be safe."

"You're quite the mood breaker," he said. "What can I say? I was hungry and needed to fuck! He was delicious!"

"Fuck you!"

"If you insist," he said and leaned over her.

She went to slap his face, but no sooner had the thought crossed her mind than he grabbed hold of her wrist.

"Mmm, feisty girl."

Coco spat in his face. Kenan ducked out of the way and clamped his mouth over hers. Coco's instinct kicked in, and instead of fighting against him, she leaned into his kiss. When she felt him react, she yanked him to her and then flipped him over so she straddled him and held a knife at his throat.

Kenan burst out laughing.

Coco played into the game she had begun. *Make him think you're here to kill him.* She raised the knife, but just as she brought it down, she found herself being hurled across the room. When she landed, she concentrated on controlling her desire to jump up and fight, but instead she acted like the feeble Creative he thought her to be. She looked up at his cruel face.

Had Chantal not warned her of the sheer force of anger and hatred that emanated from Kenan, she might well have been unprepared. And even with the mental training from Kishu, she struggled for a split second, reeling from the depth of his evil power and his need to establish control over her mind. She focused on her breath as it touched the roof of her mouth, each inhale and exhale a measured rhythm that had become automatic through arduous meditative practice. Her mind was her only weapon against Kenan. She gently pushed back whenever his mind probed at hers.

Without warning, he had her against a wall with one hand around her neck and the other twisting her hair slowly around his fingers. She remained calm, grateful for the intensity of Ignacio's physical training and the many times he seemed to appear out of nowhere and pin her down. Ignacio had explained to her that Kenan liked to surprise his prey with sudden moves that, more often than not, led to their deaths. She needed to stay calm while Kenan played his game of cat and mouse.

He stared into her eyes as if searching for a way into her mind. "You're stronger than your mother," he said. "It was you I should have taken that day, not her."

"Why didn't you?"

Kenan drew his face close to hers, held back her hair, and ran a finger down the side of her neck as he inhaled her scent. "I was misguided." He stroked her jugular vein with his thumb. "By the time I realized my mistake, rumor spread that you had died... that the physical trauma I'd supplied had killed you. At the time I didn't care, but when your mother proved useless and held no pertinent information, I hired others to see if you were, in fact, alive. And there you were, in plain sight.

"By that time I had my dark-winged accomplice." His lips brushed across her ear. "And you, little rebel, wanted nothing to do with the Allegiance." He stood in the center of the room, and Coco stepped away from the wall.

"They fed me lies my entire life," she said. "But they were lies said to protect me from you."

"They told you lies to protect themselves," he said. "Even now the one whose blood runs through your veins feeds you lies. He sends you here to meet with the devil! What kind of man would do such a thing, knowing that your life means nothing to me? Think, dear Colombina, it's only a matter of time until I have dear, sweet, Jeremy in my arms, but that's not enough. I must have Prudenza."

His words did not surprise Coco, but his vindictive delivery disgusted her. "If it's Prudence you want, then why have you brought me here?"

"To get me into the fortress." He walked over to the wall of windows and stared out at the ocean before opening the sliding door to the *terrazza* and stepping outside. The freshness of Gabriel's blood pumping throughout Coco's body magnified her senses, and she recognized the familiar presence of an ancient vampire in the room. Silently she spoke the ancient vampire's name, *Sabine,* but the only answer she received was silence.

As Coco's eyes adjusted to the dim light, she saw the mangled body of Sabine lying in a heap on the other side of the room. Coco ran to her and saw the dagger sticking out of her side and the gash in her stomach where blood seeped in a stream onto the floor.

"Sabine," she whispered. She grasped the immortal's hand and glanced quickly over her body. She knew that what had drawn Kenan outside was an image from his past, one that he would not understand. But it told her that Arianna and Hakon had begun their torment.

A caustic chuckle broke the silence. "Oh, how cute, you've found little Sabine, the great warrior," Kenan said. "Although the poor little treasure's not looking too good, is she?"

Coco looked back at Sabine. "So, let me guess… I paint the interior of the fortress and you release Sabine."

"I make no promises. However, I hear you're one of the best, and I'm well aware of the magic in your blood—thanks, no doubt, to the talents of your great-grandmother. You will get me into that damn fortress!"

"I didn't bring my paints with me."

"No problem, dearie, I have everything you need and more." He turned toward the window, and this time Coco clearly saw an image of Ravinka outside on the *terrazza*, although she pretended not to notice. Kenan clenched his fists, but in a flash the image was gone. He walked to Coco, grabbed her arm, and dragged her over to a corner of the room where an easel, canvas, paints, and brushes awaited.

"Paint, or your precious Sabine dies!"

Coco squeezed paints from tubes onto a palette and quickly painted the outline of the main living room at Casa della Pietra. Kenan strode toward the sliding door, and Coco saw Arianna disguised as Ravinka appear. For a few moments, Kenan froze. He touched the glass with one hand before he turned to Coco.

"How long will this take?"

"About fifteen minutes," she said. "Ten if you leave me alone and give me some light."

Kenan flicked on a lamp. He opened the sliding door and stepped outside. From where Coco stood, she saw him standing on a ledge, surveying the property. In essence, she had completed enough of the painting to do what was needed, so she took a moment and observed Sabine. Her hands rested on her collarbone, and it was then that Coco saw the glint of a chain against the immortal's neck.

She glanced at Kenan, who stared at something in the distance. Carefully, she put down the paintbrush and crept over to Sabine, keeping her gaze on Kenan. When she was close enough, she freed the chain from Sabine's clothing and saw two tiny vials hanging like charms against the vampire's skin. Coco balled her hand into a fist, smashed it against the small vials, and watched as they dissipated into Sabine's skin. She walked quickly back to the easel just as Kenan fled inside.

"I'm done," Coco said.

Kenan's eyes had a glazed look, and for a moment he seemed unable to speak; seeing Ravinka had definitely had an effect on him. He blinked, and when he opened his eyes, the cruel demeanor had returned. He grabbed the painting and leaned it against a chair, then yanked Coco forward, holding on to her wrist.

"Do it!" he said.

"What about Sabine?"

"Do it, or she dies!"

Coco held out a hand, and the pigments of paint lifted from the canvas toward her fingertips.

Kenan pulled a dagger from his boot and nailed Sabine's foot to the floor. "That should keep her still until we return."

Coco stared at him. "You bastard!"

"You're right about that." He stepped forward and into the image of the main living room at Casa della Pietra, dragging Coco with him.

CHAPTER 46

SABINE KNEW THE moment Nikandros and Frederico appeared next to her—the tender touch of Frederico's hands as he pulled her to his chest, his love and fear for her safety pumping through her blood. He held her while Nikandros placed his wrist against her mouth.

For a moment she surrendered to the pain she had held off until now. Her body twitched as Nikandros eased the tainted blade from her chest and removed the knife that impaled her foot.

"Drink of the blood from which you were born," Nikandros said. His words struck her sharply and forced her to drink. "I'm not ready to lose you to the next world."

She understood that it was the ancient blood of her maker that would heal her quickly. She experienced his joy when he felt the pull of her mouth as she drank from his vein. The pain subsided, and her blood reached out to her lover. She pushed Nikandros's wrist away. Her eyes fluttered open, and her gaze met Frederico's. His fingers ran over the broken vials on her neck.

"Coco broke them open…," she whispered.

Frederico lifted her into his arms and kissed her. He encouraged her to drink from his jugular vein, and she held on to him as he offered her his neck. When her thirst was quenched, she claimed his mouth with hers, but the memory of Kenan snapped her into reality. She turned to see Hakon striding across the room with Arianna beside him.

"We do not have much time," he said. "We need to get to the rendezvous point."

Sabine turned to Nikandros, her face flushed from feeding.

"We're entering a battle like no other," he said. "We are warriors, you and I, but this time I ask that you refrain and stay here with Frederico."

Sabine shook her head and stood tall and strong beside her beloved. "We've come too far to give up this war now, Father. We'll fight this battle by your side."

Nikandros stared at her. "You fill my heart with pride." He gave a quick, decisive nod, and they stood beside Hakon and Arianna.

A mist gathered around them, and moments later the room fell empty.

CHAPTER 47

SOME SAY THAT silence can be deafening. Not so for Coco, whose mind zeroed in on the one moment she had trained for her entire life. She focused on the absolute silence, allowing the words Kenan spoke to rush over her. His exhilaration at being in the fortress was reflected in the flash of victory in his dark eyes. As his gaze fell upon the Botticelli portrait of Prudence, Coco saw him lick his thin lips and straighten the jacket of his charcoal suit. She imagined him pulling the charred portrait out of the infamous Bonfire of the Vanities in Renaissance Florence centuries ago.

The colors of his aura swirled in chaos around his body, changing from brown to pink and then flashes of red. Coco sensed the moment he realized something was amiss. The bloodied hand of a woman appeared out of the painting, followed by the rest of her body. She floated to the floor, dressed in a floor-length crimson gown of silk, her long auburn hair tumbling over her shoulders. The woman reached a hand toward Kenan, and her eerie voice filled the room.

Kenan's moment of reckoning had arrived.

"See him there?" the woman whispered. "He's the one who killed me, who stole my breath."

"What magic is this?" Kenan yelled. "Isabella is dead!" He glared at Coco and strode toward her. The stench of sulfur seeped from his body. As he reached out to grab Coco, two other women appeared.

She recognized Alessandro's grandmother and a woman who resembled Illona.

A blast of energy shook the room. A wave of women stepped out from the portrait, all dressed in identical floor-length crimson dresses. They joined in the chorus of poetry with the duchess Isabella as they drifted toward Kenan.

"He thought to quiet me, to stop me from speaking," they said in unison. "But he is one of many who thought brutality and abuse could stop my voice, one of many who sought to silence me through fear, one of many whose eyes are not only for his betrothed but for other men's wives and lovers. Then he wipes his filthy hands across my womb."

When the women were close to Coco, she lifted her hands toward a painting mounted on the wall behind Kenan. She willed the landscape to awaken. Clusters of pigment lifted off the canvas and floated toward her. All the while, the women walked forward like a tidal wave of blood. They raised their right hand and pointed to Kenan as he began his transformation from human form to pure evil.

The women's voices grew loud. "And now he looks upon my face. He cannot see the millions of women around me, the children who have died because of the cruelty of men like him. Tell him this; no, wait, I'll tell him myself, through the whispers of the dead. To you, sir—your brutality has cut us down and continues to do so; your evil cruelty spews vicious lies from your sour mouth."

Coco held on to the pigment until the women had formed a U-shaped boundary around her, Kenan, and the painting.

Isabella stepped forward and continued speaking to him. "My sisters and I have gathered our strengths, our wisdom, our courage. With heads held high, we march from the open doors of libraries and schools, courtrooms and kitchens; we rise in a tidal wave of fury built from centuries past. We walk together—warriors, women of intellect and great passion. Boudica, Joan d'Arc, Elizabeth, Hypatia, and Cleopatra. Women who have fought for our rights with blood and words—Rosa, Mary, Emmilene, Elizabeth, and Susan, and see o'er there… Harriet walks beside the antebellum sisters, Sarah and Angelina. We've heard your diatribe of poison against all that is feminine, just as we always have. Ah, but this time we are ready, assembled en masse to fight for our rights like never before. You, and others like you—men without eros and wisdom, soulless men—will fall to the ground as the blood of our fallen sisters washes over you."

Kenan rose to his full height, but that only fueled the women. They joined together, pushing him toward the painting Coco had made come alive, speaking their words of retribution.

"No longer will the curtain be drawn upon my face. No longer will others with evil thoughts get to choose when I am seen and heard. My time is now. The smile upon my face is not, as you prefer to see, one of passion. Think of this, sir. See this dress I wear? See the shades of red? The bright tone of youthful blood, the ripe cherry red of new birth, and the crimson blood of the wise and aged crone. Yes, sir, whene'er you run your fingers o'er my dress, know that you touch the blood from our wombs. This is the lure of my death painting and the artist's secret.

"What's that I hear you say? You hear the whispers of my voice? You wonder how this is possible? You cry with frightened eyes as you back away from my portrait. A swish of silk and taffeta, and my smile broadens as I step forward, released from the chains of your imprisonment. I raise a hand and point to your face. I shake my head. And as women flood into this room, you turn and run to your pawns, but they have fled like rats."

"You have no power over me, Duchess!" Kenan screamed, his voice guttural and cruel. He struck out at the auburn-haired woman, and as she fell, the women around her picked her up, and once again Isabella stood tall in front of him.

"I fear you not," Isabella said. "But you need fear me. You created my wrath. My time is now."

And with those words, the women pushed forward. Kenan

glanced back at the wall behind him. When he saw the image, he reached out and grabbed hold of Coco's arm as the women pushed him into the painting. It took all Coco's concentration to hold the image until she knew that Kenan could not escape. She did not have the strength to fight him off and knew that in his current state of metamorphic evil, she had to save her energy and hold the image.

But as Kenan pulled at her arm and the pigments fell from her fingertips, she realized that something strange was happening to her body. She felt lighter. Layers of emotional pain melted away along with memories. Her life played out before her. Images ran together. She was safe in Gabriel's arms, standing with him in a museum. She watched Christopher fall to the ground and blood seep from his body. The softness of Thalia's fur as she wound around her legs. The excruciating pain of shattered bones pulsing throughout her body. A painting of a landscape—a tree, blood, and sheer terror. Her mother and father embracing and a child crying.

CHAPTER 48

Tuscany, Italy

THE CHILD CRYING was Coco.

She stood alone in a field and watched as a man dragged her mother away from her.

"Run, Colombina! Don't look back. Run!" Chantal screamed.

But Coco couldn't run away, and instead she witnessed her mother's body as it hurtled through the air—always graceful, always gentle. Coco wondered why the tall, pale man dressed in dark clothes was hurting the woman she loved. Her mother had told her to run, but the moment Coco heard her screams, she froze.

She saw red raindrops falling over her mother's body. They seemed to hang in the air for a moment before they fell, like her mother, to the ground beneath an old willow tree. Time paused, and Coco's high-pitched scream shattered the silence.

The man dressed in dark clothes strode toward her, but she floated above her body in a safe place and watched as hundreds of women dressed in red appeared along with other people who seemed familiar.

"Enough!" the Holy Father yelled. "It's over. Kenan, put her down."

Kenan turned his head toward the Holy Father and sneered at

the members of the Allegiance who had formed a circle around him. Beyond the circle, Coco saw Flora, Sonja, Luciana, and the hundreds of souls of women adorned in red.

"Is this the beginning or the end, Holy Father?" Kenan turned to Gabriel. "If I die, so does your precious Creative. Is this how you planned it?"

The Lady and the Rose, Hakon, and Prudence stepped forward within the circle formed by members of the Allegiance. They raised their arms. The sky darkened, and a flash of lightning struck the ground at Kenan's feet. He stumbled as the ground beneath him trembled. He stared at his enemies and then plunged his fangs into Coco's five-year-old body. When he had drained her, he tossed her limp body to the ground.

CHAPTER 49

A PAINFUL SCREAM REVERBERATED as Chantal rose from her shattered body and ran toward Kenan. The circle of warriors closed in, joined by the ethereal women in red, each one chanting their own painful sorrow.

"We fear you not, but you need fear us. You created us, you created our wrath. This is our time for revenge."

Members of the Allegiance closed in on Kenan, protecting the Holy Father, who held the sacred knife in his hands. Kenan hurled a knife at Stefan, but Sabine caught it midair.

"Get out of my way!" he screamed. He caught her arm and raised his free hand, then brought it down toward her heart. Just before the tip of the blade struck Sabine, Kenan's head fell back, and he roared in pain. He let go of Sabine and reached for the sword that had severed his gnarled right hand, and as he did his eyes caught sight of Nikandros.

"Get your filthy hands off my daughter!" Nikandros said, his voice calm, smooth and serious.

The women in red began to drift into formations. A small group formed a protective halo around Sabine while others drifted over Kenan and the members of the Allegiance, all the while their words echoing in a continuous ghostly chant.

"We fear you not, but you need fear us. You created us, you created our wrath. This is our time for revenge."

Kenan bellowed at the approaching immortals. Fire erupted from the fingers of his remaining hand, and he hurled flames at his enemies. But the flames were doused with blood-tinged rain. As Kenan's severed hand began to heal, his body shuddered, sulfur exuded into the air, and he flew toward the Holy Father.

Nikandros, Stefan, Gabriel, and Alessandro leaped into the air, pounding Kenan's body with knives, but his preternatural strength tossed them away as if they were fragile butterflies. Kenan extended a clawlike hand toward the Holy Father, and Pelayo, Christopher, and Frederico collided with him, assaulting his body with an onslaught of knife strikes and sword thrusts.

In the midst of the foul curses of fighting, a woman's scream stabbed the air, rising to a crescendo and into a howl of pain. Armed with swords, Louisa flew through the air toward Kenan, Ignacio by her side. Kenan looked up and unleashed a series of curses at her, and she fell as if struck by lightning. While Kenan was distracted, the Holy Father leaped upon Ignacio's shoulders and thrust the sacred blade into Kenan's heart.

But the Holy Father hesitated, his eyes focused on Kenan's face as it registered agonizing pain; had he looked up, he would have had time to deflect the sword Kenan swung at him, severing the Holy Father's neck.

CHAPTER 50

COCO'S BODY WAS no longer that of a child but a woman of thirty-two, the Creative, Colombina. From where she floated above the field near her family home in Tuscany, she watched as Kenan ripped into her neck with his fangs and threw her young body to the ground. She saw Gabriel run forward with Alessandro, Stefan, Christopher, and Nikandros and unleash a barrage of swords and daggers toward Kenan, most of which he deflected easily.

Little by little, the color in her world dissipated until all that remained was a world of black, white, and gray, and the tones were dark and forbidding. The scene below her had vanished. She stood on solid ground, a cold, lonely highway bordered by the shadowed forms of desert flora.

In the distance a storm approached, and the rumble of thunder echoed across the landscape like a giant wave. Coco shivered as raindrops fell, gentle at first, but within moments a mass of black clouds swirled above her and opened up a deluge of harsh rain. She ran along the road, searching for somewhere to hide. In the distance she saw a car and she ran harder, through puddles that had formed on the asphalt, fighting to stand against the wind that now roared through the desolate region.

The car was fifty feet away, and through the sheet of rain, Coco could see that it was an old truck. As she approached, she saw the outlines of two figures in the cab. She raced forward to the passenger door and knocked on the window. The door opened. Coco shielded her face from the rain and looked inside. At first she couldn't make out the faces of the two people but noticed they wore worn-out clothes—old jeans and torn T-shirts, dusty and dirty. When the driver turned around, she gave him a grateful smile; it was her father, and the passenger was her mother. But when Chantal looked at her and smiled, it was not an expression of love but a sadistic grin, and her narrow, dark eyes were those of a predator. Coco slammed the door and sprinted back the way she had come. Other figures appeared in the distance, and they ran toward her. She glanced around and saw that other than the road, there was water everywhere, so much so that what was once desert had become an ocean.

She glanced at the figures approaching and saw familiar faces— Sabine, Frederico, Stefan, Louisa, Ignacio, and Pelayo. Each one looked deadly, each one hungry for her blood. She turned and saw her parents had stopped running but were close enough that they were crouched in an attack position. The vampires now gathered around her, each one looking bloodthirsty and dangerous.

From out of the water, Kenan emerged, unmarked by the rain and wind, a picture of deadly elegance. Behind him Prudence appeared, dressed in black, her eyes dull and full of grief. The other vampires bowed their heads in submission as Kenan entered the circle, trailed by Prudence.

"It's no use, Colombina," he said. "I've won. Evil has endured. Your friends and family are gone… They're mine now. You're alone, and your beloved's body is in two pieces on that godforsaken piece of hallowed ground next to the dear Holy Father, who suffered the same fate. You're mine now, dearie. All mine."

"No!" Coco fell to her knees and looked up at the sky. The rain washed over her, and she whispered one word. "Gabriel." It was then that she remembered the small jewel-encrusted dagger tucked in the back of her jeans.

Kenan chuckled. "Gabriel can't help you now, Colombina. You're on your own." He knelt in front of her, and she bowed her head. "There's a good girl. This won't hurt a bit."

When she could feel his breath on her neck, Coco reached for the stiletto dagger and slammed the blade into Kenan's heart. She watched as his head fell back, his knees buckled, and he dropped to the ground. All the while, Coco never let go of the dagger.

Gradually the rain stopped, and the ghostly vampiric images of her family and friends dissolved into a wash of scarlet.

CHAPTER 51

KENAN FELL TO the ground and a keening cry exploded into the night. Prudence recognized the sound; it was not from Kenan's lips but from an otherworldly creature. It was the tortured moan of a distraught woman. She looked up at the darkening sky as the ghostly figure of Freyja emerged—a sylphlike goddess masked in a cloak of brokenhearted melancholy. She ran across the bloodied field and knelt beside Kenan, her black wings withdrawing into the folds of her long dress.

Kenan's body was changing; gone were his gnarled and clawed hands, his yellowed teeth and bloodshot eyes. The veil of evil lifted from his persona, leaving behind the body of a mortal with dark hair and cinnamon-colored eyes.

Freyja looked up at Hakon and Prudence. "We made a deal. The Creative for my beloved."

She gazed over to where Alessandro held Chantal's battered body, and at Gabriel who uttered words of magic over the four-year-old figure of Coco, who had succumbed to the twilight of death. She raised a hand in the direction of Coco, whose body morphed into her thirty-two-year-old self.

She sought out the one woman whom she hoped would understand her sorrow. "Prudence, please, help me."

"He cannot live as an immortal," Prudence said. "And as such his life will be short-lived. Is that what you want?"

"I'll take whatever moments we can have together," Freyja said. She glanced at Hakon. "Please, I beg of you, allow him to return with me to my lands in his mortal body and live for as long as I rule my world. You have my word as a goddess that he will not leave my realm."

The Lady and the Rose stepped forward. "No, you do not get Kenan as easily as this, Freyja. Free Gunwald from your dark magic so he may walk by my side for eternity. Do you think I do not know that it was you who aimed the arrow at his heart eons ago? Do you think I am not blind to your jealousy? Release my beloved now, or Kenan dies. Remember, it is I who has the power over his destiny."

"Yes," Freyja said. "It was me who shot the arrow, but it was not because of my jealousy. I did it because you had forgotten your place in this world. Love had made you both blind to the darkness that was gathering upon this earth. With Gunwald gone, you remembered what you are, and that is a goddess. I will set your beloved free, but you must swear to continue your work, for without it we will all perish."

"I know who I am, Freyja," the Lady said. "Take your lover and return my beloved." She raised a hand, and Kenan's eyes fluttered open.

"Ravinka," he whispered. "I remember… I remember that I love you."

Freyja kissed him. "And I love you."

Prudence knelt beside her and placed a hand on her shoulder. "Will Colombina live?"

Freyja's face softened. She leaned in close to Prudence's cheek and whispered, "I saved her once with my kiss, and as such she is immortal, like her beloved."

Prudence placed a hand on the side of Freyja's face and kissed her forehead. "Thank you."

Freyja spread her wings and gathered Kenan's mortal body close to her bosom. Then she turned toward Chantal's still body and saw rose-colored tears falling gently from Alessandro's eyes. A few feet away, Gabriel clung to Coco, and she was reminded of the courage of another woman, Caprecia. Through puckered lips, Freyja blew a breath of air toward Chantal. The Creative gasped and opened her eyes.

As Freyja walked away, she turned to the Lady and the Rose. "Gunwald awaits you." She spread her wings, rose into the heavens, and disappeared.

Prudence watched as her grandmother dissipated.

The crimson rain gradually turned clear, and the first light of dawn fell across the Tuscan hills. The scent of lavender and rosemary drifted from Chantal's garden, seeping into the damp air like a healing elixir. Prudence stood at the center of the field and looked around at the members of the Allegiance, each one helping another, until her gaze focused on Birgit and Illona. She watched mother and daughter say their silent goodbyes. And as Birgit's image began to waver, Pelayo guided Jeremy and Arianna to where their grandmother waited.

"You are both the image of Elion," Birgit whispered, her voice gentle and feathery. "You have the courage of your mother and the gifts of the fae in your blood. Katja's spirit is new to our world, but soon she will adjust to her ethereal body and have the strength to enter your dreams." She turned to Illona. "Do not dwell on death. You must go on and fulfill a life of joy and love." A smile brushed her lips as her image dissolved.

"Illona!" A man called her name.

Illona turned to see a familiar figure running toward her, blood on his face and hands. Pelayo gave her a nudge, and that was all she needed. She crossed the meadow in seconds and fell into Jason's open arms.

"Jeez, I couldn't see you for all the freaking blood pouring out of the sky," Jason said. "Are you okay?"

"You're the one with blood on your face, and you're asking if I'm all right?"

He grinned and kissed her.

Prudence walked toward Stefan and Sabine, who stood beside Nikandros. The ancient immortal had placed the Holy Father's severed head with his body. One by one, members of the Allegiance sensed the loss and gathered together.

Nikandros sliced open his wrist and anointed the Holy Father's forehead with his blood as he recited a prayer for the dead in ancient Latin. "Into your hands, O Lord, we humbly entrust my son, the Holy Father. In this life he embraced your love. Deliver him now from every evil and bid him eternal rest."

Luciana approached Nikandros and gave him a white cloak, which he placed over the Holy Father's body.

Prudence stood at his side. "I will take you to his sanctuary below Rome so you can prepare his body."

Nikandros gazed into Prudence's eyes, and there were rose-colored tears on his cheeks. "I'll need Stefan and Sabine to help bury their brother. I do not have the strength to do this on my own, and we are family."

Out of the mist, a woman appeared, dressed in a crimson cape. Her image flickered as if the flame of a candle burned inside her body. She raised a hand and whispered, "Walk with me, Holy Father."

A ghostly image of the Holy Father rose from beneath the white cloak that covered his body. There were only a few who heard the words he spoke as he floated toward the woman and grasped her hand. *Beatrice, my love.*

Prudence watched as the two spirits were swept away in the ether. "They are now free to love each other."

CHAPTER 52

Tuscany, Italy—July 16, 1576

A S THE LARGE party employed by Isabella's husband, Paolo, approached Cerreto Guidi, an air of impending doom hovered around Isabella, made more repressive by the nightly dreams she'd had of late—dreams of her much-loved cousin, Leonora, who wandered along a lonely windswept beach where waves pounded onto the shore. The more recent of Isabella's dreams had shown Leonora walking closer to the shoreline, ignoring her pleas to turn away. However, it had been another dream that caused Isabella's sense of doom—the appearance of her much-loved, deceased brother Giovanni standing underneath the arches inside the church of San Lorenzo, beckoning to her.

Isabella pushed the image of her recent dream beneath another that in essence gave her joy; by now her infant son would be safe with Marguerite and her mother, away from Tuscany in a place where the Medici heir's life would not be in danger. In her daze, Isabella was guided to her rooms with the help of her ladies-in-waiting, where she rested until her respite was interrupted and the duke summoned her to his room.

Isabella did not hesitate but went to him as ordered, wearing only a chemise and robe, followed by one of her ladies and the dwarf, Morgante, whom she had known since she was a child. When she reached Paolo's room, she asked for her attendants to wait for her. They begged her not to enter, as if even they sensed a cloud of impending darkness approaching. But Isabella had already accepted the fait accompli.

The duchess entered Paolo's room and walked toward him, stopping when she realized they were not alone.

She gasped. "I should have known you were as dark as each other," she said. A hand over her mouth quickly shrouded her suffering. Her gaze went from her husband, who was approaching her with madness in his eyes, to the figure of Kenan standing in the shadows. In the darkness that followed, a familiar hand clasped hers, pulling her out of the pit of pain to the tranquility of the chapel at San Lorenzo. She sat between Giovanni and Leonora, taking in the splendor of Brunelleschi's architecture before resting her gaze upon the bronze pulpits and the work of Donatello.

"It is true then," she whispered. "Art is where we find sanctuary."

Giovanni turned to her and smiled. "And thanks to your selfless courage, in years to come this city of ours will once again experience a rebirth, and hope will rise through the arts under the guidance of the Medici bloodline."

CHAPTER 53

Los Angeles, California—UCLA Campus

AFTER CHECKING THE time on her cell, Coco picked up a cardboard box full of items from her desk and left the building. She walked briskly down the stairs and through the sculpture garden, giving a quick glance to the statue of Freyja as she passed by. Students were lying on the grass, enjoying the warmth of the morning sun as the blue sky beckoned forth another beautiful day in the city of angels.

The smells of toast and coffee lingered on the streets, and the hissing of air caused Coco to turn her head toward a blue bus. She watched as people exited and made their way through the Village, darting off into different directions—some toward the campus or hospital, others mingling with the morning rush along Wilshire Boulevard.

When she reached her building, Coco unlocked the gate and raced up the stairs to her apartment. She entered, looked around, and walked over to a painting of a landscape leaning on an easel. With the box in one hand, she held out the other toward the canvas, noting the rush of excitement flooding her body as pigments of paint gathered at her fingertips. The corners of her mouth broke into a smile at the sight of the familiar scene that lay hidden beneath the landscape. She stepped forward, leaving the sounds of Westwood behind her.

He stood waiting for her, leaning against the bench in the kitchen, arms folded. His golden eyes ignited her soul, causing her to trip as she stepped forward. He caught her, placed the box on the kitchen bench, and claimed her mouth with his own. When he released her, he settled an arm around her shoulder and guided her out of the kitchen.

"Am I too late?" she asked.

Gabriel shook his head and grinned. "It's about to happen. Sabine, Illona, and Prudence are with her now."

He lifted Coco into his arms and rushed up the staircase at vampire speed, lowering her to her feet when they met Christopher standing in the hallway and looking somewhat nervous.

"I was worried you wouldn't make it," he said. "She's been in labor for a few hours now. She'll be happy to see you."

Coco and Gabriel followed Christopher into the bedroom. The group that had gathered around the bed parted when they saw her, allowing her access. Coco approached the bed and sat down.

"It won't be long now," Sabine said. "I think she's been waiting for you."

"Hey, beautiful lady," Coco said, running a hand over her friend's head. "How are you feeling?"

"Nervous," Layla said. "I can tell you that from experience, *mi amo.*"

Coco turned to see Layla standing with Christopher, holding their baby daughter in her arms. At the sight of the newest member of the family, Coco's eyes brimmed with tears, but the image was disturbed by a strange howling emanating from the bed. She turned to Thalia and watched the feline's fluffy body shudder as the rhythmic spasms of labor seized her body.

"It's okay to stroke her belly," Sabine said and checked her patient.

"The sounds she's making—grunts and cries—are quite normal, all part of the feline birthing process."

"Does she need something for pain?" Coco asked.

"She's doing fine. Cats are resilient and strong, and Thalia is extraordinary." Sabine glanced at Coco's barely pregnant belly. "Don't worry, you're not a cat, and I promise you won't suffer. Besides, I don't wish to bear the brunt of Gabriel's protective instincts."

"Glad to hear it," Gabriel muttered. He rubbed Coco's shoulders. "We'll get through our child's birth together."

"Spoken like a true man," Sabine said with an edge of sarcasm. She winked at Coco. "Don't worry, I've got you covered."

An ear-piercing meow was followed by grunting noises and the birth of a kitten.

"You're a clever mommy. Look what you've done all by yourself," Sabine said. "A word of warning—cats eat the umbilical cord. Best to look away if you're queasy. Thalia will clean her kitten, and then the little one will suckle, allowing Thalia time to rest between births."

"And you said there are two kittens?" Gabriel asked.

Sabine nodded. "Yes, both females."

Coco kept her hand by Thalia's side while the new mother took care of her kitten. "She looks like she has tabby stripes."

"I'm not surprised," Gabriel said. "I know the father."

"Another stray you've adopted?" Prudence asked.

"He adopted the villa," Gabriel replied. "Besides, Maria tells me he's earned his keep."

A whimper at the door caused the gathered crowd to turn to Max—Gabriel's German shepherd—sitting at the door with a large tabby cat beside him.

"Ah, here's the proud father." Gabriel walked over to Max, patted him on the head, picked up the tabby, and brought him over to Thalia. The tomcat curled up and licked Thalia's coat. Moments later he began purring in an equivalent decibel range of a Fiat. "Now he's a happy father."

As soon as the kitten began suckling, another shudder ran over Thalia's body. She howled and grunted and then gave birth to the second kitten. When she had cleaned her, Thalia lay back and both kittens suckled.

"Look," Coco said. "She has a gray mask like her mother and little white paws."

Chapter 54

COCO GAZED OUT the car window at the ocean, placed a hand on Gabriel's thigh, and sighed. Considering the stress of the past ten months, Gabriel had insisted on taking her for a short vacation, and although she thought it odd that the area he had chosen was close to Kenan's villa at the edge of Circeo National Park, he had assured her that the place had been thoroughly cleansed by Prudence, Hakon, and Sonja.

"Why did you really choose this place?" she asked.

He grinned but his gaze never left the road. "Always questions."

"Damn vampires and your secrets."

She went to move her hand, but he covered it with his own and stroked her wrist with his thumb.

"Patience," he said.

Coco rolled her eyes, grinned, and then returned to the ocean view. In the distance, shrouded by fog, islands appeared, and Gabriel, who seemed to be enjoying playing the part of tour guide, let go of her hand for a moment and pointed in the direction Coco was looking.

"The Pontine Islands," he said. "You've been to one, although I'd rather that had never happened."

"Can't say I remember much about the actual island, but I'd love to see it again. Maybe we can go over there?"

"It's on our agenda, I promise."

Thirty minutes later, Gabriel pulled the car up to the front of a hotel in Borgo Grappa. As he was helping Coco out of the car, Pelayo pulled up next to them in a black Range Rover. The car door opened, and Arianna hopped out, joined shortly after by Pelayo and Jeremy.

"I can't believe we're on vacation in Italy together," Arianna said. "And I've actually been here before."

Coco stood back and watched the twins and Pelayo as they gathered their bags and walked into the hotel. Gabriel began to follow, but when he saw Coco was not beside him, he glanced back at her.

She crossed her arms and raised an eyebrow. "What's going on?"

Gabriel walked back to where she stood. "Nothing. Just here to relax."

"Bullshit—you're hiding something."

He grinned and nodded. "You're right, I am. Now let's go."

"You're not going to tell me?"

"No." He placed an arm around her shoulders, kissed her cheek, and guided her forward. "Patience, *mi amore.*"

They were greeted in the foyer by the manager of the hotel who suggested they enjoy a cool drink on the patio.

"*Perfetto,*" Gabriel said. They followed Pelayo, Arianna, and Jeremy to a table outside.

It was then that Coco sensed something unusual—a buzz in the air, an indicator that something unique was about to happen. She gazed at Gabriel, and he squeezed her hand and then poured her a glass of Pellegrino. Doing her best to act nonchalant, Coco perused the mix of people on the patio, but none seemed to be at the root of the tingling sensation that wavered in the air.

Arianna excused herself and made her way across the patio and into the main lobby, and Jeremy strained his neck to follow his sister as she walked away. He reached for Pelayo's hand.

"Is everything okay?" Coco asked.

Jeremy stared at his drink, and as a smile tugged at the corners of his mouth, he looked across the table at Gabriel. "Is that why we're here?"

"What?" Coco cut in. "Please, tell me what's going on."

"Unless you want to sleep outside, Gabriel, you'd better spill the beans," Pelayo said.

Gabriel nodded. "One of the properties Jason and Arianna viewed has been owned by a local family for generations. They recently put it on the market, and it just happened that while their villa was being shown—to Arianna and Jason—the owner insisted his grandson bring him here for drinks and a game of chess, something they do regularly.

"Pelayo and I waited in a suite upstairs, remotely viewing via a tiny camera on the necklace Arianna wore, and we noticed that when she entered the lobby, she halted midstep. Because Pelayo and I had access to what Arianna saw, I knew instantly that a certain young man had caught her attention."

"The young man with his grandfather!" Coco blurted out.

"Ah, but you see, *mi amore*, he is not just any young man—"

Coco's eyes grew wide. "Oh my god! It's him, isn't it?"

Gabriel grinned.

"Did you know he'd be here that day?" she asked.

"Not at that time. We had a lot going on," he said. "And members of the Allegiance have protected his family since we moved Isabella and Troilo's son out of Florence. Believe me, Colombina, I was perhaps the most surprised when we saw him in the video, but more so by his reaction when he saw Arianna."

"Did she say anything to you?" Jeremy asked.

"I remember exactly what she said," Pelayo chimed in. "She asked Jason if he'd ever experienced a feeling that you've met someone before. When they arrived upstairs, she seemed a little hesitant to leave. That's when Gabriel suggested we all come back one day."

"So you know him?" Jeremy asked.

Gabriel nodded. "I've not spoken with him, but I feel I know him well, and I've wondered for the past few months if your sister and he were destined to meet each other."

"So that's why we're here," Coco said. "You have my full approval, Gabriel, but is being here kind of pushing destiny?"

"They found each other earlier," he replied. "And I had no idea that he would be here that day."

Coco looked up and saw Arianna walking toward the table with a young man about her own age and an elderly man. "Don't look now, but they're headed this way."

Gabriel rose as they approached, noticing the glow around Arianna and the young man.

"Gabriel," Arianna said. "This is Vito and his grandfather, Lorenzo. They own one of the villas Jason and I looked at when we were here before."

"*Ciao*," Gabriel said, and continued to introduce everyone in Italian.

Coco no longer struggled with the language as she had prior to becoming blood-bound with Gabriel. He gathered two more chairs, and Vito and Lorenzo joined them.

Gabriel leaned forward. "So, is the villa still on the market?"

Lorenzo shook his head and smiled. "No. I don't know what I was thinking. I love the villa and plan on leaving it to Vito." He looked at Arianna. "Did you and your brother find a place?"

"Actually, I'm not sure where I'll be living in the near future."

"Are you currently living in the States?" Vito asked.

Arianna smiled. "I've been in Italy for a while."

"Do you like it here?"

"Very much so," she said. "But I'd like to go to grad school."

Vito sipped on his drink. "What is it you're interested in?"

Arianna pushed a stray lock of her hair behind her ear. "My undergrad was in languages and social justice, but I'm also interested in history and the arts. I'm not sure I want to go back home quite yet. What about you?"

"I recently finished doing a grad course on art during the Renaissance in Florence. Like you, I'm not sure what to do next."

Coco squeezed Gabriel's fingers. "Did you enjoy the course?"

Vito nodded. "Yeah, I did, but it made me a little sad to see the support the city—well, the Medicis—gave artists during that period, and how my friends who are artists struggle now. Not just here in Italy, but everywhere."

"I feel the same," Coco said. "Perhaps it's time for another Renaissance."

"Perhaps," Vito replied. He spoke to Arianna. "Are you staying here, at the hotel?"

"For a few days, yes," she said. "And I think we're spending time on one of the islands."

Lorenzo gestured to Gabriel, "Join us at our villa for dinner this evening. We have beautiful views of the islands."

Gabriel looked at his iPhone and checked the time. "I think Colombina and I can manage that, but there's something we need to take care of first." He pushed back his chair and encouraged Coco to stand.

"What is it?" Coco asked.

"A surprise," he replied. "I apologize for our hurried departure, and by no means is it the company. I'll leave Pelayo to make the arrangements for tonight."

"Go, *amigo*, I've got you covered." Pelayo winked at Gabriel. "We'll see you in the lobby in a few hours."

Gabriel reached out and shook Lorenzo's and Vito's hands before guiding Coco across the patio, through the lobby, and into the elevator.

When the door closed, Coco turned to him. "Another surprise?"

"You have five minutes to change."

"Into what?"

The elevator door slid open.

"Your outfit is waiting for you in the bathroom." He took her hand and strode along the hallway to a door that opened with a wave of his hand. He pointed to a room off a living area and patted her backside. "Go—it's that way. I'll meet you out here in five."

"Ten!"

"Eight. Now go. I'm counting."

When Coco emerged from the bedroom, she wore an elegant black cocktail dress with shoestring straps and a pair of black suede pumps. She had thrown her hair up in a french twist and did her best to control the flush of color that spread across her cheeks when her gaze met Gabriel's, for he undoubtedly had chosen the silk underwear that she wore under the dress and the garter belt that held up her sheer black stockings.

Gabriel stood waiting for her, looking for all the world like the delicious vampire-wizard that he was. Her gaze lingered over the tailored charcoal suit, white shirt, and black oxfords, wondering if there was a chance he might consider foregoing whatever he had planned and instead head back into the bedroom.

"Tempting, yes, but the night is young, Colombina, and I have a promise to keep."

"You do?"

He strode over to her, clutched her hand, and tossed his runes into the air.

⁓

Wherever Gabriel had brought her, it was dark, but as her eyes adjusted Coco recognized the location. She turned and kissed him, taking her time to luxuriate in his love.

"I promised to bring you here on our first date," he said. "And I'm a man of my word."

"Are we alone?"

"Of course, *mi amore*," he said. "Well, except for the waiter."

The lights rose to a soft glow, and a trail of rose petals led out of the foyer. She looked back at Gabriel, and he raised an eyebrow and urged her forward. Hand in hand, they followed the petals through to the galleries where Coco sensed the pull of paintings by Goya, Rembrandt, and Degas, to the hall where Picasso and Braque held court. They continued through to the large gallery that held her favorite Picasso. To Coco's delight, a table had been set up with a white tablecloth and champagne glasses, directly across from Picasso's *Bust of a Woman* in oil with fixed black chalk on canvas.

Coco eased herself onto a chair and stared at the image. A waiter appeared with champagne, the bottle of which appeared dark, and all she could see of the label beneath his hand was the letter *K*, but the scents that rose from the liquid as she brought the glass to her mouth made her think of lemon and vanilla and gingerbread. As quickly as the waiter appeared, he was gone.

"There's a scent I can't place," she said.

"Heliotrope."

Coco took a large sip and held it in her mouth for a few moments, then turned toward Gabriel and grinned. "Did Sabine say I could have this?"

"One glass, *mi amore*. Enjoy it."

"This is orgasmic," she whispered, "I'm in heaven. Picasso, incredible champagne, and you. You've outdone yourself."

She placed the glass on the table and walked around the room, clasping her hands behind her back to remind her she was not alone in case she was tempted to see if any of the paintings held secrets. She turned to Gabriel.

"Shall we go and visit Sandro?"

Gabriel gathered the two glasses and walked with Coco back the way they had come. The path of rose petals formed a new path to the gallery that housed Botticelli's works. They sat together and stared at the *Madonna and Child with Adoring Angel*, sipping champagne and snuggling into one another.

"I'm filled to overflowing with love for you, Gabriel…"

He cupped her chin and kissed her, and when he broke away she saw his eyes brimmed with tears.

"Best first date ever," she said, "but can we please go back to the hotel now?"

"Me, over Picasso and Sandro?" he said. "I'm feeling lucky."

"And can we bring the champagne please? I've only had a few sips."

Gabriel raised an eyebrow as his gaze drifted over her body, pausing at her delicate pregnancy bump before returning to her amethyst eyes.

Coco gasped as the sensation of butterfly wings beating softly fluttered in her belly. "Did you feel that?"

He grinned. "You are an extraordinary woman."

Gabriel picked up the glasses, and a moment later the gallery fell empty.

EPILOGUE

HIGH ABOVE A jagged fjord, fierce crashing waves announced the place where the ocean meets the River Styx. Towers of granite ascended into the infinite heavens, and the glow of candlelight ebbed into the curtain of darkness. Between fine cracks in the rocks, shards of life pushed upward, nourished by the luminosity of goodness that for eons had been lost to all life.

Within the candlelit rooms, a couple sat amid rumpled bedsheets. The human, Kenan, pulled a brush gently through Freyja's long raven-hued hair, marveling at the joy the simple act brought to his heart. And she, the goddess of the underworld, leaned into him, luxuriating in the warmth of his humanity.

Across the world, a celebration was taking place.

Helen was in the midst of preparing a birthday party for Frances. She grinned as she watched her children instruct Sam in the strategy of blowing up balloons. When the doorbell rang she walked through to the front entrance of Sabine's New York home and opened the door.

"Happy Birthday!"

Frances handed her a newspaper. "We did it," she said. "And the phones are ringing nonstop at the office."

Helen unfolded the paper and read the headline. She hugged Frances and allowed her tears of relief to fall.

"It's okay," Frances said. "It's done, you and your children will be protected always."

"Thank you," Helen said. "So others like me are coming forward?"

Frances nodded. "By the hundreds, and I just received a text from a prominent politician's secretary requesting an interview. He apparently wants to make it clear to the public—the voters—that he's for changing the legal age of marriage in his state. Your courage made this happen."

A loud pop followed by laughter made the corners of Helen's mouth turn upward. "We'd best rescue Sam from the kids."

In a valley deep in the heart of the northern Alps of Slovenia, the ancient vampire Nikandros tended to his garden. A ripple of magic brushed against him, he looked up and stared for a long moment at the somewhat ordinary scene playing out before him, for it was not something he'd ever thought possible. His two daughters—one of his blood, both raised with his heart—placed dishes of food on a table. He watched as Sabine turned toward Frederico and knew by the passion of their kiss that she had finally come to peace with her past, and in so doing had found eternal love.

Nikandros sensed Luciana's gaze upon him, and a warmth flowed throughout his blood, for she was his beloved. He walked toward his family and sat at the table where they would celebrate life together before Flora departed for Florence. There she would work beside Marilyn and Marco searching for lost paintings of her grandfather, Sandro Botticelli.

At Casa della Pietra, Prudence stood with her beloved Stefan on the tower overlooking the Dolomite Mountains in Northern Italy. For centuries the fortress had protected her and the loved ones who were her family of blood and friendship. She laid her head on his shoulder, and a smile crossed her face as he drew her into an embrace.

"It is so quiet here now without our extended family," Prudence said. "I became used to having everyone here."

Stefan kissed her forehead. "We all have our lives to live, *tesoro*, and they've promised to return for the winter solstice and through to the new year."

"The little ones will both be toddlers by then, and I sense another on the way," she said. "Of all the names I've had over the years, I believe nonna is my favorite."

Stefan chuckled. "You don't look like a grandmother."

"Looks can be deceiving," she said. "Maria has her hands full with little Sofia, although I've noticed Gabriel is not apt to let his daughter out of his sight, for her magic is strong."

"It will be good for Maria to have Isabel close by; they've become good friends," Stefan said. "And I hear Eduardo has organized for Isabella to give dance classes at his studio. You and I could attend… It's been a while since we danced. Perhaps Chantal and Alessandro could join us."

"I would like that," Prudence said. "Caprecia would be happy for Eduardo, she wanted him to be loved and to love. Have you heard from Ignacio?"

"I have." Stefan nodded. "He says Louisa is well, and for now they have decided to live in Occitanie. She loves the area as much as he."

"Ignacio is drawn to his family's roots, to the brave souls of the Cathars. A tragic piece of history." She gazed up at Stefan. "And what have you heard from Christopher? How are Pelayo and Jeremy, and Jason and Illona?"

"All is good in DC." He raised an eyebrow. "Well, with our family at least. And before you ask, Kishu is content with his life of solitude in Hawaii but will return for winter solstice."

He squeezed her shoulder and cleared his throat. "I wrote a poem for you, *tesoro*. 'Twas a while ago."

She gazed into his dark eyes. "Will you share it with me, my love?"

He brought his lips to hers, and when their kiss was complete, he held her hands in his…

"One taste of thou and life's burdens lift,

Sorrows fade into joy and my youth is restored.

Thine breath against my skin and my heart is quiescent.

A tender touch and the withered sinew that

girds my wretched soul is hallowed.

I bethink the wisdom from this dance of life,

The stillness of death and rebirth,

the drops of rain upon the leaves of scarlet, umber
and gold,

and the fractured moonlight sparkling upon virgin snow,

each snowflake a glittering gem.

The hoot of the owl,

the sweet scent of life and goodness.

I want for nothing with you by my side.

Fairest nymph,

Beloved rose,

Wife and mother,

My divine Prudence."

❧

As day melted into twilight, Arianna stood beside Vito at the top of the tower at Palazzo Vecchio in Florence. They witnessed the sky become a wash of pink, orange, and indigo, and when the lights of the city began to glow, Vito kissed Arianna's fingers and draped his arm around her shoulders.

"Do you think we can do it?" he asked.

"You mean rebirth the humanities?"

Vito nodded.

"I believe that with art as our superpower, we can do anything," she said.

A baby's giggle made them both turn around in time to see Coco step onto the tower, followed by Gabriel carrying a contented baby in his arms.

"You guys finally made it," Arianna said. "Old age getting to you, Gabriel?"

"No," he said. "But it's a slow process navigating through any building in Italy with two Creatives in tow. And Sofia is intrigued with celestial beings. I'm waiting for the day she brings one to life."

"Our clever little girl," Coco said. She leaned forward and kissed her daughter's cheeks.

Sofia reached a chubby little hand toward her mother, and rays of gold emanated from her fingertips.

Coco looked at Gabriel. "Did you see that?"

"One could hardly miss it," he replied. "Perhaps it's time we returned home, let her rest before we attempt the Uffizi tomorrow."

Gabriel turned and headed back down the narrow stairs. Coco hugged Arianna and Vito before turning to follow Gabriel. At the top of the stairs, she looked once more at the silhouette of the two young lovers and smiled as she caught the scent of roses and frankincense in the air.

AUTHOR'S NOTES

LATE APRIL 2017 found me revisiting Florence with my sister, Suesie. My first trip to Italy was in 1987 while working as the wardrobe mistress for David Bowie during his *Glass Spider* tour. I'd previously been employed by director Julien Temple as the costume designer for Bowie's music video *Day In, Day Out,* and it was during this time that his management asked me if I'd be interested to go on tour as the stylist. At first I declined as I had concerns about leaving my clients in Los Angeles and I had recently become sober; however, after careful consideration I accepted, and a few weeks later found myself in London working with the head costume designer and getting to know the rest of the glam squad (hair, makeup, wardrobe) before heading out on the tour.

I truly believe that in life there are no accidents, that everything we do—the places we go, people we meet, every experience no matter how inconsequential it may seem—plays a part in our destiny. And it is with this in mind that I have Julien Temple to thank for introducing me to David Bowie, for without that introduction, I might have waited years to visit what would become my favorite city in the world: Florence.

While in Florence, we stayed at Villa la Massa, a stunning property that sits on the banks of the Arno River among a superb twenty-two acres of beautiful gardens and a small chapel. As stated on their website, "Villa la Massa is a sixteenth-century Medici dwelling on the outskirts of Florence. It was turned into a luxury hotel in 1948." It was there that my soul awakened to the history of Tuscany, and although my personal library is filled with books on the area and the Florentine renaissance, it would be thirty years before I returned. I will add that Villa la Massa is the model for Antonia's Florentine home in The Creatives Series—I can see her touch of elegance in every detail of the estate.

Fast-forward to Florence 2017. As soon as Suesie and I arrived, we dropped off our bags, ate dinner at a neighborhood restaurant, and walked along narrow streets, both of us charmed by the beauty and charisma of Florence and her people. Veering off our path, we turned down an alley, and I froze when I saw the familiar dome of the Cathedral of Santa Maria del Fiore a couple of hundred feet ahead. I remember catching my breath at the wonder of it all. But it was more than that—everything around me seemed innately familiar.

We hurried to the end of the alley and stepped into the deserted square where we stood on the aged cobblestone and stared at the magnificent architecture of the Duomo. My heart opened just as it had thirty years before while at Villa la Massa, and whispers of stories yet to come caught me unaware. Pushed by a cold wind, we wandered around the square, me taking videos and stills for future reference. My senses were on overdrive.

During the following week we explored alleys, art museums, gardens, rooftops, and restaurants before we picked up a car and drove to our second destination, a 1,100-acre organic farm, Tenuta di Spannocchia, built in 1225 and located on a nature preserve in the hills of Tuscany.

For those of you who follow my blog and social media posts, you will already know that Spannocchia is the property I envisioned as Gabriel's villa outside of Florence. At Spannocchia, we hiked to ruins of ancient monasteries, dodged wild boar, and wandered along centuries-old roads covered in moss while my sister pointed out various types of flora.

From Spannocchia we drove to Sienna (best pesto gnocchi ever!), then explored the beautiful city of Verona. A few days later we visited friends in Asolo before driving to the Marco Polo Airport and catching a water taxi to Venice. We had initially planned to explore Lake Garda and farther north to the Dolomite Mountains but with limited time, a storm approaching, and Florence tugging at our hearts, we drove south to Tuscany, stopping along the highways to enjoy espressos with other caffeine-needy travelers at the counters of numerous gas stations. We returned the rental car and hightailed it to the apartment where we customarily dumped our bags, then headed out to the Uffizi (again). We spent that evening in the tower of the Palazzo Vecchio watching the sun set. It was pure magic and would later be the setting of the last scene in *The Immortal Muse*.

During that research trip, I felt like I was being pulled by an invisible force into particular areas and buildings within Florence, and often synchronicity stepped in. For example, when we arrived at the Palazzo Riccardi Medici, I had my heart set on seeing Lorenzo's room on the lower floor; however, we found it closed due to construction. So instead we explored the rooms opposite, and voilà, an exhibition of photographs, books, and artworks salvaged from the devastating floods of 1966 had me rewriting a back story.

The moment we stepped into the rooms where the exhibition was displayed, a certain character named Gabriel began whispering prose about a tale of two women. He then ushered me back to previously seen locations. It took five visits to the Palazzo Vecchio and another to the Pitti Palace and Boboli Gardens before I realized that it wasn't Eleanora di Toledo I needed to investigate but her daughter—the princess of Florence—Isabella.

Perhaps the beauty of Florence lies within her ability to captivate the soul and have us consider slowing down, for it is then that we breathe in her magic. When Suesie and I stepped up to the counter at the Santa Croce Church and Museum all set to explore the venue on our own, a gentleman stepped forward and suggested that if we could wait a few minutes, one of their English-speaking volunteers would be available to give us a free guided tour. We figured why not? A few minutes turned into five and then fifteen. I approached the gentleman again, and he suggested we step inside and wait by the door as the volunteer would be with us shortly. Once inside, we waited for another fifteen minutes, and just as I was ready to take off on my own, a gentleman approached, apologizing profusely for keeping us waiting.

We instantly liked Umberto, who waited patiently while I asked questions and wrote notes, filling one notebook and starting another. He gave us his "extended tour" (around ninety minutes), which consisted of not only historical information but also anecdotes about the Florentine people. At the end of his tour we stood in the courtyard and I asked him what the consensus is among the locals about Lorenzo. He puffed out his chest, and with a grand gesture of his hands and a sparkle in his eyes, he gazed at the buildings and then to me and said "Look around… See what he gave us, what he did for the arts? We are grateful to Lorenzo and the Medicis for this. We Florentines are proud of our art and architecture."

The next day we explored the Duomo and Museo dell'Opera del Duomo on a private tour with Alexandra Lawrence. Alexandra is American and lives in Florence. She is fluent in Italian and an excellent guide. She has a degree in political science, studied Italian literature at the graduate level, and has completed an eight-hundred-hour journey through Florence's art and history to become a licensed guide for the city and province. Two more notebooks were filled with information gathered during our time with Alexandra, whose knowledge of the Medici family, art, and the culture of Florence during the renaissance is remarkable. I highly recommend booking a private tour with Alexandra via her website at exploreflorence.net.

During the research and writing for The Creatives Series, I have devoured many books, but one that captured the story of Isabella de' Medici best is Caroline Murphy's *Murder of a Medici Princess.* My copy of this detailed book contains multiple sticky notes, has been read many times, and will no doubt be read again.

While I understand the subject matter of my books is at times dark, it is not without purpose. Although my books are fictional, the stories are based on articles I've read in newspapers, one being a piece in the *New York Times* (March 31, 2017) titled Missing Girls in Washington DC Widen City's Racial Divide. That article sparked the impetus of Kenan's depravity in *The Devil and the Muse*. Likewise, the subject of child brides in the United States (backstory of *The Immortal Muse*) has been and continues to be covered by journalists from a variety of reputable newspapers, and I invite you to google "child brides in the United States" for more information.

I trust you've enjoyed The Creatives Series as much as I have enjoyed writing Coco's story. I truly believe that art has the power to heal and bring about change, and every day when I write or paint, I say the words "without courage all is lost," because it takes immense courage to put your heart and soul out into the world. To my fellow Creatives: remember, art is our superpower!

See you soon.
Mandy

Acknowledgements

IN THE WORLD of book publishing, it takes a team to transform a manuscript into book form so it can be displayed in a bookstore or online in its final stage of presentation. With this in mind, I would like to thank the following people for being part of my team.

Thanks to my beta readers Ciara Byrne and Maria Mitzi David. Also thanks to Ciara for double-checking the Spanish translations, and to Åsa Thuvesen for the Scandinavian and Italian translations. To the awesome design team at Damonza for creating the covers and formatting my books. To Nikki Busch for your developmental edit, and to Anne and the ladies at Victory Editing for the line edit and Oops Detection. Thanks to Alexandra Lawrence for your detailed tour of the Duomo and Museo dell'Opera del Duomo and for answering all my questions regarding Lorenzo and the Medici family.

To my husband, Brian Beverly, thanks for making my stories come alive through your music and production, and likewise to my sons; Jack Beverly for your work on my promos and the endless conversations about history, and Angus Beverly for your "you've got this, Mom" support. The three of you are my anchor. Thanks also to my sister, Suesie Shaw, for holding my hand during the tough times and for being a fabulous travel buddy on our jaunt around Italy. Hopefully we'll share many other journeys and art museums in our future.

Thanks to you, the readers, book bloggers, and reviewers for taking the time to read my books and post photos on social media. Your reviews and messages are truly appreciated.

AUTHOR BIO

MANDY JACKSON-BEVERLY WAS born in Pyramid Hill, Victoria, Australia—population 419—and grew up around the rugged coastline and rolling hills of Tasmania. Upon moving to England, she discovered the tantalizing London fashion scene and fell in love with the concept of the creative collective. Later in Los Angeles, she found her own creative freedom among the thriving, no-holds-barred visionaries of the music video world.

Mandy has worked as a costume designer and stylist for an amazing array of creative dynamos including photographer Herb Ritts; directors Joel and Ethan Coen, David Fincher, and Julien Temple; and music icons David Bowie, Madonna, and Tina Turner. She taught art and theater in public high school, is a contributor to *The Huffington Post,* and reviews books for *The New York Journal of Books.* These days she lives with her family in Ojai, California, and spins stories for her readers' pleasure as well as her own.

When Mandy's not writing or reading (she has a fascination with Jung), she's cooking, painting, or on walkabout—preferably in Italy.

Mandy loves to hear from her readers. You can find her via her website at *www.mandyjacksonbeverly.com.*

Author of *A Secret Muse, The Devil And The Muse,* and *The Legend of Astridr: Birth,* and *The Immortal Muse*